NO QUARTER

A TOM ROLLINS THRILLER

PAUL HEATLEY

INKUBATOR
BOOKS

Published by Inkubator Books
www.inkubatorbooks.com

ISBN (eBook): 978-1-915275-86-8
ISBN (Paperback): 978-1-915275-87-5

For Aidan

PROLOGUE

The cabin is not big enough for the dozen people held captive within.

It's been a hot day. Early June. It's been a hot start to the summer. The night is cool, but the cabin is stifling. There's no air inside.

The people are too tired to protest. They have spent their days working in the field beyond the cabin. Hard, backbreaking, exhausting work. From the moment the sun rises until it sets. They break once at lunchtime. Rice and beans. Always rice and beans. They each get a two-litre bottle of water to see them through the day. They don't get a drop more unless they pass out. After lunch, work doesn't stop again until evening. More rice and beans. The portions are never big. Just enough to get by.

They were brought here with the promise of work. Day laborers, picked up from corners in Sacramento. Promised good hours. Promised pay.

Then they get here, and they're promised something else. Promises that sound a lot more like threats, until they become just that. Until they *are* threats. So the workers get in the field, and they do what they're told, and they're grateful for their small bowls of rice and beans twice a day, and they're grateful for the thin, uncomfortable mattresses they get to sleep on in a hot, cramped cabin. Because they know the alternatives. And they know what the alternatives mean for the people they care about.

Mateo Garcia is not sleeping. He's the only person in the cabin still awake. Everyone else is deep in a heavy sleep.

He's tired, though. His back aches. His bones are weary. He can barely keep his eyes open, but he bites his tongue, bites the back of his hand. Doles out sharp pains upon himself that keep him awake, until he can taste blood, until the crescent shape of his teeth is so deep, it's almost to the bone.

Mateo lies on his back and stares at the ceiling and doesn't move except to raise his hand to his mouth. The sweat sits heavy on his brow. It stings his eyes. His shirt is soaked to his chest. It feels like a second skin.

He waits. In his head, he counts off seconds. He doesn't have a watch, so he's had to grow accustomed to where the moonbeams fall. He listens to the outside, too. His bed is near a window. He listens to the footsteps of the armed men who patrol outside. Learns and memorizes their rhythms, their routes.

When they take their breaks.

By his count, there are four men on guard outside. He recognizes their footfalls. He knows how one of them drags his leg a little. How one is heavy-footed, and one is light. How one of them doesn't so much patrol the outside of the cabin as stop at every window and peer in. This is the one for whom Mateo feigns sleep. This one checks that the door is locked, too. Mateo hears how he shakes it in its frame. None of the other guards do this.

The windows are built into the cabin. They do not open. They don't need to be checked, not like the door.

Mateo waits until a moonbeam lands on his face. That means break time. The guard who checks the door makes sure it is locked. All four of them step away from the cabin. They go to the side. They have cigarettes or a drink, or they eat something. Mateo can hear them as he slips from the bed, as he creeps closer to the nearest window. He hears their low, distant voices. The occasional burst of laughter.

Mateo does not have long. He reaches under his mattress, to where he keeps his 'tool.' A spent bullet. He found it in the field. Made sure none of the guards were looking and slipped it into his pocket. He doesn't know who fired it, or when. Doesn't know if it hit its intended target. He scrapes its point into the wood beneath the frame. He catches the slivers of wood that fall away in his hand and puts them in his pocket. Tomorrow, out in the fields, he will dispose of the waste.

He's working the window loose. Scraping through the wood, weakening it, until he can push it through. It won't be long now. He's getting closer every night.

Soon, he'll be free.

1

Tom wakes with the dawn. It's going to be another hot day.

He stands on the porch of his ranger station, and he looks out through the trees, sipping water from his canteen. He spends most of his nights in the station. His days are out in the forest. It's quiet right now. Peaceful. Inside the station, his bed has been made. Drumskin tight. He's showered and shaved. He's eaten a light breakfast. He's ready for the day.

A small radio rests on the railing near him. It tells him the weather. This summer has seen a record-breaking heatwave for northern California. The day's temperature will reach up to 110 degrees. Despite his shirt being open, he can already feel sweat prickling his brow and trickling down his spine.

Tom closes his eyes, and he breathes deep. It's a clear, beautiful morning. The air is clean. He can smell the blossoming flowers, the lilies, the phacelia, and the bowers. He looks out through the trees, the ash and the redwoods, and he takes another sip of water. He wipes the sweat from his brow. Soon, he'll head out. He'll check the dry areas for risk of fire.

Most of his job so far this summer has been ensuring a wild-fire has not broken out. It's been very hot. It's been very dry. After he's done that, there is an area he's still clearing where an ash afflicted with dieback was cut down to prevent the spread. Most of the tree is gone, but there are still some blocks of wood and chippings that need to be cleared.

Tom has been here for a year now. The North California National Forest. He likes it. He likes being a forest ranger. Ron Judge, the head ranger, took a shine to him in the interview. Liked the fact Tom was a veteran, and figured that what he lacked in ranger experience and training could be made up for from his time in the Army. Tom likes the work. Likes being outdoors. It keeps him busy. When he's on shift, he's able to spend his nights in the ranger station. When he's off shift, he books into one of the motels or hotels in the nearest town of Oak Hills. There are a surprising number for such a small town. They cater to tourists and students from Sacramento who come to visit the forest. This time of year, it can get busy. He imagines the motels and hotels do a decent business.

A lot of the time, when he's working, Tom can go days without seeing another person. The forest is 607,000 acres – approximately forty-three miles long, and twenty-three miles wide. Tom can busy himself deep in the trees in the quadrant he watches over and never see a hiker or another ranger.

He hears from them, though. Hears from them regularly, on the radio. They always make sure to check in. Even now, he hears it squawk to life. It's Monica Boyd. She's checking in. She makes a joke of it. "Rollins, you still breathing? Ain't heard from you in a while."

Tom answers, "I'm still breathing."

She chuckles down the line. "Glad to hear it. Gonna be another hot one today, huh?"

"Feels that way."

"Make sure you've got plenty of water, lather on that sunscreen, and wear your cap."

Tom grins. Monica isn't much older than he is, but she takes her role as the rangers' matriarchal figure very seriously. "Roger that," he says. "Already accounted for."

"Glad to hear it. Have a great day."

Tom carries the small radio back into the station. The weather report is over. It's playing music now. Mark Lanegan's cover of 'Death Don't Have No Mercy.' He lets it play through while he buttons up his shirt. The sleeves are short. The bottom half of the Santa Muerte tattoo on his left shoulder is visible. He got her before he got the job. He was in Saxton, the nearest town to Oak Hills. He gifted the Santa Muerte pendant Alejandra had given him to someone he felt needed it more. Part of him felt like maybe he still needed her protection. Felt, too, like having her on his skin meant he was keeping Alejandra nearby.

It was in Saxton he found out about the North California National Forest. Saw that they were looking for rangers. He applied. The rest is history.

Heading out, cap on and SUV keys in hand, he gets another call on the radio. It's Ron Judge this time. "We're gonna need a cleanup near you, Tom."

"Sure," Tom says. "What's happened?"

"Ah, just some kids or picnickers or something. Maybe a campsite. A hiker just called in, let us know about it – said there's some leftover food. Need to get it gone before we find ourselves with a bear problem."

"I'm on it. Whereabouts is it?"

Ron gives him the directions. Five klicks from his station, heading west. Tom goes back into the station. He grabs a shotgun. A 12-gauge Remington 870. He loads it with rubber rounds, in case a bear has already caught the scent of the abandoned food and trash. There's already a litter picker and a roll of trash bags in the SUV.

Tom drives out. Starts his workday. When he reaches the area, he waits a moment in the SUV, looking it over. There's no sign of any bears. A couple of birds, finches, peck at a mostly empty bag of chips. They promptly take flight as Tom exits the SUV.

As well as the bags, there are a couple of discarded beer bottles and a greasy rotisserie chicken bag. There are bones in the bag, as well as some leftover meat. In the early morning heat, it smells. There's no sign it's been a campsite. No sign that whoever left the mess stayed here overnight. They likely came, had their small party, and moved on.

Tom narrows his eyes and gets to work. At least, he supposes, whoever left this mess wasn't stupid enough to try to have a fire. He's been called out to a few occasions where groups have not heeded the dry-conditions warnings and have attempted to start a campfire. The college students are the worst for it. They come out into the forest and seem to forget everything they've ever learned about preventing fires. It's likely the alcohol they sometimes bring with them that makes them so mentally impaired. Or perhaps the weed he often smells clinging to their clothes and in their hair.

He's had a couple of occasions where people have gotten belligerent with him. They've tried to cuss him out or step up to him. Tom makes sure they always back down. He holds their eye. They turn to water under his glare. They see the look in his eyes, and they understand he isn't the kind of man they've mistaken him for.

Tom finishes clearing the area and ties the bag tight. As he's putting it in the back of the SUV, he gets another call. It's Ron again. "How you getting on with the cleanup, Tom?"

"Just finished," Tom says.

"Well, I'm sure you had things you were planning on doing already, but seems we've got a busy morning for you."

"Okay."

"Just had a distress call here at headquarters from a hiker. The hiker himself isn't in trouble, but he's seen a couple of people he thinks are. Says they aren't dressed for being so deep in the forest, and they're swaying all over the path, look like they're about to pass out from dehydration. Figured it was probably a good idea to let us know so we could go check on them."

"Sure. Where are they?"

"You still at the cleanup site? Two klicks north of where you are now."

"Got it."

Tom places the sealed bag in the back of the SUV and heads north in search of the two ill-prepared hikers. He's expecting college kids. They come out here, think nature isn't something to be concerned about. It's happened before. More than once he's had to pick them up, either on a trail or lost in the trees, then get them rehydrated and back to headquarters. It's rare they ever need any assistance beyond some water, maybe a snack to get their blood sugar back up. Then it's just a case of letting them recover in a cool room while they get their strength back up, and sending them on their way with a pamphlet about staying safe while hiking.

Ron always performs medical checks, though. Makes sure they're safe to leave. That they're not going to keel over from heatstroke just a few steps away from the headquarters. They've never had to call anyone an ambulance. Not while Tom's been here, at least. It's happened in the past, of course. Tom has been told some stories. But it seems they've had a lucky year. Nothing serious.

He reaches a point on the trail where the SUV cannot pass and parks it. Continues on foot. He takes a couple of bottles of water with him, just in case. It doesn't take him long to find the two hikers. They aren't dressed for the occasion at all. Jeans and heavy work boots, checkered shirts and jackets tied around their waists. One of them is wearing a bandana. The other is wearing a frayed trucker's cap. They're walking slowly. The one with the bandana is propping the other up.

Tom follows, waiting to get close enough to call to them. He notices something strange as they stumble along. It makes him slow, watch them, make sure he's not imagining what he's seeing. They keep turning their heads, looking into the trees. The trees on their right are thicker. They pause, look in, then they'll shuffle on. After a few paces, they might do it again. One of them will tap the other, point. They'll confer. Then they continue.

It doesn't seem like anything at first. The kind of movement that could easily be missed. It's the regularity that catches Tom's attention. How often they do it. How rarely they actually look straight ahead. Their tired heads are on a swivel. They're searching for something.

Tom gets close enough to call out. "Excuse me."

They both freeze. They go stiff. This isn't the kind of reaction Tom was expecting. He thinks they're almost about to raise their arms in surrender.

He speaks again to put them at ease. "You two all right?"

They don't turn. Tom pauses, doesn't want to get too close. They're like animals, ready to either bolt or spin and attack. "My name's Tom," he says. "I'm a ranger here in the forest – we got a distress call about two guys matching your description who may be in some trouble."

The one with the trucker cap cautiously turns his head, peers back over his shoulder. He sees Tom, and some of the stiffness goes out of him. He says something to his friend. They're speaking Spanish.

"I have water," Tom says, holding up the two bottles.

They both turn. There's not a canteen or a bottle of water between them. No supplies of any kind. They look at him blankly. At first, he's not sure they speak English. The one wearing the bandana blinks. The other pushes the trucker's cap back on his forehead and wipes away sweat. "Water will be good," he says. His English is heavily accented. Tom thinks Mexican.

Tom smiles at them, tilts his head back toward where he's parked the SUV. Trucker cap looks willing, but bandana is reticent. Tom goes to them. He hands the water over. They drink greedily. It doesn't take long for both of the bottles to be drained completely.

Tom takes the bottles back from them. "I've got more," he says. "If you need it." He makes a show of looking them both over. "For being so deep in the forest, neither of you are dressed for it."

Trucker cap shrugs. Bandana says nothing. He watches Tom, watches his lips moving when he speaks, but Tom isn't sure he understands.

"Two of you need a ride anywhere?" Tom says.

They both stiffen. Bandana perhaps understands more than he's letting on.

Tom takes a step back. He places his hands on his hips. "Two of you out here looking for something?" he says. He keeps his tone friendly. "Trying to find your way back onto an easier trail, perhaps?"

Trucker cap latches onto this. "I think we have maybe got lost."

"Maybe got lost and ended up deeper in the trees than you expected?"

"I think so, yes."

Tom nods. "Neither of you look like you're in a bad way. Just tired and thirsty, I reckon. But I don't think I can just leave you out here in the forest to wander, as ill prepared as you are. Might end up getting yourselves more lost. Or hurt. Or maybe worse. So how about I give you a ride back to your car, and you can go back to wherever you're staying and rest up, and if you wanna come back to the forest, you can think about getting some better supplies. There's a store in town has everything you're gonna need. How's that sound?"

They hesitate. They put their heads close together and confer, speaking Spanish. Their voices are hushed, and Tom only knows a little Spanish. He's not sure what they're saying.

Trucker cap speaks up. "Okay," he says. "Back to town. When we come back, we'll come back better prepared, like you say."

They follow Tom back down the trail to where he's parked the SUV. Trucker cap sits up front. Bandana goes in the back. Tom gets them each another bottle of water, then takes a long drink from his own canteen. He starts up the SUV and turns it around, taking his time heading back out of the forest.

"It's hot today," Tom says, making conversation. It feels like there's more to these two lost men. He's not sure how much they'll be willing to share, but he can't help trying to tease some information out of them.

"It's nice and cool in here," trucker cap says. "It feels good."

The air conditioning is turned up, blasting them with cold air, drying the sweat on their skin. "You have names?" Tom says.

Trucker cap goes to speak up, but bandana reaches forward, places a hand on his shoulder. Trucker cap shrugs it off, then says, "I'm Gabriel. My friend is Luis."

"How long have the two of you been hiking today?"

Gabriel hesitates. Again, Tom is curious. Their answers are thought out, guarded. He can feel the tension from Luis in the backseat.

"A few hours," Gabriel finally says.

"Uh-huh." Tom side-eyes him, looks him over. "You've started to burn. You were lost and almost severely dehydrated. At a guess, I'd say you got started a lot earlier than a couple of hours ago. Maybe dawn? Maybe before that, even."

Gabriel shrugs.

"You just come to admire the scenery? Get back to nature?"

Luis speaks up from the back. He speaks in Spanish: "¿Es crimen?" Tom understands it. *Is that a crime?*

Tom responds in kind: "No es crimen." *It's no crime.*

Luis falls silent, perhaps not having expected Tom to know any Spanish. Perhaps worrying that maybe what they were earlier saying to each other was heard and understood. Tom reverts to English, his Spanish only able to stretch so far. "I'm just curious, is all. You've put your lives in danger. The forest is a big place, and it's easy to get lost. A lot of people don't seem to understand that."

They pass by the main ranger headquarters. A large building with redwood panelling and a couple of ranger SUVs parked down the side. Tom can't see anyone outside it, or at the windows, but he knows Ron will be in there. Monica too, more than likely. The headquarters isn't far from the exit. A dozen kilometers more, and they're at the main road.

Tom pauses, the SUV idling. "Where've you parked?" There's a parking area to the left, where most people leave their vehicles, but not everyone uses it.

There's a moment before Gabriel answers. "We did not drive here."

Tom frowns. "You come here from Oak Hills?"

"Yes."

"Then how'd you get here?" It's five miles from Oak Hills, the nearest town, to here.

"We got a ride."

"Taxi? Uber? Friend?"

"We did not know them."

"You hitch?"

Gabriel nods.

Tom feels his frown deepen. "It's a strange kind of determination you have to get to the forest."

"Will you take us back to town?"

Tom nods. "Sure." He turns onto the main road.

"When we come back, we will be better prepared," Gabriel says.

"Sure," Tom says. He's thinking. Thinking about what they've done. Thinking about what they've said, and more importantly, what they haven't. He has questions, but he knows he'd be wasting breath. They won't answer.

"Take it easy today," Tom says, trying a different approach. They may not talk to him, but he wants them to know he's available. He doesn't want them running off again on whatever fool's errand they're attempting and getting themselves killed. "And tonight. Get plenty of rest. Plenty of fluids. You start to feel sick, call a doctor."

Gabriel nods. Tom sees it out of the corner of his eye.

"Next time you come to the forest, even if you decide to come back so early in the day, maybe give me a call. I'll be up. I'll be more than happy to take you out on one of the trails, make sure you're not putting yourselves in any kind of danger."

"Maybe we'll do that," Gabriel says.

"Just go to headquarters," Tom says. "Tell them you're a friend of Rollins. They'll let me know."

Gabriel grunts. He and Luis have both fallen silent.

They're not far from Oak Hills now. Most of the journey on the main road has been in silence.

"Where do you want me to drop you off?" Tom says.

"We don't know the street names," Gabriel says. "I'll point. Just head toward the center of town."

They enter Oak Hills. It's already midday, and it's busy. Or, at least, as busy as Oak Hills gets. A couple of groups of people walk together on the sidewalk. Tom is held up by other vehicles on the road. They pass by the outdoor shop, and Tom points it out. "You plan on getting some decent gear, that's where you want to go."

Gabriel grunts. They get a little further down the road, and he points to the left. "This turn," he says.

Tom takes it. It leads them off the main strip. They don't go much further when Gabriel points again. "Here will do."

Tom pulls to the side, lets them out. Gabriel thanks him for the water and the ride.

"I meant what I said," Tom says. "You come back to the forest, ask for me."

Gabriel nods. Luis is already walking away. Gabriel turns and follows him. They go down the block. They head towards the corner. There's a small gathering already there. Tom watches. Gabriel and Luis go to them. There aren't many people there. Maybe half a dozen. They look like day laborers. Gabriel talks to someone when they reach the corner. He and Luis glance back toward Tom's SUV, then they leave the group, disappear around the corner. The man they spoke to watches the SUV a little longer, then leans back against the wall.

Oak Hills can be a busy town, especially in summer, but it is not a big town. Not the kind of town where he would expect to find day laborers waiting on a corner. Fifty miles away in Saxton, perhaps, or further, in Sacramento. But not here. He can't imagine there's much work for them.

And is that what Gabriel and Luis are? Day laborers? Perhaps they got tired of spending their day on the corner, waiting for work that may never come. They decided to hitch a ride to the forest and to go for a hike. They were searching for something, though. Looking in the trees like they'd heard there was a secret trail, and they'd spent the day trying to find it. Except, across 607,000 acres, they weren't going to find anything. Not without help, or a map, and they had neither.

It's lunchtime. Tom could eat. He pulls the SUV forward and circles down the road to get back to the main strip. There's a diner he likes at the end of it. He'll go there. Get himself something to eat. He knows, however, that all the while he'll be thinking of Gabriel and Luis.

2

The diner has the imaginative name of 'Clyde's Diner,' after its owner, Clyde Watson. The man himself must be in his sixties, but he's in there every day. If he's not working the register, he's on the grill.

Tom pulls into the parking lot. There aren't as many other vehicles as he was expecting. It's lunchtime. There should be a rush on. There are a couple of other diners in town, as well as a Chinese restaurant, but Clyde's has been here the longest. It's considered an Oak Hills institution. As such, it's often people's first choice when they come out for lunch. Tom was expecting to have a wait. Expecting to maybe struggle to find a parking space. As he gets out of the SUV, he looks toward the entrance, almost expecting a flock of vehicles to follow him in, to fill up the spaces, rush inside the building, and make it look how he's expecting it to.

That doesn't happen. Tom is confused. It's been a couple of months since he last came to Clyde's. He's wondering now if something has happened. If there was an outbreak of food poisoning. If there's a reason people appear to be giving it such a wide berth.

There are four other cars in the parking lot. As Tom approaches the door, the one nearest him catches his eye. A Honda Civic. There's someone inside. He keeps moving, but he cuts his eyes in its direction, watching. The woman inside isn't getting out. Isn't making any attempt to. She's sitting, pretending to be on her phone, pretending to be casual, but she's watching the building. Watching a corner of it. The front right-hand corner. There are windows there. From where Tom is, sunlight is glinting off the glass. He can't see what, or who, is on the other side.

The woman is Japanese American, and Tom realizes he knows who she is. He's just not used to seeing her out of uniform or in a civilian vehicle. She's Reiko Miller. The only cop in town. Dressed like she's off duty, but acting like she's on.

Ordinarily, Tom would wave. He'd say hello. Maybe go over and talk to her. In this instance, he doesn't. He keeps walking to the diner's swing door. Makes like he hasn't seen her. She's keeping a low profile, and that has to be for a reason.

Inside, the diner is quiet. The last time Tom was here, it was at a similar time of day. The waitresses were rushed off their feet. The bell on the pass-through was ringing incessantly, to announce that food was ready. There was a steady low murmur of voices from the crowded tables and booths. The occasional clatter of dishes being cleaned deep in the kitchen. Now it's almost silent, save for the steady hum of fans that attempt weakly to circulate the hot, heavy air.

Tom goes to the counter. Clyde is there, a newspaper spread out before him. He looks up, hopeful. When he sees just one man approaching, he can't disguise his disappointment. "Hey, Tom," he says. "Been a little while since I saw you last."

"Looks like it may have been a while since you last saw a

lot of people," Tom says.

Clyde's expression is sour, but he doesn't say anything to this. He pulls out a pen and a pad of paper from his top pocket and presses it down on the counter. "What can I get for you?"

Tom orders a panini with salad to go, then takes a seat while Clyde goes through to cook it himself. Tom looks to his left. An old couple sit in a booth at the window. The husband is reading his newspaper while the wife dips her last few fries in ketchup. Near them, a young guy sits alone at a table. He's eating a burger and sipping on a milkshake.

Tom turns to his right. There's one booth occupied on that side, but it's full. Four men. They sit by a window. The right window. The window Reiko was watching from outside.

Tom doesn't stare. He gets up from his stool and goes to the bathroom. He doesn't need to use it. He washes his hands. Hangs around long enough it's plausible he might have taken a piss. He heads back out. He's looking right into their booth. Gets a better look at the four men. They're Hispanic. Three of them have shaved heads. The fourth has short, tight curls. One of them is wearing a vest, his jacket hung over the back of the booth, and Tom can see the tattoos that run up and down his arms and across his chest. The guy with tight curls has two black teardrops tattooed below his right eye. Tom assumes he, and the other two who are wearing long-sleeved shirts, are tattooed similarly to the guy in the vest.

Tom passes close by to their table. He gets a good look at the tattoos on the vest-wearer's arms. Recognizes some of them. He knows what they mean. The most obvious is high up on the guy's left shoulder. It spells it out, plain as day.

MS-13.

Tom returns to the counter, back to his seat. Clyde is already leaving the kitchen, the panini made. Tom's mind races while he pays. MS-13? In Oak Hills? Tom spends most of his time in the forest, it's true, but he spends at least a couple of nights a week, or a couple of nights a fortnight, staying in town. He's never seen any sign of MS-13 before, nor any sign of why they might be here.

It used to be easier to spot them. Their faces used to be covered in gang markings. Branded for life. Once in, no getting out. Save for the one with a couple of teardrops, they didn't have any face tattoos. He wonders if maybe the logo was just for show. Posturing. It would be a deadly game to play, but people have done dumber things when desperate to look tough.

It's been a while, but the last Tom had heard, the face tattoos were being phased out a little. Make it less obvious who the gangsters were, and what they might be trying to do. That could be the case here. But, again, why? What's in Oak Hills? Of course, he could be overthinking it. Maybe they're just passing through. Stopped for a bite to eat. Going on to Sacramento.

"You all right, Tom?" Clyde says.

Tom's been too lost in his thoughts. "I'm fine," he says. "Just thinking about something."

"Yeah," Clyde says. "It sure looked that way."

Tom thanks him, then picks up his bagged food and leaves. Outside, he notices Reiko is still in her car. She's still watching the window while pretending to be on her phone. The window where the four potential gangbangers are sitting. If Reiko's watching them, he doesn't think they're just passing through. He thinks she has to have some concerns.

He reaches the SUV, and she turns her head to him. She smiles at him, raises her eyebrows. Tom nods back, not wanting to make her presence too obvious. He gets inside and pulls out, but he's not as hungry as he was before. His food sits beside him on the passenger seat, untouched. He's too busy thinking.

3

R eiko Miller watches the diner. She can't remember the last time she went on a stakeout. There isn't much call for them in Oak Hills. Isn't much call for any kind of police work, truth be told. She's the only cop in Oak Hills, and there's never been more than she can handle. There's the occasional domestic disturbance. Kids drunk in public. College kids getting rowdy. By and large, the people in town know her, and she knows them. The only real trouble comes from outsiders.

The outsiders she's watching now haven't caused any trouble. Not so far. None that she's aware of, at least.

She's here out of uniform, in her own car, because she knows they won't know her. When they eventually leave the diner, they won't recognize her, and she doesn't want to spook them.

She can see them, faintly, through the window. When she first got here, she couldn't. The way the sun was hitting the glass, she couldn't see inside. She knew they were in there, though. Knew they were sitting in the booth by the window, same as they always do.

Clyde told her about them. She'd popped in for a cup of coffee. She was surprised how quiet the diner was. Clyde didn't hold back in telling her how it had come to be so. "It's those fucking gangbangers," he said.

Reiko wasn't sure she'd heard him right. "Gangbangers," she repeated. "In Oak Hills."

"That's what I said." Clyde nodded to himself. "I see their tattoos. They try to hide 'em, but I see them, and I know what they mean."

He had Reiko's attention. Her coffee was forgotten. "You're being serious."

"Of course I'm being serious! When've you ever known me not to be serious?"

Reiko leaned on the counter. "Tell me about them," she said. "These gangbangers."

He did. The four Hispanic guys who came in almost every day now. Except, he thought maybe there were five, because sometimes one of the guys would be different. One of them had teardrop tattoos on his face, but that wasn't the big deal. It was the tattoos he spied on their arms, on their shoulders if they took off their jackets and shirts on a hot day. MS-13.

"MS-13?" Reiko frowned. "In Oak Hills? You're sure?"

"That's what I said. They only used to come in a little, but now it's every day, almost. You see what they're doing to my business? I'm not the only one who sees them, and I'm not the only one who knows what those tattoos mean. It keeps people away. Scares them off. Only customers I get now are the ones so loyal I can consider them friends. The ones who've been coming to me since the day I first opened, practically." He pursed his lips, shook his head. "You know, there's two other diners in this town." He held up two gnarled and oil-scarred old fingers. "*And* a Chinese restaurant! Why've they always gotta come to me?"

"How long have they been coming?"

Clyde thought about that. "A few weeks now. Four, at the most."

"They cause any trouble?"

"No. They keep to themselves. Always in that booth over there." He pointed into the corner of the room. "They don't hassle anybody, but that's not the point. Sometimes it's the way they look at people, you know? It's the way that if they come in and someone's already in that booth, they'll wait, and they'll watch, until the poor folks sitting there get up and leave, half their damn meals left uneaten."

"They pay?"

"Yeah. And always in cash."

"They tip?"

"Yeah. Nothing major. Reasonable amount."

"Uh-huh. I can't arrest them just for existing and scaring off your customers. What if they're not MS-13 at all? Or what if they're *former* MS-13. On the run from their old lives. Lying low, trying to start over? Oak Hills would be as good a place as any. Quiet. Out of the way."

"And what if they *are*?" Clyde said.

"I'm considering every possibility," Reiko said. "I don't want to jump to conclusions. There hasn't been any major crime in Oak Hills in decades."

"And you remember what that was? I've lived in Oak Hills my whole life. I remember it. I remember what happened, and I remember when it happened, and it was long before you were even born."

"David Lovett killed his wife."

"That's right," Clyde said. "She'd been sleeping with his best friend. Lee Polanski, he was called. Lee managed to fight him off. Lee left town soon after. Lost his lover and his best friend in one fell swoop." Clyde shook his head. "It was a bloody business. You do your research on that case, or did your father tell you about it?"

"I did my research," Reiko said. "Soon as I got transferred to Oak Hills, I did my research. It didn't take long. There wasn't much to read up on." She paused, then added, "Dad didn't talk to me about his work."

"It was your father who arrested David. He was a good cop. An even better chief."

"I hear that a lot."

"People don't wanna forget him."

Reiko cleared her throat. Her father had been dead five years.

"He'd look into every possibility," Clyde said, "a little like what you're talking about."

"I know that," Reiko said. "Just because he didn't talk to me about his work didn't mean he didn't teach me what he knew. He wanted me to be a cop. He said it was his proudest day when I graduated. So I know what you're trying to do, Clyde. And yes, I'll approach your concerns the same way he would have."

"Just because it's been decades since we last had some crime doesn't mean we're never gonna get any. Could be we're overdue some."

Reiko looked at him. Her coffee was cold by then. Clyde noticed. He took it away without a word and poured her a fresh cup.

He leaned in close to her over the counter, spoke in hushed tones as if the men he spoke of were present. "I'm just alarmed, okay? If they are who I think they are, that worries me. Because if they're here, there's gotta be a reason why."

Reiko took her coffee. "The possibility worries me too, Clyde."

Now, Reiko shifts in her seat, her lower back feeling tight. The men have been inside the diner for almost two hours now. So far, they haven't done anything worth monitoring. They've eaten. After they finished, they've sat and drank and talked. One of them, when he laughs at something, he throws his head all the way back. Reiko almost thinks she can hear him through the glass and across the parking lot.

She's seen only a couple of other people go inside. It's a far cry from Clyde's usual busy days. Most people who do go in come out with takeout. Only a few have taken seats within – Clyde's most loyal regulars – but now it must be empty save for the men she's watching. The men Clyde is concerned about.

She saw one of the forest rangers earlier, too. Tom. He came to town about a year ago. Although saying *he came to town* is the wrong way to phrase it. He doesn't spend much time in town at all. Not that she sees, at least. He's always at the forest. The others who work there, she knows them well. Knows where they all live. Tom's a little harder to get a handle on. Ron has told her he's ex-Army. A hard worker, but he keeps to himself. Only leaves the forest when he absolutely has to. Will spend a couple of nights in town, then promptly returns to work, like being away from it has been almost painful.

The first time she met him, Ron making introductions, she'd thought he'd potentially be trouble. There was a look about him. The way he carried himself. A look in his eyes and his face. He smiled as they shook hands, and he was pleasant and charming, but Reiko picked up a vibe. She wasn't at all surprised to find out he'd been in the Army.

When he emerged from the diner, she'd worried he'd maybe come over. Talk to her. At the least, wave. Make it obvious she was there. He didn't though. She appreciated that. Seemed like he was able to read between the lines.

There's activity in the diner, through the window she's watching. The men are standing. They're getting ready to leave. Reiko slides down in her seat. She's been pretending to play on her phone. Now she presses it to her ear, pretends to be on a call.

The four men leave. One of them is in a vest, and she sees his tattoos briefly before he pulls his shirt back on. She didn't get a good look at any of them. Wasn't able to see what had spooked Clyde so much. Another of them is carrying a bag of takeout.

They cross the parking lot in the opposite direction to where she's parked. They get into a Ford. It's not shiny or new. It's six years old and in need of a wash. Perfect vehicle for not wanting to stand out. To keep a low profile. The one with curly hair drives. They pull out of the parking lot. Reiko waits a beat, then sits back up and starts her engine. She watches them in the mirror. Sees which route they take into town, so as not to lose them. They're heading down the main strip. When they're halfway gone, Reiko turns her car around and follows them. She keeps her distance, always watching up ahead. Two cars get in between them. She watches where they turn, where they go. She doesn't lose them. The two cars in between turn off, go elsewhere. Reiko keeps her distance.

They leave the main strip, head to the outskirts of town, to the suburbs there. They enter a cul-de-sac. Reiko doesn't go in after them. She stays by the entrance, parked under a tree. She watches where they go. They park at a small house at the end. They all get out of the Ford. A fifth man meets them at the door. He's frowning, looks annoyed. He taps his watch and says something. The others laugh at him. They hand over the take-out meal. This seems to placate him. He turns and goes back inside the house, and the others follow.

Reiko makes a note of the car and the registration. She'll run the plates when she gets back to the station. She makes a note of the house, too, though she's not likely to forget where it is. She'll keep an eye on it. Watch it from a distance. Hopefully, nothing happens. Hopefully, they're not up to anything she needs to concern herself with.

But she'll find out. She'll watch, and then she'll know. And when she knows for sure, and if she has to, she'll do something about it.

4

When Tom gets back to the forest, he stops at headquarters to fill out a report about the two men he rescued. He details where he found them, and what condition they were in. Writes about where he dropped them in town, at their request, and that they were in good health when he left them.

He's still at the headquarters as the others are checking in, getting ready to leave. He wants to get back to his station. The others don't see much of him, and whenever they do, it's as if they want to make the most of his presence.

Ron and Monica are already at headquarters. Monica is waiting for her husband, Jay, to pick her up. "Always pleasant when you come in and spend an afternoon with us, Tom," she says. She's only a couple of years older than Tom and has a lean, strong build from years spent working outdoors. She wears her dark hair tied back in a ponytail. Tom isn't sure he'd recognize her if he saw her with it down. "Don't be afraid to make it a regular thing. You don't have to be a stranger."

Tom smiles, his report finished. He's ready to leave. "I'll see you next time, Monica."

A couple of other rangers have entered the headquarters. The last two in are Stephen Summers and Freddy Lowe. They cover the area about five miles away from Tom's station. Their area is closed off. It's been closed off for a while now – as long as Tom has been in the forest, and longer than that, from what he's heard. Seems like it's a dangerous area. Something always going wrong. At first, there'd been some bad storms shortly before Tom started, and more than a few of the trees were at risk of toppling. Just as that issue got dealt with, there was a risk of crumbling rocks. Stephen and Freddy were working on getting those rocks secured so hikers could return to the area. Then the heatwave came, and they've deemed the area excessively dry and too much of a fire risk. No one is allowed in.

Tom sees them sometimes, when he's checking the outskirts of his own area to make sure there's no fires. One of them is usually standing guard at the entrance to their quadrant, to make sure no one ignores the signs and comes wandering in. Stephen is older, mid-fifties. Friendly and talkative. If he and Tom cross paths, they'll often stop and talk for a few minutes. Small things. They talk about the weather. Or about recent happenings in the forest.

Freddy, on the other hand, is entirely different. Tom doesn't care for him much. In fact, Tom thinks he's an asshole.

He's a younger guy. Early thirties, same as Tom. His manner is grating. An angry man with a chip on his shoulder. Pissed at the world for no discernible reason. Tom avoids him when he can. Isn't interested in hearing his voice, or his views.

Tom remembers the first time they met. It was at the overgrown entrance to Stephen and Freddy's zone. Back when they were having trouble with loose rocks. Tom was walking the perimeter. Acquainting himself with this area of land he had become the keeper of. He kept his head down, got on with his work. He'd spotted Freddy trying to hide among the trees. Knew he was watching him. Tom left him to it. Figured maybe he wasn't a talkative guy. Was just staying out of the way so they didn't have to converse. Tom was fine with that. If anyone wanted to talk to him, he'd talk. If not, he wasn't going to lose any sleep over it.

"Hey, newbie."

Tom had turned directly to where Freddy was standing, and he could see how this surprised Freddy. He'd expecting a couple of minutes of frantic searching, desperately trying to find the source of the voice. Freddy was caught by complete surprise that he'd been watched this whole while.

Then Freddy recovered himself. Cleared his throat and stepped out from the trees. He had long hair, which he wore loose, and a wispy beard. "You know this is our area, right? Me and Stephen. We can keep an eye on things."

"Sure," Tom said.

"You see the signs?" Freddy jerked a thumb back at the loose rock warnings.

"I see them."

"Good. I don't want you to come wandering in not paying any attention to where you are or what you're doing, and then I've gotta clear your crushed fucking brains up."

Tom looked at him. "Okay," he said.

Freddy held up his hands. "I'm just saying, man."

Tom moved on.

Bumping into Freddy at *any* time led to a similar kind of conversation. The kind where he'd prod and needle, try to get a rise out of whomever he was talking to. Tom often wondered if he'd been teamed with the more affable Stephen in an effort to get him to calm down.

Stephen stops as he enters the headquarters and spots Tom. "How you doing?" he says. "Been a while, good buddy."

They shake hands. Freddy slinks into the building behind Stephen. He spots Tom, and his eyes light up. Tom knows nothing good can come of this expression.

"I'm good," Tom says to Stephen. "You keeping busy out there?"

"Every day." Stephen laughs. "Last thing we want is for a damn forest fire to break out. We've had a couple of close calls before, when it's been hot – but I can't remember when we've ever had heat like this. Anyway, you keeping yourself busy, too?"

Freddy grunts. "Ain't you heard?" he says.

Stephen glances back. "Heard what?"

"About the two spics who got themselves lost," he says. "Tommy here had to go and pick 'em up, make sure they didn't drop down dead on the trail."

Tom grits his teeth. He glares at Freddy. The air goes out of the room. Stephen picks up on it. He takes a step back. He can probably guess what it is that Freddy has said wrong, though perhaps not why Tom would be so affronted by it.

"Don't use language like that, Freddy," Tom says. He keeps his voice level, his tone even. He stares a hole right through Freddy's eyes.

Ron and Monica enter into the foyer where Tom, Stephen, and Freddy are. They've either heard some of what's been said, or they've picked up on the change in atmosphere, too. "What's going on here?" Ron says.

"Everything all right?" Monica says.

The other rangers in the headquarters don't concern themselves. Likely they know exactly what Freddy is like, and they're not interested in wasting any time on him.

Freddy can't hold Tom's eye, but he feigns looking away by laughing, shaking his head. "Nothing," he says to Ron and

Monica. "Nothing's going on. Figure I may've just touched a nerve for Tommy here." He makes to walk by. He passes close. He's doing it on purpose.

Tom knows he shouldn't, but he can't stop himself. His hand snatches out, and he grabs Freddy by the arm. Digs the tips of his calloused fingers into the barely there muscle of Freddy's biceps.

"Ah, Jesus – get off!" Freddy says, trying to pull his arm back but unable to.

"Apologize," Tom says. "And don't use that language again."

Out of the corner of his eye, he can see how Ron and Monica look at each other. Monica speaks to Stephen. "What'd he say?"

"Uh," Stephen says. "I'm not – I'm not sure..." He says, copping out, covering for his colleague. "I didn't – I didn't quite hear..."

"I didn't say anything!" Freddy says, flailing, looking around for support. "This psycho's just fucking grabbed me, and –"

"You know exactly what you said," Tom says. "And so do I."

Freddy stops flailing. He looks back into Tom's eyes. He smirks. When he speaks, his voice is low so only he and Tom can hear. "What, you prefer 'beaner'? 'Wetback' maybe? You sweet on them or something?"

Tom thinks about Alejandra. He thinks about Carmen, and Rosa.

His eyes narrow. He takes a deep breath in through his nose. People are watching. He wants to grab Freddy by the throat. Wants to squeeze an apology out of him. But he knows it would do no good. Even if he gets what he wants, it would just be lip service from Freddy. It would just be Freddy telling Tom what he wants him to hear. It won't change who he is as a person. He'll still be garbage. And besides that, two people present didn't hear what he said, and one is pretending he didn't.

Tom lets go of his arm. He was holding Freddy tight, and he takes comfort in knowing that he's sure to have left a bruise. He keeps his eyes on Freddy's. Freddy rubs his arm. He has some confidence now, knowing Tom won't escalate things further. Knowing that people are watching. It makes him feel safe. As brazen as when he dropped the extra racial epithets.

Stephen steps in, gets between them. He bundles Freddy away. "Get through there," he says. Freddy grins as he leaves, misplaced swagger in his stride. Tom made his point, though. That will have to be enough.

"He can be an asshole, Rollins," Monica says. "But try not to let him get to you."

Ron grunts. "That's true," he says, then he turns and walks away. Ron is old. He's closing in on his retirement, and that's all he's waiting for. Until that day comes, he just wants a quiet life.

Stephen hangs back. "I don't know what he said to you, Tom, but I'm sorry. Like Monica said, just try to ignore him. I mean, think yourself lucky – you don't have to work with him every day!" He grins.

"Mm," Tom says. "How'd you handle it?"

"A lot of deep breaths," Stephen says, smiling. "And long walks in nature." He laughs, and Tom smiles back, feeling some of the previous tension leave both his shoulders and the room.

"I did hear about the two people you picked up, though," Stephen says. "Were they all right?"

"Not when I found them," Tom says. "But they'll be fine. Water and rest, they'll be right as rain."

"Good," Stephen says, nodding. "That's good to hear. I'm

glad. Last thing we want is someone getting hurt on one of the trails – or worse. What were they doing out there, anyway? I heard they were pretty deep, and they weren't dressed for the occasion."

Tom shrugs. "I don't know. They weren't saying much."

Stephen scratches his chin. "Oh, really? Nothing at all?"

"Just that they were hiking." Tom remembers how he felt like they were looking for something, the way their heads were turning, their eyes were searching. He doesn't share this information, though. He keeps it to himself. Can't guarantee Stephen would understand what he was talking about if he were to tell him.

"They weren't far from me and Freddy by the time you found them, that right?"

"That's right," Tom says. "Not far at all."

Stephen thinks about this. "Could've left them to wander a little longer, and we would've saved you the trip." He smiles, then takes a step toward the door. "You heading back out?"

Tom nods. "You?"

"Yup. I got fire watch tonight. Just came here to drop Freddy off."

Both men leave together, head to their respective SUVs. On the way, Tom sees a car parked to the side, the engine idling. He recognizes it. Recognizes the driver. Jay Boyd, Monica's husband. Tom doesn't know much about him. Just what he looks like, and who he is. He's a skinny guy, unshaven, with dark hair. He sees Tom and Stephen, and he waves. Stephen is already waving back. Tom nods, once. He climbs in his SUV, and he drives back to his station.

5

B ull Draven drives his pickup truck through Oak Hills, Clyde's Diner in mind. It's early evening, and the sun is low. Golden hour. His favorite light of the day. Shadows stretch. Where the light touches, everything glows. Up ahead, where he can see the diner, the sunlight shines like fire upon the glass.

The parking lot is empty. He parks near the entrance. Gets out of the truck and stretches. Enjoys the light for a moment. The warmth. It's been a hot day. He's been in the house, sweating through his shirt despite the air conditioning and the open windows. He's taken a shower before he came out. Got changed. Though now, out of his truck and standing in the parking lot outside Clyde's Diner, it feels like it's only slightly cooler than it was earlier.

He goes inside. There are fans running in here. A few of them. Their steady hum fills the air. Bull goes to the counter near Clyde and sits right next to one. "Quiet, ain't it?" Bull says, enjoying the feel of the cool air blowing straight onto his skin.

Clyde gives a start, looking up from his crossword. "Bull!"

he says, his face splitting into a grin. "Didn't hear you come in."

"Light on my feet," Bull says, grinning.

"What can I get for you?"

"One of your burgers sounds real good right about now."

"Consider it coming right up." Clyde slides off his stool behind the counter and shuffles off to the kitchen. "Cheese with it?"

"Sure, why not? Let's live a little." Bull watches him go. He peers through the pass, sees how Clyde gets to work by himself. Bull looks around the rest of the diner. He's the only patron. There isn't a single waitress in, either. Clyde's working solo.

Bull turns Clyde's crossword around. Takes a look at it to kill some time while he waits for his food. It doesn't take long to come. Clyde promptly shuffles back through, places the plate in front of him. "Hope you weren't filling any of the answers in for me," he says, perching himself back on his stool.

"Only in my head," Bull says, popping a fry in his mouth. "I wouldn't take your little joys away from you, Clyde. You the only one working?"

Clyde's expression turns sour. "I'm the only one I can afford to pay," he says.

Bull picks up his burger in both hands. Takes a bite. "Something happened? I know it's been a little while since I was last in. Everyone been missing my sparkling personality?"

"I wish it were as straightforward as that. *Gangbangers*, Bull. You believe that? Goddamn gangbangers."

Bull raises his eyebrows. "Oh?"

Clyde nods. "Never thought I'd see the day. Not in Oak Hills."

"That certainly surprises me, too."

"I saw them, though. Saw some of their tattoos, and I know what they mean. I'm not an idiot. I've heard stories. Seen things on the news. Sacramento ain't that far, and I know they have trouble sometimes. I had to tell Reiko. The cop, you know."

"I know her," Bull says.

"And she made sense, y'know. She said they aren't causing any trouble. And that's true. They're keeping to themselves, sure, but I got a right to worry, don't I? Like I said, I know what those tattoos mean."

Bull chews. He listens. He thinks.

"Maybe you don't wanna talk about it, and that's fine," Clyde says, holding up his hands, "but back when you were in Sacramento, you ever have any run-ins with MS-13?"

Bull smiles. He swallows. "When I was *locked up* in Sacramento, you mean?"

Clyde nods, sheepish.

"You can just come out and say it. It's been two years since I got out. I ain't precious about it. I've been in Sacramento lots of times, and you've gotta be specific with what time exactly you're talking about."

"I meant when you were locked up, yes."

"Man, I had run-ins with *all* kinds when I was locked up in Sacramento. Aryan Brotherhood. Mafia. Hell's Angels. Bloods. Crips. You'd better believe MS-13 were among them."

"You have trouble with them?"

"Not trouble per se. Not me, Clyde. You know me. People come looking for trouble, I'll always do my best to calm them down, see if we can just talk it out." He finishes his burger. Puts the last bite into his mouth. "I get along with everybody." He swallows. Takes a long drink from the iced glass of water Clyde brought him with the burger. "Let me tell you something I learned inside, Clyde. Hell, let me tell you something I've learned from life in general."

"I'm all ears," Clyde says.

"People like that – gangbangers, or any other kind of people you might be scared of, they all fall under this umbrella I'm talking about – you've just gotta know how to speak to them. That's all. And sometimes that means you've gotta learn how to speak their language, or at least some kind of language they're going to understand. It's the same whether it's MS-13 or Aryan Brotherhood. Find what they want, and speak on their level."

Clyde mulls this over, his brow furrowed. "I'm not totally sure how that's gonna help my current situation." He gestures to the empty diner.

Bull takes another drink. "Well, perhaps not. You said you'd told Reiko about your worries though, right? Guess now you've just gotta try to be patient. I'm sure things will work themselves out."

Bull rests his elbows on the counter, clasps his hands together. He smiles. His mind is still working. Still thinking. It always is. It never stops. Always searching for an opportunity. A solution to his problems. It's what got him through prison. It's what kept him alive. It's what's kept him thriving in the two years since he was released. "Besides," he says, unable to help himself. "I'm sure there's gotta be more dangerous things about here than some gangbangers with their tattoos." He grins.

6

Tom sits on the porch of his station. He has his KA-BAR out. He leans forward on the railing where he has a whetstone resting, and sharpens the edge of the blade along it. It keeps his hands busy, but his mind is still free to observe the woods. When he's done, he puts the knife and the stone away. Sits back and watches as the shadows draw out, grow longer, spread. Until all is in darkness. It's peaceful. It's his favorite time of day. As the night draws in and the air slowly cools. As the animals that hide away during the day come alive. He hears birds calling to each other. Small creatures rustling in the underbrush.

Heat continues to rise from the dry ground. Tom sits outside to keep an eye on it. To watch for any glow that might suddenly appear in the distance. A glow that may spread, grow bigger. A glow that could potentially engulf the entire forest.

The shotgun is nearby, resting against the railing within easy arm's reach. It's loaded with rubber slugs. In case of bears. Tom doesn't believe in being too careful. Doesn't think there's any such thing.

He breathes in deep. Breathes in the cooler night air. Soon, he'll get up and stretch his legs. Take the shotgun with him while he takes a look over his area, checks for fire. Checks, too, for anyone who may have sneaked in and decided to have a picnic without clearing up after themselves.

For now, though, before he gets up and goes back to work, he enjoys the peace. The nature sounds. He breathes in deep. Breathes in the fresh forest night air. He can't smell anything burning. That's a good sign.

He picks up the shotgun and steps down from the station porch. It's dark now. It would be hard to see, but his vision has already adjusted to the dark through being seated outside as it drew in. He steps lightly, though. Watches the ground for snakes. Sure enough, it doesn't take him long to find one. A California kingsnake. He sees its bands of black and white moving across the ground. It hasn't picked up on his approach. It slithers toward him. Tom stands still. He stomps his right foot down a few times so it picks up on the vibrations. It momentarily halts, then just as quickly changes direction. It moves away from him. Tom continues on his way.

Snakes aren't his biggest concern. It's bears. Bears and, of course, fire.

He's seen two bears while he's been here. Both of them were black bears. The first one he saw was two months into starting the job. It walked right by the station one morning. Tom was inside, brushing his teeth, when he saw its fur passing by below his back window. He waited until it was past, then leaned out the window and watched it go. It never looked back.

The second bear was a month ago. At the time, he was relocating a hornet's nest that was too close to one of the trails. A couple of people had been stung, and a few others had been run off. Luckily, when he spotted the bear, he wasn't handling the nest. He saw it coming. Saw how it stopped and watched him, almost curious. He knew it was unlikely the bear would attack, but he also knew he couldn't risk that assumption. Slowly, he turned to face it. The shotgun was nearby, resting against a tree. He could easily grab it, but he didn't want to have to. He didn't want to hurt the bear. He spread his arms wide and took a couple of steps forward. Toward it. He shouted at it. It sat up, startled. Tom didn't want to get any closer. Wanted to stay near the shotgun, just in case. He shouted at it again, and it finally turned. It fled, pausing only once to look back. It looked him right in the eye, and then it turned and disappeared through the trees. Tom put a call out to the other rangers, let them know the bear's location and the direction it had run, and then he returned his attention to the hive.

Tonight, he can't see any bears. No dark shapes coming curiously toward him through the trees. Thankfully.

He's come far now. He's been walking for a while, in a loop. He walked about a mile south from his station first, then cut a mile west. He estimates he's gone about three miles north. Two miles past his station. He'll loop back now. Rest. If he doesn't feel like sleeping yet, he can always come back out in an hour or so.

He hears something in the distance. Something familiar. A tight burst of gunfire from an automatic rifle. He stops and turns toward the sound. It's too distant to be of immediate concern. He steps behind a tree just in case. Peers out behind it. There's another tight blast. He pinpoints the direction it's coming from. North. Directly ahead. He looks that way, listening.

A third burst, then a fourth, in quick succession. Getting closer. Getting *real* close.

Then he hears something else. Something crashing,

tumbling, flailing through the forest. Something falling, then scrambling back to its feet and continuing on.

Something getting closer.

Tom sees it. A man bursting through the trees, coming his way. Frantic. Running for his life. Even at distance, Tom can hear his hard, ragged breathing. He gets close enough that Tom can see the whites of his eyes. He hasn't seen Tom yet. Too busy running for his life. Desperate to get away from whoever is in pursuit. Whoever is firing at him.

The man is coming toward Tom's tree cover. Tom reaches out as he gets near and grabs him across the chest, drags him behind the tree with him. Presses him up against it with his right hand clamped over his mouth and his left forearm across his chest. He can feel the guy's heart pounding through his skinny rib cage. The guy's eyes are wide. He thinks he's been caught. He's terrified. He smells of stale sweat and fear.

Up ahead, from the way he came, others are following. Tom peers back around the tree. More than one hunter. Three of them. They pause when they see their prey has disappeared. When they realize they can't hear him anymore, they look around, searching the area, thinking he's dropped and hidden behind a bush or a tree. They move carefully. They're still in a rush, but they've slowed down. Enough for Tom to get a good look at them. He doesn't recognize them, that much is certain. They wear dark sweaters and combat trousers. One of the pairs of trousers is camouflage style. Two of the men are white, and one of them is black. They all carry automatic rifles, but they're all different. One of the white guys has an SG 553. The other has an FN FAL, and it is this that Tom thinks he heard firing earlier. The black guy is carrying a G3.

Tom pulls his head back behind the tree. He looks into the panicked eyes of the man he's holding. He leans in close, still pinning him, still covering his mouth, but sticks up one of his fingers and uses it to press to his lips. The man nods that he understands. Tom feels him go limp against the tree. They slide down it together. Tom lowers himself to a knee. The man sits on his backside with his back against the bark. Tom uncovers his mouth. Lets go of his chest. The man is breathing hard, but he's trying his best to be quiet.

Tom tilts his chin toward the three men. He whispers. "Who are they?"

The man shakes his head. He swallows, and Tom hears a dry click.

Tom takes a breath. Appraises the situation. He doesn't know who any of these men are, nor why they're in the forest. Three of them are heavily armed, and if he didn't know any better, he'd say they were mercenaries, judging by their clothing and mismatched weaponry. The man breathing hard beside him, however, is scared, tired, and emaciated. It's clear who needs his help, and who needs to answer some questions.

Tom is outgunned. Armed with only the shotgun loaded with rubber slugs, he's no match for their mixed weaponry. The best they can do is lie low and try to escape. Get back to the station and call for help. At least at the station Tom has his Beretta, though that's still no match for the automatic rifles.

"Follow me," Tom says. "Stay close, and stay low. Do you understand?"

The man looks at him blankly, though it's clear he's trying.

"Habla espanol?" Tom tries.

The man nods.

"I only speak a little Spanish," Tom says.

"I speak..." the man says, still catching his breath. No

doubt if Tom's arm were still across his chest, he'd feel his heart continuing to hammer. "I speak...*little* English."

"Then we make a hell of a pair," Tom says, and does his best to repeat his earlier instructions in pidgin Spanish. The man understands well enough. This time, there is understanding in his face. He nods.

Tom peers around the tree again. The men are getting closer, but they're still searching. Holding the shotgun in front of him, Tom crawls to the next tree. The man follows. They continue to the next, then the next, pausing just long enough for Tom to look back and see what their three pursuers are doing. Then they continue on. Tom is heading for where the trees are thickest and darkest. When they get there, they can break into a run, but they'll have to remain quiet.

They don't make it to where the trees are thickest. The man following is faltering. He can't keep up the pace. He starts falling flat on his face, all energy gone. He's making noise. It draws the attention of the three looking for him.

"Over there! He's over there!"

Tom hurries on without him. He's not leaving him behind, but the three don't know Tom is with him. He gets to a tree and stands up behind it, his back pressed into it. He preps the shotgun. He can hear the three coming closer. They aren't firing. Either they can't see where the other guy is, or the short bursts earlier were to scare him. If they weren't trying to kill him, they were trying to get him to give himself up.

Tom presses the stock of the shotgun into his shoulder and spins around. He fires. The rubber slug catches the white guy with the FN FAL high in the left shoulder. Right on the front delt. It spins him around and renders his arm useless. He falls to the ground. If Tom was right, if he was the trigger-happy shooter earlier, it was important to take him out first.

The other two stagger to a halt, caught off guard, not expecting to be fired upon. Expecting only to be doing the firing.

Tom doesn't stay behind the same tree. Slamming another slug into the chamber, he crouches low and runs to the next tree. In position, he fires upon them again. The slug misses, but it passes by close enough for the blond guy with the SG 553 to panic. "*Fuck!*" he says. "He's got cover – let's go! Fuck this guy, *let's go!*"

The black guy doesn't need much persuasion. The unexpected fire has caught them off guard. They grab their fallen buddy, who is groaning on the ground. Drag him along. They don't check to see if he's bleeding. Don't check to see what has actually hit him. Tom fires again to hurry them on their way.

The three men disappear back the way they came. Into the darkness. It won't take them long to realize that what their friend was hit with wasn't lethal. That while it may have hurt like hell, it was rubber, and the worst he's likely to end up with is some severe bruising. And then what? Do they come back, guns blazing? Are there perhaps more of them out there in the trees, in the dark? Will they come back with reinforcements?

Tom isn't waiting around to find out. He goes to the fallen man he's been defending. The man is still on the ground. He's trying to push himself up, but his arms are shaking. His body has given out on him. He's crying. He keeps apologizing.

"Save your breath," Tom says, ducking low and scooping the man up, draping him across his shoulders. He carries the shotgun down by his side. The man's apologies turn to gratitude.

"Thank me later," Tom says, and he sets off at a run, back toward the station.

7

The man's name is Mateo Garcia. He's very hungry, and he's severely dehydrated.

When they reached Tom's station, Tom didn't bother taking him inside. Went straight for the SUV and sped down to headquarters. The ranger on duty nearly shit himself as Tom came barrelling in with Mateo slung over his shoulder, barking at him to call the cops. The ranger clearly wasn't expecting any kind of excitement this night.

They've given Mateo water and some fruit. The other ranger doesn't speak much Spanish, either, but they've at least managed to get his name.

Tom told the ranger to call around to the others. The ones still in the forest, on fire watch duty. Warn them of the armed men. Ask them if they've seen anything. The ranger comes back a few minutes later and says none of them have.

Tom has stood by the window in the entrance most of the time, keeping an eye through the trees. There hasn't been any sign of anyone approaching, not until the red-and-blue lights of a police cruiser pull up in front. Reiko Miller. It hasn't taken her long to arrive. Ron Judge turns up shortly after her. The other ranger insisted on calling him, telling him what had happened.

Reiko steps into the headquarters, her hands on her belt. It's late, and Tom thought the call would wake her, but she's in uniform and doesn't have a hair out of place. "What happened?" she says.

Tom gives her a quick rundown of events. Her eyes narrow as he tells it. He lists off the weaponry they had. Leaves out his theory they could be mercenaries. It would just lead to questions he doesn't have the answers to, such as mercenaries for *who*?

"You're sure those are the weapons they had?" Reiko says.

Tom nods. "Pretty sure."

"It would've been dark out there."

"I'd been in the dark a while. My eyes were used to it."

"Where is he now?" she says, meaning Mateo.

"In the break room," Tom says, tilting his head back toward the closed door. "He's in a bad way. Looks like he's had a rough time."

"Has he said anything? Who they were, why they were chasing him?"

Tom shakes his head. "He doesn't speak much English, and neither of us" – referring to the other ranger – "speak much Spanish. I'm not sure it would make any difference, though. He's still catching his breath. It's taking up all his energy to stay conscious."

"Well, *I* speak Spanish," she says, heading toward the door. Over her shoulder, she says, "Have you been standing watch?"

"Haven't seen them," Tom says. "Unless they have vehicles, I'm not sure they'd come this far."

Tom follows her into the break room, back to Mateo. He's slumped in a chair in the corner, his eyes fluttering. He looks pale. He manages to sip from a bottle of water. Reiko looks him over. Sees how dishevelled he is. How ragged and tired, how underfed and bone-weary. "Jesus," she says, breathing the word. She takes a step forward. She speaks in Spanish. The only part Tom understands is her opening question – *Mateo?*

Mateo looks up at her through heavy eyelids.

She speaks to him.

"What are you saying?" the other ranger asks.

Reiko doesn't answer straight away. She gives Mateo a chance to respond. He doesn't take it. She sighs and says, "I'm asking him who he was running from. Who the men shooting at him were."

"What's he said?" the ranger asks.

Reiko looks at him. "Have you heard him respond?"

The ranger looks from Reiko to Mateo, then back again. "Uh," he says.

Ron Judge sits silent to one side, his brow furrowed, while he watches things transpire. In stark contrast to how neat and orderly Reiko was when she arrived, it's clear he dragged himself out of bed and fell into his clothes. They're untucked. His hair, which is thinning but usually combed back over his bald spots, is wild.

Reiko turns to him. "You all right there, Ron?" she says. "You maybe have any ideas?"

"About armed men chasing a Mexican in the dead of night?" he says. "No. Surprisingly. No, I don't have any ideas."

"Never had anything like this happen before?"

"You'd know about it if it had."

"I mean before I was here."

Ron shakes his head. "Been here all my working life. We've had trouble with folks bringing guns in, sure. Poachers, that kind of thing. Those poachers were never hunting a *man*.

And they never had automatic rifles. And they were never stupid enough to set them off during a dry season."

Reiko turns back to Mateo. She crouches in front of him, brings her eyes level with his. She speaks. Tom makes out a little of what she says. She's repeating her earlier questions. Asking him who those men were. Why they were chasing him. She asks him if he's in any kind of trouble.

Mateo understands her. Tom can see it in his eyes, which aren't as tired as he's pretending they are. They're alert, really, wide awake behind his façade. He's pumped full of adrenalin. And he may not have all the answers to what she's asking, but there's no doubt he has some of them. He's just not sharing.

Reiko sees it, too. "Creo que tu me entiendes, Mateo." *I know you understand me,* she's saying. "No puedo protegerte si no me hables." *I can't keep you safe if you won't talk to me.*

Mateo opens his mouth. His lips are dry. His tongue flickers out over them. He can't speak. Gestures for water. The ranger hands him a fresh bottle. Mateo takes a drink. He swallows hard, and when the water is down, he looks pained. He's able to speak, though. He's able to lie. In English, even: "I don't know who those men were."

Tom doesn't believe him. It's clear Reiko doesn't, either. She sighs, getting back to her feet. She and Tom exchange a glance.

"What are you going to do?" Tom says.

"I can't do much," she says. "He doesn't have any papers, no passport, and he won't speak. I'm gonna have to go off the assumption he's here illegally and take him into custody, unless I hear otherwise. But if he is in trouble and he won't talk about it, this may be the only way I can keep him safe."

They both turn to look at Mateo. He avoids their gaze. He drinks more water.

Reiko takes him gently by the arm, lifts him to his feet. Tells him he's going to have to come with her. Mateo doesn't protest. Still doesn't talk, either. He holds the bottle of water he's been given with both hands, a thumbnail tearing at the sticker on it.

"You not gonna send anyone out to find those shooters?" the other ranger says.

"I'll make a call to Saxton," Reiko says. "But come on. You know as well as I do, they're not gonna be in a rush to send anybody here."

Tom frowns. "Why's that?"

She looks at him. "You had the displeasure of meeting Chief Grice?"

"No."

"I'll be sure to tell you all about him some time."

"I look forward to it," Tom says as she guides Mateo past him, leading him to the door.

Mateo pauses as they pass Tom. He looks into his eyes, reaches out to him like he wants to clasp his arm or his hand. The bottle gets in the way. Tom feels the warm plastic against his bicep. "Thank you," Mateo says, in English. "*Thank you.*"

Reiko takes him outside, to her cruiser.

The other ranger stands with his hands linked atop his head. "She's gotta be kidding me, right?" He looks between Tom and Ron. "They could still be out in the trees! What're we supposed to do?"

Ron looks up at Tom. He holds his eye. Tom nods.

"I'll look into it," he says. "It's nearly dawn. I don't think they'll still be out there. Not in the daylight."

"You have a theory why they may have been out there at *all*?" Ron says.

"I have one, but it doesn't hold much water."

"Share it anyway."

"I could imagine bringing someone out into the forest to execute them," Tom says. "But you wouldn't do that with three automatic rifles."

"What *would* you do with three automatic rifles?"

Tom thinks about this. "You'd stand guard," he says. "And you'd give chase if someone ran away from whatever it was you were guarding. Especially if it was maybe the *person* you were guarding."

8

Reiko takes Mateo back to Oak Hills. The sun is up by the time they reach her small station. Doris, her receptionist, isn't in yet. It's still a few hours before she starts.

The station is on the outskirts of town. It looks like a house at first glance, but upon further inspection, there is a Saxton police department sticker in both of the front windows. Inside, the station is an open space save for the corner where Reiko's office is. The kitchen is next to this, and opposite is the desk where Doris sits. There's a radio next to Doris's desk.

She guides Mateo to the door at the rear of this open space, then takes him downstairs to the cells. There are only two. It was last summer since anyone was last in either of them. A drunken college frat boy causing a ruckus in one of the diners that doesn't belong to Clyde. "You're gonna have to wait in here," she says. She notices the bottle of water he's been clutching the whole drive over is empty. She takes it from him. "I'll get you some more," she says, then locks him inside.

Mateo stumbles across the ground and collapses face-first onto the cot in the corner. A moment later, she hears him snoring. He's exhausted. From the chase. From lack of food and water. Reiko watches him for a moment, wondering what he's involved in. Wondering who the men chasing him were and, most importantly, why he wouldn't tell her anything about them.

She returns upstairs and goes to her office. Before she sits behind her desk, she peers out the window. The sun is coming up. The town is slowly coming to life. A retiree, Gerald Patterson, passes by on the sidewalk on his regular morning walk. He's like clockwork. He looks up, sees Reiko. Smiles and waves. Reiko returns the wave.

Her nerves are on edge. The thought of men armed with automatic rifles running around the forest, under her jurisdiction, makes her uneasy. It gets her mind to racing. Creates a lot of questions she doesn't like not being able to answer.

She sits down and picks up the phone on her desk. She calls through to Saxton. To the main police headquarters.

Oak Hills is a satellite town. The main station is in Saxton. It's where she should be. Where the action is. Or at least, more action than here. Instead, she's been stationed as the only cop in this tiny town where nothing ever happens, wasting away the prime years of her life and her career. All because Chief Linden Grice is a petty, vindictive, jealous little prick.

She gets through to the Saxton station and tells them what has happened. The chief isn't in yet. She's glad to hear it. Means she doesn't have to speak to him. The officer on the other end tells her they'll send some men over to help her out.

"I don't know how long they'll be, though," he adds as a warning.

"Thanks," Reiko says into the phone, and hangs up.

His warning was one that Reiko was already expecting. Chief Grice begrudges sending anyone over to Oak Hills. She can imagine just what he'd say to her request. The disbelief and condescension in his tone. *Come on now, Reiko. Automatic rifles, in Oak Hills? Are you sure? You're going off the word of some no-doubt-traumatized ex-Army Ranger, who claims he can see exactly what those guns were in the dark? I'm sure this won't turn out to be anything you can't handle yourself.*

She won't hold her breath on her backup getting here any time soon.

9

Tom drives the SUV back to his station, then backtracks through the forest. He takes his Beretta and KA-BAR with him, as well as the shotgun. Tucks the handgun down the back of his trousers, pulls his shirt loose and hides it under the flap. He doesn't start at the beginning. Not where he first became aware of the gunfire and saw Mateo fleeing. Instead, he walks to where it ended. Where he fired upon the potential mercenaries with the shotgun and chased them away. Looks the area over. He finds some spent cartridges. 7.62 mm. The kind used in the FN FAL. As he suspected. He pockets the cartridges, then continues on. Doesn't have to walk far to where he first spotted Mateo.

He looks around. Eyes on the ground, on the trees and the bushes. Searches out signs of movement. Of pursuit. The dried branches and twigs work in his favor. He can see where they've been stepped on. Where they've snapped from the pressure. He sees on the bushes where some of the branches hang loose, broken as someone – like Mateo – has brushed past them at speed. He spots scars on trees where bullets have grazed them. Finds where one has embedded itself. He digs it out with the KA-BAR. Another 7.62 mm, its tip crumpled from the impact.

However, on the ground, there are no more spent cartridges. He double-checks this. Makes certain. There aren't any. They're all gone. Collected. Picked up and taken away. The armed men either came back for them, or else they gathered them up as they chased Mateo. Or they grabbed them as they made their escape. Potentially it was this last option, otherwise why would they have left the cartridges back where Tom fired upon them? They were worried about being fired on again. Worried that maybe he had something stronger than rubber slugs, and these were just warning shots.

Tom continues on. He picks up on two trails. One is heading back the way he just came. Mateo's pursuit. The other cuts off to the side. A shortcut back the way they came, perhaps. Tom sticks with Mateo's route. Follows it to its source. To, hopefully, whatever Mateo was running from.

The forest is peaceful. He can hear cicadas. Spots a couple of dragonflies hovering above the ground. It doesn't seem like the same place where, just hours before, there was a shoot-out. It's like it never happened. Time passes, and nature continues about its business. The insects and the animals, the trees and the bushes, the birds – none of them care about the men with the guns or the man they were chasing. They don't care about Tom. Don't care what he's doing. All they know is they need to stay out of his way.

As the sun rises, the day gets hotter. Tom begins to sweat. He pushes the cap back on his head and wipes sweat from his brow. He pauses to take a drink from his canteen, then continues on. The trail is strong. Made by a panicked chase, it's one of the easiest he's ever followed.

He follows it a few miles north. By his estimate, he's travelled about four miles from the area where he first saw them.

Five miles from his own station. It doesn't take him long to reach the entrance to Stephen and Freddy's area. To the left of the entrance is a steep rocky outcrop that rises up about twenty meters, lined with gnarled, spindly, hardy trees. To the right, through the thick trees, there is a sudden drop down to a ravine below. The entrance to the area runs only a couple of dozen yards, curving to the left, before it opens up into the quadrant beyond. The tunnel-like entrance is perpetually in darkness from the canopy of trees reaching overhead, their branches pressing up to the rocks to the left. Mateo's trail leads inside.

Freddy is leaning against a tree. He watches what Tom is doing. Watches his approach. "What're you doing?" he says, eyeing the shotgun.

"Following the trail from last night," Tom says. He stops, looks at Freddy. "I assume you heard about it."

Freddy grins. "Yeah, I heard about it," he says. "Stephen told me all about it. Heard you were playing at being spic savior again."

Tom knows Freddy is trying to piss him off. It's obvious from the look on his face. The way he grins, showing all his teeth. The way he lets his tongue flicker out, run over the top row of them.

Tom doesn't rise to him. Doesn't react to what he has said, but he does file it away. Compartmentalizes it in a small box at the back of his mind, labelled 'Freddy.' Tom won't forget. One day, perhaps when Tom is ready to move on from here, the two of them will have serious words, apart from everyone else. It may even take place at Freddy's home. Tom will discuss with him the many aspects of Freddy's life where he feels he could improve himself. Then they'll see if Freddy feels like grinning.

Tom points beyond Freddy. "The trail leads in there."

Freddy makes a show of looking at the ground. Of

following where Tom is pointing. "Well, shit. I wish you'd told me sooner. Chances are I've gone and walked all over it without even realizing."

"I'm sure I'll pick it up again," Tom says. He takes a step forward.

Freddy stumbles back, not expecting the movement. He almost falls. He holds up his hands, opens his mouth, but before he can respond, they both fall silent at the sound of footsteps approaching. They're coming from behind Freddy. They both look. It's Stephen.

"Oh, hey, Tom," he says, stepping out into the clearing. "You still up?"

"Looks like you are, too."

"It was an eventful night," Stephen says. "Don't think I would've got to sleep if I'd tried." He looks between Tom and Freddy. His usual casual smile falters somewhat, picking up on the tension in the air between the two men. He turns back to Tom. "What can we do for you this morning?"

"Says he's following a trail," Freddy says.

Stephen speaks to him over his shoulder. "I'm sure Tom can speak for himself."

"It leads into your area," Tom says.

"I tried telling him –" Freddy begins, but Stephen holds up a hand and motions for him to be quiet. He rolls his eyes at Tom. Shakes his head a little.

"Nothing to see, I'm afraid, Tom," Stephen says. "I've already looked the area over myself. Can't see any sign of anything. No armed men, no other runaways – not even any spent cartridges. My best guess is something happened on the road, and they chased him through here. We got damn lucky they didn't start a fire, that's all I'll say. It's *real* dry back there. They couldn't have picked a worse place to come racing through, especially if they were shooting at that point."

Tom grunts. He's about to press. He wants to get inside

the area, to take a look around. Maybe he'll see something Stephen missed. Before he can, he hears a vehicle off to his left. They all turn. A ranger SUV. Monica is driving. She sees them and turns, comes toward them. Gets as close as she can. She opens her window. "You're far from home, Rollins," she says.

"He's tracking," Freddy says, smirking.

"That so?" Monica says, looking impressed. "Find anything?"

"Trail dies back there," Stephen says, jerking a thumb back into his and Freddy's area. "Nothing to find, unfortunately. I already looked it over."

Monica nods along. "I see. Well, it sounds like you've hit a dead end, Rollins. You want a ride back to your station?"

Tom doesn't answer straight away. He looks to where the trail goes. "It's all right," he says finally, turning back to Monica. "I'll walk. I don't mind."

"No, come on, I insist," she says, waving him in. "Besides, I wanna talk to you about last night."

This gets his attention. She sees how he raises an eyebrow.

"Maybe nothing like that," she says, laughing. "I don't have any inside scoop. Come on, we'll talk on the drive."

Tom spares a last parting look at Stephen. At Freddy. At the trail. Then he goes around the SUV and gets inside.

10

From the direction Monica has come, they have to take the long way around to get back to Tom's station. They drive for about a mile before Monica says anything. "Y'know, I've worked here a long time," she says. "Ten years now. That's a lot longer than you've been on the scene."

Tom's window is down. Monica drives slowly, being careful on the trails, and so the air that comes in is still warm.

"And I don't mean to sound like I'm being condescending or anything," she says.

Tom nods. "Sure."

"I'm just trying to make a point, is all. And my point is this – in ten years, I've seen some downright *weird* things happen in this forest. I've seen some things I don't even know how to explain. Real strange shit that I can only put down to the heat and the solitude, when you're out there in the trees without another soul around, and maybe what you *think* you saw was just a trick of the light."

"Mateo being fired upon was no trick of the light," Tom says.

"No, I get that, I get it. I'm just setting the scene, is all. Gone a little off topic. Let's leave the spooky, maybe-all-in-the-mind stuff alone. Let's talk about tangibles. Things in this wood can get weird, and this I know. Especially when the college students start flooding the place. They get up to some shit. Some bacchanalian-type stuff, and I know that happens, I know it's for real, because I've had to clear it up. And sometimes we catch them in the act, and we've had to chase them on out, or help Reiko make some arrests. Something about the forest can just make people straight up lose their damn minds."

Tom listens, though he isn't sure where she's going with her story.

"I've used a lot of breath to make a short point," Monica says. "So I'll make this part fast." She glances at him. "Don't worry about Mateo." Her eyes return to the trail. "Don't worry too much about what you saw. Truth is, you'll likely never see any of them ever again. They chased some poor guy through here with their guns, and they went a little wild, but now they've moved on. And luckily, no one got hurt. But they ain't gonna be coming back here."

Monica makes a few tight turns. They're not far from his station now. Tom can see it up ahead.

He shrugs one shoulder. "I hope you're right about that."

Monica pulls to a stop in front of his station. The engine idles. She turns to him. Her hands rest on her right thigh. Tom takes his time getting out, thinking she has something else to say, something to wrap up with. She doesn't speak. Just watches him. He picks up his shotgun. She still hasn't said anything. He slides out so she can't see the Beretta tucked down the back of his trousers.

"Trust me," Monica says finally, leaning over before he can close the door. "You think on it too much, you're not gonna be able to sleep tonight. Gonna be jumping at every shadow and every little sound. Don't let it eat you up." She smiles at him. Being friendly. Reassuring. "They won't come back. As long as you're here, you'll never see anything like that again, trust me."

Tom nods, then closes the door. Monica turns her SUV around, then rolls away, taking her time as she goes. Tom watches her leave. He starts walking to his station, but then he stops. Something catches his eye. On the bottom porch step, there's some dried dirt. It's not a big deal, except Tom knows the last time he looked it wasn't there. He keeps the station clean.

Casually, he shifts the shotgun from where it's slung over his shoulder, so that he's holding it down by his side with his hand near the trigger. He doesn't inspect the dirt more closely. It's just a small clump of it, knocked loose by someone's boot. He circles around the station instead. Goes to the back, where the small bathroom is. There are some broken twigs directly below the window. What little grass there is has been flattened. In the dry dirt, he's able to make out a slight print impression. It looks like the sole of a combat boot. Someone has been looking in the window.

He goes back around the front, taking his time. Looking around, but not being obvious about it. He goes up onto the porch and stops by the main window. On the glass, there's a slight greasy smear. Someone has tried to wipe it away. It's where they've pressed their face to the glass with their hands cupped either side to block the light out. The imprint is likely from their hands.

Someone has been here. Someone has been looking in, front and back. It could have been a hiker in need of assistance or directions. Looking to report something, perhaps. What he's thought was a combat boot imprint could actually have been a hiking boot. If they knocked and there was no answer, they'd then press their face to the glass. That doesn't surprise Tom. What surprises him is that they'd then go around the back and try to look in there, too.

Tom runs his tongue around the inside of his mouth. Over his teeth. He unlocks the door, then glances back over his shoulder, through the trees, as if some kind of answer might be waiting there for him.

There isn't. There's nothing. Just the trees.

11

R eiko is in her office when Doris calls through on the intercom. Doris used to be Reiko's father's receptionist, back when he was the chief and she still lived in Saxton. She could be retired a few times over, but she claims she likes to keep busy. Reiko thinks a lot of the reason Doris sticks around is out of loyalty to her father. She can't help him anymore, so she'll help his daughter instead. She even moved here, to Oak Hills, when Reiko was transferred. Doris claims the town is so quiet it's like she *is* retired.

Doris only ever uses the intercom if someone is in the station and she's trying to look professional. The rest of the time, the space is so small she just turns her head and hollers. The call coming through instantly lets Reiko know that someone is present. She expects it to be her backup from Saxton. She's already been waiting long enough.

"I've got two gentlemen here to see you, Reiko."

"I'm coming through," Reiko says, standing. She has the blinds closed on her office door and can't see whom Saxton has sent.

She steps outside and sees it's not any of her fellow officers from Saxton. Instead, it's two men she doesn't know, wearing bulletproof vests with ICE printed across the front. One of them has a shaved head. The other has blonde hair, gelled and combed. Reiko frowns. "Hello?" she says, caught off guard.

One of them nods. The one with hair. He speaks. "Officer," he says, "we're from Immigration and Customs Enforcement. We received notification that you have an illegal immigrant in custody?"

"A call from who?" Reiko says.

"Saxton PD," the man says. "We're here to collect him from your custody and transport him to a holding facility."

Reiko blinks. "Saxton called you? They never told me."

The one with the shaved head shrugs. "You'll have to take that up with them."

Doris remains seated at her desk. She looks up at Reiko and the men, her head turning from side to side as she follows the conversation.

"I will," Reiko says. "But first I'm gonna need to see some ID."

"Of course," says the one with hair. They both pull out their IDs, hand them over. Reiko studies them. Everything is in order. She hands them back.

"I think I'd best call Saxton –" she says. She doesn't like the situation. It's off in a way she can't necessarily articulate. She feels it in her gut, though. It's telling her something isn't right.

"Ma'am, we heard there was a shoot-out," says the one with hair. "We've been led to understand that this individual has been chased and fired at. We don't have time to hang around. We need to get him somewhere secure, now, where he can be interrogated and we can find out what has happened, and what he might be involved in."

"He's part of an active investigation –"

"And we'll let you know where we take him," the agent says. "And we'll pass on any information that he may happen to share with us. But we're going to need you to take us to him right now."

Reiko hesitates. She looks them both over. Calling in ICE is the kind of thing Chief Grice would do. To fuck with her. Always trying to fuck with her.

"Officer?" the one with the shaved head prompts.

"I'm calling Saxton PD," she says, standing her ground. "I'm sure you understand."

Neither agent protests, but it's clear they're not happy to be kept waiting.

Doris has already dialled through. She holds the phone up to Reiko. Reiko takes it, tells the operator on the other end who she is, and that she needs put through to Chief Grice immediately. She's put on hold. Grice is in no hurry to answer. He's content to keep her waiting. Reiko tries not to let her rising annoyance show. The two ICE agents watch her. She stares back at them.

Finally, Grice answers. "Miller," he says.

Reiko gets straight to the point. "Chief Grice, I've got two ICE agents here wanting to take away my witness from the shoot-out in the forest, and they say you called them."

There's a brief pause, then Grice says, "That's right."

"That's right? Well, did you think maybe I should know about it?"

"You know about it now, don't you?"

Reiko can hear his grin. He's enjoying playing with her.

"I expect you to assist them in any way you can," Grice says, "and not to waste my, or their, time with inane phone calls. Hand over your prisoner – or *witness,* if that's what you want to call him – and send them on their way."

"Sir –"

"That's enough, Miller," Grice says, snapping. "I've made

myself clear enough, haven't I? You have your orders. Follow them. Oh, and tell the agents there I commend them on their response time. They've turned up quick." He hangs up before Reiko can respond.

She puts the phone down and looks at the two agents. Without a word, she leads them down to the cells. Mateo is awake now. He's sitting on the cot, his back against the wall. He stands up when he sees them enter. His eyes narrow when he sees ICE on both of the men's vests.

"Open it up," the one with hair says.

Reiko hesitates, but she does. She doesn't like it. She gets a bad feeling from the situation. She can't be sure an agency like ICE will have Mateo's best interests at heart.

The agent with the shaved head pulls a plastic zip tie from his pocket and steps into the cell. In Spanish, he tells Mateo to turn around and face the wall. Mateo does. He looks scared. Reiko can't watch his face. His expression makes her stomach sink.

They bind Mateo's wrists together and lead him from the cell. Mateo is too weak to object. He just lets them lead him along, up the stairs and back through the station to their waiting car outside. Reiko follows them. She speaks to the agent with hair. "When can I expect to be updated?"

"When we have anything to share," he says, glancing at her idly. "We have your number. We know where you are." He gets into the car.

In the backseat, Mateo watches her. Watches until the car pulls away and she can't see him anymore. She goes back inside.

"Well," Doris says. "I didn't care much for them."

"Mm," Reiko says.

"It doesn't surprise me at all that Linden would put a call in to immigration without giving you a heads-up first."

Reiko nods. "Same."

She has a bad feeling. The situation has made her feel sick. With a little time, she's sure she could have gotten Mateo to talk to her. He knew more than he was letting on. Why wasn't he sharing? What was he so scared of?

"Call Saxton," she says, heading for her office. "Ask them when I can expect my backup to be here, or if they've just decided against sending them and figured it wasn't worth telling me *that*, either."

Doris picks up her phone. "I'm on it."

Reiko closes her office door. Stands with her back against it, and presses her hands into her face. She thinks about Mateo. There are still butterflies in her stomach. She dreads to think where they're taking him. What they might subject him to, and where they'll spit him out when they're done with him.

She takes a deep breath. Calms herself. Focuses on her breathing. It helps. A little.

12

Tom writes a letter.

His shift ended not so long ago. He's taken a shower, gotten changed, then sat down at the small desk in his room and pulled out a sheet of paper and a pen. This is the fourth letter he's written this year. He sends them all to the same person. Taylor Hendricks, in Portland, Oregon.

He remembers her response to the first one he sent. She opened with:

This is the first letter I've ever written in my life. You really are old school, aren't you?

She was pleased to hear that he'd found work in the forest. Was glad he enjoyed it. She told him all about her new school. About her friends. How her brother and his wife were doing. They didn't talk of the past. Of what they had been through together in Washington. They spoke only of the present, and sometimes of the future.

Tom pulls out her last letter. It arrived a couple of weeks ago. He reminds himself of what she wrote. The last letter he sent, he also sent her a parcel. He'd gone along to Saxton to a small bookstore there and bought her a copy of *Crime And Punishment* by Dostoevsky. They'd talked about it while they travelled together. He'd told her he'd buy her a copy if they came across a bookstore. That hadn't happened, but he'd remembered saying it, and eventually kept his promise.

In her response, she thanked him for the book. She said she'd waited until she'd read it to respond. She enjoyed the book. She went into great detail about all the things she liked about it, and said she understood why it was one of his favorites. The rest of her letter was telling him about school. She said she enjoyed English most. This didn't surprise him, especially not after reading her in-depth analysis of *Crime And Punishment*.

Tom puts her letter back into his bag where he pulled it from. Tucked safely into an interior pocket with his picture of Alejandra. Absently, he scratches at his Santa Muerte tattoo. He turns his attention to the blank piece of paper in front of him. He isn't sure where to start. His mind is still racing with the events of the night before, not to mention his earlier discovery that someone had been looking in and around his station. These kinds of things aren't appropriate to tell her about. He likes telling her about his work in the forest. About the trees. About the animals he sees. About finding peace in nature, a light breeze prickling his skin and the sun shining down on the back of his neck. He doesn't want to tell her about rescuing a man from a gang of other men chasing him with guns. Taylor has already been in enough gunfights of her own. More than someone her age should ever have to endure.

Tom taps the end of the pen against his teeth. The page

remains blank. It feels like being back in school and having no idea how to answer a question that has been posed. Usually, it's not so hard to write the letters. Usually, it comes so easily. Right now, his mind is elsewhere.

He presses the pen to the paper, and he begins.

Dear Taylor,

I'm very glad you enjoyed the book. I deliberated for a long time between that and something by the Beats. As strange as it may sound, Crime And Punishment seemed the more appropriate option.

I also very much enjoyed your analysis of said book. You pointed some things out to me I'd never noticed for myself, and others that I'd long forgotten. You clearly have a talent for such things.

Speaking of, I'm glad to hear you're enjoying school. I'm glad to hear your brother and Tilly are well.

He pauses, reading over what he has already written. It's not a lot. This may end up being a short letter.

He leaves it as it is for now and pushes away from the desk. He steps outside onto the porch and takes a look around. The signs of someone creeping around have perturbed him. Put him on edge.

It's early evening. Not yet dark. Everything is quiet and calm. There's nothing to see. Nothing to be worried about. Not yet. He goes back inside. The shotgun is loaded with rubber slugs. He doesn't have any other ammo for it. He keeps it near to where he is at all times. The Beretta, too.

He sits back down at the desk and puts the unfinished letter to one side. He's going to sleep on it. He hasn't written enough yet. Too preoccupied. Can't focus the way he'd like. Instead, he does something he doesn't have to think too much about. Something that comes second nature. He strips and cleans the Beretta. It keeps his hands occupied. Keeps his mind clear, though it's free to wander. He turns his head to where he has put the letter on the bed, and reads over his lines. Thinks what else he might have to say. Thinks how he can finish it.

13

Reiko is frustrated.

Her backup from Saxton still hasn't arrived. She stands in the doorway to her office as darkness creeps in around her, and looks toward the station's entrance, almost willing them to appear. Saxton is fifty miles away. It shouldn't take a full day to get here. ICE made it in seemingly no time at all. She isn't sure what she might say when her backup finally does get here. *If* they ever get here. She knows it's not their fault. Any delays will come from Chief Grice. She can't help feeling annoyed, though.

Doris had gotten through to Saxton. They'd reassured her that backup was on its way. Would be with her any minute now.

Doris went home a few hours ago. Backup still hasn't arrived. Doris's parting words were, *Don't stay here all night, Reiko. Go home. Get some rest. If they turn up and you're not here, they have your number. Make them wait for you this time.*

Reiko nodded, but she knew she wouldn't take her advice.

She goes to the kitchen area and makes herself a cup of coffee. It's too late to make a fresh pot, so she just drinks what's left. It's burnt and bitter. She grimaces at the taste, but the taste isn't why she's drinking it.

Headlights cut across the front of the station. Reiko doesn't get her hopes up. There's an intersection directly opposite. Lights have been cutting across the front since it first started to get dark. This pair keep coming, though. They get closer. There's a second pair. Another vehicle is following. They come to a stop directly in front of the station. Reiko allows herself to get her hopes up, and those hopes promptly turn back to annoyance. She puts the coffee down and steps outside to meet them.

Two vehicles. A Saxton PD cruiser, as expected. The other is an SUV. She frowns at it. Two men get out. They're wearing vests that say ICE across the front.

The Saxton officers get out of the cruiser. One black, one white. She doesn't know the white guy. The black guy, however, is Greg Noble. An old friend. They went to the academy together. She's pleased to see him. At least, she *would* be pleased if it weren't for the extra set of ICE agents.

"Reiko," Greg says. "Good to see you."

"Good to finally see you," Reiko says.

Greg raises an eyebrow at this. "Finally?"

"I called this morning."

Greg looks at the other cop. The other cop just shrugs, raises his eyebrows. "We were told about two hours ago," Greg says. "Then we had to wait for the agents here to arrive."

"That's another thing," Reiko says, pointing at the two immigration agents. "Why are they here now?"

"What do you mean?"

"Two ICE agents came by earlier."

Everyone falls silent. Greg looks at the ICE agents. One of them takes a step forward. "We're the first ones here, ma'am," he says. "No one else has been here before us."

Reiko looks back at the agent who spoke. "Two came by

earlier," she says. "And took away my witness. I checked their IDs. I spoke to Chief Grice, and he told me he'd sent them."

"Chief Grice called us," the agent says, "and we're here now. I assure you, we're the first to get here."

Reiko's mind races. She grinds her teeth. Without another word, she turns and races back into the station. She throws herself down behind Doris's desk and brings up the security footage from the front of the building. She starts rewinding back to when the earlier pair of agents arrived and took Mateo away.

"*Shit*," she says. Something had felt off. But their ID was in order. Saxton told her they'd called immigration.

The four men have followed her in. "Tell me what's happened," Greg says. He comes around the desk behind her.

Reiko gets the car and the men up on screen, motions for the ICE agents to come around and look. "I don't recognize them," the speaker from outside says. "But that doesn't mean anything. Let me make a call. Make sure there hasn't been some crossed wires somewhere." He pulls out his phone and steps to one side.

Reiko looks at Greg. "I think I know how that call's going to go," she says.

Greg nods grimly. "No crossed wires."

"No crossed wires." She turns back to the screen, jots down the model and license of the car, along with a brief description of each 'agent,' as well as Mateo. "Either he knew them already," she says, thinking of Mateo, "or he didn't know them at all, and he's in a world of trouble right now."

The ICE agent returns, slipping his phone into his pocket. He shakes his head. "We're the first here."

Reiko reaches for the phone. "Then we need to put out an APB." She starts dialling. "*Fuck.*"

14

Tom has returned to his letter to Taylor. He'd thought he might sleep on it, but he decided to get back to it. To get it done.

It's late. It's warm in his station, and he has his bedroom window open a crack. It doesn't let in much in the way of cool air. There isn't much of that going around at the moment. Not during this heatwave. Instead, he gets to hear the sound of the cicadas. The occasional rustling of a bush as a predator stalks its prey. It's a soothing kind of background noise. One that he's grown accustomed to over the last year. It calms his mind. Helps him to concentrate on the letter to Taylor. Clears away his racing thoughts of the gunfight and Mateo, and the mystery therein. Makes him think that maybe Monica was right. Maybe he'll never see or hear anything about Mateo and the others again. It'll become like it never happened at all.

The loudest cicadas, the ones nearest his window, fall silent. Tom almost doesn't notice. It's not uncommon. But then he hears a dry twig snap. He stiffens, but he doesn't move from the desk where he sits. The sound was near his window. Whoever is out there could be looking in right now. Could be looking directly at him.

Tom keeps the pen in his right hand. Keeps it to the paper like he's still writing. His left hand slides up the desk, to where the Beretta is. He listens to the window. To the shifting in the air there. The difference in the sounds. How some of them are blocked out by someone stepping right up to where the window is open.

Tom grabs the Beretta and pushes himself off the chair. He rolls to the side and comes up on one knee, pointing the gun out in front of him, toward the window. There's a shadow there, only partially lit by the lamp in his room. The shadow panics at his sudden movement. At his being armed. Tom spots a rifle. It's not pointing at him. Tom can't fire. Can't take the risk. He doesn't know for sure who this is.

"If you don't want to get shot, you'd better tell me who you are," he says.

The shadow doesn't respond. Not verbally, anyway. It swings the rifle toward him. Tom fires. Glass shatters. The shadow drops from view. Tom isn't sure he hit it.

Tom presses himself against the wall along from the window. He gets close, gun pointing. Looks outside through the broken glass. There's no one there. No body.

Through the window, he can hear further noise. Further movement. It's coming from around the front. He hears voices. There's more than one of them. Just like last night. Tom grabs his bag, slings it over his back. Grabs the shotgun. It won't do as much damage as he'd like, but it can at least subdue them. Slow them down. Maybe scare them off again.

The window at the front of the station smashes. It wasn't a big smash. They threw something small. Something that he can hear rolling over the floorboards. Tom recognizes the sound. It could be a grenade.

His knee-jerk reaction is to jump out the window. That

would be a mistake. They could be waiting for him. Expecting this. Standing to the side, ready to pick him off. Instead, he dives down the side of the bed. Pushes the frame up onto its side so the mattress and the frame will take the brunt of any of the explosion that manages to get through the wall.

This all happens in the space of a few seconds. He was right. It was a grenade. It explodes. Tom feels the station shake. It's not strong enough to bring down the wall. He doesn't hear another one thrown in. The men outside are going to come in after it. They'll think he's dazed. Easy pickings.

Tom goes to the bedroom door. He waits. Listens. Keeps one eye on the bedroom window. He hears them come up the porch steps. Hears them kick the door open. They'll come in hot. Guns raised, waving. Searching him out. He gives them a second to cool down. They're coming to his door. Tom throws open the door, fires the shotgun. There are two guys. They're wearing ski masks, despite the heat. The rubber slug catches the one at the front in the chest. The impact throws him back into the one behind him.

There are two more men on the porch. They open fire. Tom throws himself down. The bullets tear through the walls. Chunks are blown out of the wood above and behind him. Splinters rain down around him. He crawls toward the bedroom window. He grabs his bag on the way. By now, the gunfight at the front should have drawn away whoever might have been standing on guard there. In case it hasn't, he pulls out the Beretta.

The men in the front are leaving the station. The gunfire has stopped. Tom peers out the window, looks both ways. He climbs out and drops to the ground, staying low.

"*Light this motherfucker up!*"

The voice comes from the front. Tom knows it can't mean

anything good. He starts running for the trees. Behind him, the men fill the station with grenades. They explode. Flaming pieces of wood sail through the air, risking a forest fire. There's nothing left of the station.

Tom looks back. They won't be satisfied with blowing up the station. That was just to flush him out. They want his body. They've come to kill him. If he runs, they'll chase him like they chased Mateo.

He doesn't run. He circles back, using the trees for cover. He knows this area well. Moves from cover to cover with ease. Gets the drop on them. There's four of them. Tom fires. Catches one of them in the shoulder. He cries out, goes down. The others are caught by surprise. They panic. Start firing back. Their shooting is wild. They can't see him. They lay down suppressing fire.

Tom takes cover behind a wide redwood. He peers out. One of the men keeps firing. The two others are hauling up the one he shot. They flee. When they're far enough away, the shooter turns and hurries after them.

Tom wants to follow. He starts to, but he stops himself as he draws alongside the burning station. Left unattended, the fire will spread. There's no one else here to stop it. He has to let them go. Right now, stopping the fire is more important.

15

Reiko feels herself being pulled in all directions. She's never experienced anything like this before in Oak Hills.

There's been another gunfight in the forest. It involved the ranger again. Rollins. This time, there's been an explosion, too. They've blown up his station. Risked a potential forest fire.

Reiko is racing there now. She's left Greg and the other guy – Johnny, he was called – behind. The ICE agents left soon after the APB was put out. They didn't seem impressed, but Reiko doesn't care about that right now, or about them. She's not impressed, either. If Grice had kept her informed, kept her up to date, none of this would have happened. If two strangers who look the part turn up and they have the appropriate ID, and Saxton PD is telling her right in front of these 'agents' that *yes*, they did call immigration, then what the hell else is she supposed to do?

She gets to the forest and follows the smoke. Even in the dark, she can see it rising to the sky through the trees. When she gets to the scene, she sees half a dozen rangers hurrying

around, as well as the volunteer fire department. The nearest
fire station is in Saxton, but with Oak Hills being so close to
the forest, it was necessary to form a volunteer department.
Together they've managed to contain the flames, prevent
them from spreading.

Reiko gets out of her cruiser, rushes over. She can see
Rollins. He's standing with Ron, Stephen, and Monica.
There's a bag on his back. He doesn't look spooked, like she'd
expect from someone whose workplace/home has just been
attacked and blown up. Instead, he looks focused. He barely
blinks. He stares off through the trees, like he's searching.

"Another close call," Reiko says to him, stepping up. She
looks him over. He's dishevelled, and he smells of fire, but he
looks otherwise unharmed.

He grunts, his eyes narrowed.

"You get a good look at them? Same men as last night?"

"They were wearing masks," Tom says. "And there were at
least four of them this time."

"They say anything to you?"

He shakes his head.

"What kind of people are running around my forest?"
Ron says, exasperated, posing the question to no one in
particular.

Monica reaches out to him with a sympathetic expression. She squeezes his shoulder and strokes his back.

"Two nights in a row?" Ron goes on. "What the hell is
going on here?"

Monica takes Ron by the arm and leads him to the side.
He's more worked up than Tom is. Stephen pats Tom on the
back, then follows them. Reiko is left alone with Tom. "How'd
you scare them off this time?" she says. "The shotgun again?"

"Beretta," Tom says.

"The rangers don't carry firearms," she says. "I assume it's
your own personal weapon?"

He nods.

"Do you have a permit for it?"

"I got it from the government," Tom says. "When they needed me to do their dirty work."

"There's no need to sound so touchy," Reiko says. "I'm just asking. Under the circumstances, it's a lucky thing you had it. But you understand I have to ask. I need to understand every angle. It's my job."

Tom finally tears his eyes away from the darkness through the trees to look at her. He blinks, and it's almost like he's realizing for the first time whom he's talking to. "Sure," he says.

"Walk me through it," Reiko says. "Tell me what happened."

Tom does. Tells her how he'd noticed signs people had been looking in on his station earlier in the day. How it got late, and they came back.

"Any idea why they came after you?"

Tom shrugs. "Far as I can guess, it'd be because of last night. I saw their faces. They've got to know I saw their faces."

"Seems excessive," Reiko says.

"I agree," Tom says. "It's *very* excessive, especially for what I've theorized."

"Maybe there's another reason," Reiko says. "Something we haven't considered. Something we don't know about."

"Maybe so," Tom says. "Or maybe it could be they're pissed that I helped Mateo get away."

He must see how her face darkens at the mention of Mateo's name.

"What?" he says. "What's happened?"

Reiko tells him. Before he can respond, Reiko gets a call on her radio. It's Greg. They've found Mateo. It's not good news.

"I need to go," she says.

Tom heard enough of the radio conversation. "I'm coming with," he says.

"I can't let you do that."

"I've been shot at twice now," Tom says. "They've tried to blow me up. They've nearly burned the forest down. All because I helped Mateo."

Reiko shakes her head. "They all sound like more reasons why you shouldn't come."

"Then how about this," Tom says, changing tactic. "You already know I used to be in the Army. After that, I did some specialist stuff. I'm highly trained, Officer Miller. Whatever you're heading out to, I could be of use. Maybe I could see something others wouldn't."

Reiko considers this. There are definite pros to what he has said. "All right," she says. "But when we're out there, stick close to me." She goes to her cruiser, and Tom follows. He swings the bag from his back into the footwell.

"Do you still have the Beretta on you?" Reiko says, turning the car around and heading back out of the forest, toward the outskirts of town, toward where Greg told her they'd found Mateo.

"Yes," Tom says.

"Keep it hidden. I can't guarantee who the other cops on the scene are going to be, and they might not take kindly to you open-carrying."

Tom doesn't answer. He looks straight for a long time, until they're on the road, the blue-and-red lights flashing overhead.

"Is Mateo dead?" he says finally.

Reiko doesn't lie. "Yes," she says. "I think he is."

16

There's a car burning by the side of the road. There's a fire truck nearby. There is only one volunteer truck in Oak Hills. This one must have come from Saxton. It's still working on putting out the fire. Reiko tells him the burning car is the one the fake ICE agents drove away in.

They're on the outskirts of Oak Hills, about ten miles west. The smoldering car is parked under some trees near a picnic area. The trees look dry enough that, again, this burnout could have caused a potentially dangerous fire.

The area is lit up blue and red by the spinning lights on the tops of the cruisers already present, as well as the fire truck. There are half a dozen police officers standing around. The area has been cordoned off. A couple of them are standing away from the others, by some trees, looking in on something. Their faces are pale and grim.

Reiko gets out of the cruiser, and Tom follows. Another of the cops comes toward her, eyeing Tom warily.

"He's with me, Greg," Reiko says. "This is Tom Rollins. He's the guy whose been shot at these last two nights."

"The guy who found Mateo in the first place?" Greg says.

"That's right."

Greg nods at him, and Tom returns it.

"Is Mateo here?" Reiko says.

Greg nods, then motions her to follow. Tom keeps up. The other cops notice him, but they don't pay him much attention. He's with Reiko, and that's good enough for them. Greg leads them to the area of trees where Tom spotted the two cops looking in. It's his and Reiko's turn now.

There's a body there. It's Mateo, but it takes them both a moment to realize it. The body is naked. It has been dismembered. The arms have been severed at wrists, elbows, and shoulders; the legs at ankles, knees, and hips. They've been laid out like some kind of bloody anatomy deconstruction. Mateo's head has been cut off and propped up. There's something in his mouth. Tom sees a gaping hole in his chest and realizes they've cut out his heart. This is what's in his mouth.

"Jesus," Reiko says.

"Yeah," Greg says.

"There's a lot of blood," Tom says. "He was still alive when they started cutting." He's looking at Mateo's neck, where the blood from there has spilled over his shoulders and the top of his chest. "They might've started with his arms. The extremities. So he could feel it and see it. Tourniquet it off to keep him alive. They didn't do the same at his legs. Too many important veins and arteries in the legs. They killed him before they did that. There's not so much blood on his lower half. They cut off his head. That's what killed him. By the time they got to his heart, there probably wasn't anything left in it."

Greg looks at him sideways. "Who's this guy?" he says to Reiko.

"He's ex-Army," Reiko says, though she's frowning, like

maybe she wouldn't expect him to have this kind of knowledge from the military.

"I've had some experience with cartels," Tom says. "This looks like their kind of handiwork."

Reiko frowns at this, staring at the body. She's thinking, most likely about the men in the diner that Tom saw her watching. She looks at Tom, though, catches his eye. They're both thinking MS-13.

"Cartels," Greg says. "Reiko, you said the guys who picked him up were white? You think they were crooked agents, on a cartel payroll?"

"The two you brought with you didn't recognize them," Reiko says. "We can check further, but I don't think they are. I think they were convincing frauds, likely with cartel money to *make* them look so convincing."

"Mateo didn't look like a runaway cartel member," Tom says. "Too malnourished, for a start. They'd been working him, likely with a gun to his back." Tom gets down on his knees, gets in closer to the body without touching it. Gets close to one of the severed hands. The left. "Did you notice this?" he says, pointing at the hand and turning to Reiko. Reiko comes in next to him, looking at the hand. "It's not so obvious now, but when he still had circulation, his hands were covered in bruises. Lots of little cuts and scrapes, too. And his fingernails, you see them? They're chipped, and look at the dirt under them."

Reiko nods, then stands back up. "The guys you saw in the forest were white too, right?"

"The ones last night, yeah," Tom says, moving away from the body. "One of them was black when I saw them chasing Mateo." He divulges his theory. "I think they were mercenaries. Could be ex-military. Ex-security forces. Could be they just like playing tough and getting paid for it. I'd reckon at least some of them have to have some kind of background and training. I followed their trail back through the forest earlier today. Save for where I chased them off, every area where I could find evidence of gunfire, they'd picked up their spent shells."

"That denotes some kind of professionalism," Reiko says.

"Like I said, they didn't get them all. The ones I found are in my bag. They're yours, but I'm not sure they're gonna be able to tell you much."

"Everything's worth checking," Reiko says.

Tom keeps looking down at Mateo's dismembered corpse. Remembers the last thing Mateo said to him as Reiko was leading him away. *Thank you.*

"If I'm right, and they're mercenaries," Tom says, "they could be working for a cartel."

"Why dump him by the side of the road?" Greg says. "Why burn out the vehicle?"

"Burn out the vehicle to get your attention," Tom says. "Not just yours. Everyone's. Mateo is a message. A message to anyone else who might try to run away. Could be a message to the whole town – the whole county. If I'm right about Mateo being used for labor – slave labor – we don't know where they're getting these workers from. We don't even know where they're putting them to work. Mateo was Mexican, and maybe they transported him up here, but that's not to say all their workers are. They could be people from the towns. Their families could be under observation. Told to behave themselves and keep their mouths shut. You know how they operate."

Reiko and Greg nod.

"It's a warning to everyone."

17

Reiko gives Tom a ride back to the forest. They left the scene just as forensics were arriving.

"You have much cartel activity in the area?" Tom says as they drive.

Reiko shakes her head. "Other than the men you saw me watching in the diner, none."

"And what do you make of them?"

"I've been watching them," Reiko says. "But I can't be certain they're MS-13."

"I saw their tattoos," Tom says. "That's usually a certifiable sign."

"I know plenty of people who've regretted past tattoos," Reiko says. "Right now, all they're guilty of is killing Clyde's business. He's pulling his hair out."

"Anything else? Anything other than them?"

"No," Reiko says.

They reach the forest. Reiko comes to a stop in front of headquarters. Tom doesn't get straight out. "You've got two active crime scenes," he says. "Which one are you going back to?"

"Neither," Reiko says. "There's nothing for me at either of them right now. Forensics are at both. I can read what they find later."

"What're you gonna do instead?"

"I'm gonna do my job," she says. "I'm going to investigate."

Tom grabs his bag from the footwell and prepares to get out of the cruiser. "You have a starting point in mind?"

Reiko doesn't answer, but she nods.

Tom doesn't push his luck. Reiko isn't the kind to share. She's a good cop. She knows what she's doing. He wants to know, though. Wants to know what is happening, and who's behind it. Wants to know who has killed Mateo. Who has taken a shot at him.

Tom leans in before he closes the door. "Good luck," he says. He closes the door. He fully expects to see her again soon. Their paths will cross. They're heading for the same destination, just neither of them knows what it is.

Tom heads into headquarters. He needs a shower.

Ron is waiting for him inside the foyer. "Tom," he says. "I saw the cruiser. I figured it was probably dropping you back off."

Tom nods. Before he can say anything, Ron continues.

"Come on into my office a minute, Tom," he says. "I just need to talk to you real quick."

Tom follows. Ron closes the door to his office once he's inside and motions him to take a seat. Then he goes around the desk to the other side. His hands fidget on top of the paperwork he has spread out in front of him. He hesitates. He has something tough he needs to say, but he doesn't want to say it.

"Listen, Tom, I'm real sorry about this," he says. "But these men, whoever they are, they came back looking for you. Presumably, they were trying to kill you." Ron shakes his head, like he still can't believe he's having to say this. "Makes me sick, it really does. Feel like I've gotten an ulcer since this whole damn thing started. But they came back here, after you, and... I'm real sorry, but I'm gonna have to place you on leave, Tom. For your own safety. For the forest's safety, too. Those crazy bastards nearly started a damn wildfire last night. I can't take a risk on anything like that happening again, or on any of my other rangers getting hurt or killed. I'm sorry, Tom. I truly am. But I believe the safest place for you to be right now is away from here."

He sighs, shakes his head. "At least until the police have done their job. Once they've got to the bottom of it all and cleared this whole mess up, then you can come straight on back to us."

Ron looks at Tom like he's worried how he's going to react. He's bracing himself.

Tom takes a deep breath. He nods. "I understand, Ron," he says. "That makes sense. I don't want anyone else to get hurt, either."

Ron sighs with relief. "Thank you, Tom," he says. "I'm glad you understand. And listen, Monica is just outside, in the break room, I've spoken to her already, and she's waiting to give you a ride back into Oak Hills."

"I appreciate that," Tom says, standing. "I'll get going now. No point in hanging around."

"I *am* sorry about all this, Tom," Ron says.

"I know," Tom says, leaving the office.

Monica is standing in the break room door, waiting. She shakes her head and holds out her hands. "This sure is a heap of shit, Rollins," she says. "Just nothing we can do about it."

"There's one thing we can do," Tom says.

Monica tilts her head to the side. "Yeah?"

"We can get me into town so I can take a damn shower."

Monica grins. "Let me grab my keys."

18

Reiko thinks she's managing to hide it, but she's shaken by what happened to Mateo. It's not so much what she saw. She's prepared for such gruesome sights. She steeled herself a long time ago, knowing that such horrors could potentially come with the territory. Of course, she never expected to see anything like this in Oak Hills. Being here for so long could have softened her, but she doesn't think it has.

No, what has shaken her is that it happened right under her nose. They took him from her, and she let them.

She's angry. Not so much at herself. She did her job. She did it right. Did everything she was supposed to. Their IDs were in order. Saxton told her they'd called immigration. They never told her when they'd reach her, same way they never told her when her backup would arrive. Same old story. Chief Grice leaving her to rot, except this time his wilful negligence has caused a man's gruesome death.

It's *him* she's angry at. Chief Linden Grice. A grade A asshole. Her father used to say the exact same thing about him.

She knows how it's going to go. Grice, despite speaking to her on the phone and telling her directly that he'd called immigration, won't shoulder any personal responsibility. He'll put it all on her. The only question now is when he'll do it. Soon, no doubt. Always desperate to cover his own ass.

Reiko drives across town. She goes to Bull Draven's house.

Bull was released from California State Prison in Sacramento two years ago. He moved in with his two nephews in Oak Hills. Josh and Kai. Their father was Kurt Draven. Bull's brother. He died five years ago, while Bull was still locked up.

When Reiko found out he was coming to town, she did her research. Bull had been arrested for large-scale cultivation and distribution of hydroponic marijuana. He'd served eight years of his sentence. Got out early for good behavior. Reiko had been surprised at the length of his sentence. Turned out he'd been running a *large*-scale operation. The judge had decided to make an example.

For two years, Reiko has kept an eye on Bull Draven. For two years, he's behaved himself. He barely leaves the house. Goes out in his truck only to get food or to pick up his nephews when they get back from their jobs as cross-country truckers. He's kept his nose clean. So far as she can tell, he doesn't even touch weed. Not anymore.

She stops the cruiser in front of his house. Wipes sweat from her eyes. Even with the air conditioning running, the car still feels like a hotbox. She takes a deep breath. Considers what she's doing here.

When she works a case, she likes to approach it from all angles. To look at it from every possible perspective. Consider every outcome. Sometimes, looking from every angle, considering every outcome, means using a different set of eyes.

She knocks on Bull's door.

When he answers, she has a feeling he's already noticed her cruiser out front. He opens the door with raised eyebrows and a ready smile. "Officer Miller," he says, "this is an unexpected pleasure, and so early in the day. What can I do for you?"

"Is it all right if I come inside?" Reiko says.

"I guess that depends what for," Bull says.

"Just to talk."

"Just to talk, huh?" His smile never fades. "Am I in trouble?"

"You tell me," Reiko says.

Bull chuckles. "Come on in, Officer." He steps aside, holds the door wide.

Reiko has seen the outside of the house plenty of times, but this is her first time inside. It's modest. It's also a lot cooler than it was in her cruiser. She can hear the hum of fans running in the living room. On their way there, she sees framed pictures of Bull's dead brother on the wall along the hallway. Some of them are of Kurt and his kids, Josh and Kai. Some are of Kurt and Bull – as kids and as men. Some are of all four of the men together. Reiko can't help but notice that here in the hallway there are no pictures of the Draven women. She supposes the absence of Josh and Kai's mother makes sense. She ran out when they were still young. So far as she's aware, though, Bull's nephews are still in contact with their sister. Reiko guesses maybe there's pictures of her in the rest of the house.

In the living room, there is a sofa against the rear wall. Two chairs, one either side. She takes a seat in the one nearest the window and the television, so she can see the door. Bull lowers himself into the corner of the sofa, spreads his arms along the back and the armrest. There are four fans plugged in and running. They all point toward the sofa, but Reiko catches enough of a breeze from them.

"What can I do for you, Officer Miller?" Bull says. "Or would you prefer Reiko?"

"Officer Miller is just fine," Reiko says. Before she can say anything else, he beats her to the punch.

"I don't suppose this has anything to do with that messy business just outside town?" he says. "Or the gunfights in the forest?"

Reiko is caught off guard, but she manages to hide her surprise. Keeps her composure. "Why would it be?"

Bull shrugs.

Reiko watches him. "How do you know about all that?"

"Oak Hills is a small town," he says. "News travels fast. Big news travels fastest of all. A shoot-out in the national forest two nights running? Well, that's the biggest news Oak Hills has ever had. Except, then along comes a dismembered body." He raises his eyebrows. "Now that's some *big* fucking news, wouldn't you say?"

"And why would I come to see you about it?"

"That's what I'm wondering myself," Bull says. He looks at her for a long time before he answers. "At a guess, I would say you're here to see me looking for some insights. Because of my background."

Reiko returns his look. "All right, then," she says. "I won't beat around the bush. You ever deal with cartels?"

"Dangerous business, cartels," Bull says. "Always made sure to steer very clear of them. While I was on the outside."

Reiko picks up on the pause before his last statement. "And while you were on the inside?"

Bull holds up his hands. "On the inside is a different matter altogether. You do your best to avoid all kinds of undesirables, but do you really think that's achievable?"

He waits so long she figures this is a question he wants her to answer. "Sacramento State Prison is a big place."

"Not big enough, believe me."

"Then what was your experience with them while you were inside?"

Bull leans his head back a little, looks up into the corner of the ceiling. He drums his fingers on the armrest. Thinking. "Nothing that I could imagine would help you. Although, cutting a man up is certainly their style." He smiles. "So ask the questions you want to know, and I'll answer them. Though like I say, I'm not sure how I can help."

"MS-13," she says.

"I've seen them around."

"In Sacramento, or here?"

"Both. You're talking about the boys who like to take up space in Clyde's Diner."

"You consider they could be ex? Maybe they've come here to get away from it all?"

Bull smirks. "No such thing. You're in, you're in for life. That's why they used to tattoo their faces. They don't all do that so much anymore. Try to avoid attracting so much attention to themselves. Come to a small town like this, might as well have a neon sign that says *Look at this illegal thing I'm doing.*"

"They could still be hiding out."

"Less than one hundred and fifty miles from Sacramento? They ain't very smart if they are. They'd wanna get themselves a lot further east. A *lot.* And even then, they'd be looking over their shoulders the rest of their lives."

"You keep in touch with anyone from prison?"

Bull shakes his head. "No, ma'am. I got out, and I'm staying out. Keeping my nose clean, you know me. I won't waste another single day of my life behind bars, and you don't accomplish that by keeping in touch with people who're still there."

"So you have no way of finding out that, *if* there is cartel activity in this area, what exactly they're up to?"

Bull shakes his head. "And I'm afraid, Officer, that I'm not going to offer to ask around, either."

Reiko holds his eye. "You moved some big-time product back in your day," she says. She's about to push some buttons, and she knows it.

Bull's affable expression doesn't falter. "Can't deny that," he says. "What's done is done. But I've paid my debt."

"And that was in Saxton. Whole family came from Saxton, didn't they?"

"That's right."

"And now here you are, in Oak Hills."

"Moved in with my nephews. You know that, Officer."

"Why'd they move here?"

Bull smiles. "Their daddy died. And they were escaping the taint of my being arrested. The Draven name isn't worth dirt in Saxton. At least Oak Hills offered them a chance to start over. Plus, their sister was already here, and she was settled and happy, so why not?"

Reiko leans back in her chair a little, mimicking Bull's relaxed posture. "When I was transferred here, I made sure to acquaint myself with Oak Hills and its history. I like to know the place I'm protecting. And I won't lie, it shocked me how few records there were. I mean, I'd been told Oak Hills was a peaceful place. I'd been told I'd be bored out of my head most of the time. But until I sat down and read through the records and the history and then realized it had taken me no time at all – well, that's the only real way to do it any kind of justice. There's been crime. Of course there has. No place is untouched by at least *some* darkness. But the sheer lack of *major* crime is truly mind-boggling. Y'know, at first, I thought maybe this peace and quiet was a sign of something else. Some grand conspiracy. Thought maybe my predecessor here had been dirty, and he was hiding some things. But that was just the boredom talking. It really was. I looked into Oak Hills. I asked around. And the truth is, it really is just as peaceful as it seems. Picture perfect, isn't it?

The kind of American town people wrote songs about back in the fifties and sixties. The kind of town you'd find on a postcard.

"I don't know, maybe it's how close we all are to the forest. Maybe there's something calming about it. Soothes the desires of otherwise dangerous people. I talk to the rangers, of course, and I know they would disagree. They say they get to their busy season, and it's like people come here just to lose their minds. But in all honesty, it's never anything that can't easily be handled. Nothing in Oak Hills ever is. Until recently. Until the last couple of days, in fact. And all of a sudden, seemingly out of nowhere, we have gunfights in the forest and a dead body by the side of the road. And if we go back a little further, although not too far, from what I've been led to understand – maybe just a month or two – we have some potential MS-13 gangbangers show up. It just makes you scratch your head and ask, *What is going on in Oak Hills?*" She looks at Bull. "What do *you* think is going on in Oak Hills?"

"I honestly couldn't say, Officer," he says. His posture, his expression, never changes.

"You're the only man in this town has a background matches up to anything like this."

"I've never killed anyone."

"I'm sure if I were able to talk to the head of a cartel, they'd tell me the same thing. There are heads of any number of violent gangs across the United States who would likely brag about that."

Bull starts to chuckle. "Officer Miller, if you think I have any kind of sway over MS-13, or whomever may be responsible for what's happening here, you give me too much credit. Any power I may have had, I lost the moment I was arrested." He changes position for the first time. Sits forward and clasps his hands together, but he's still smiling. "I've been in Oak

Hills for two years now, Officer," he says. "Two years. And in all that time, there hasn't been any trouble. Isn't that right?"

Reiko doesn't answer. She doesn't have to. Bull already knows he's right.

"But then you're all worked up about these MS-13 showing their faces, and you've got bullets and bodies. So I'm afraid I can't help you," he says. "Whatever you may think about me, I don't know anything about anything. And I like it that way." He leans back into the sofa, returns to his earlier pose. "But I think you already know who could be responsible, really. You just came here to confirm your suspicions."

He looks at Reiko, and she looks back. Neither of them says anything for a while.

Finally, Reiko stands. "Thank you for your time, Bull," she says.

"Don't mention it, Reiko."

She shoots him a look. He grins. "Don't get up," she says. "You look comfortable. I'll show myself out."

19

Monica hasn't said much on the drive into Oak Hills. It isn't like her. She's usually very talkative. Tom doesn't mind, though. He's appreciated the silence. It's given him a chance to think about things. To go over the events of the last couple of days. To consider what his next moves may be.

She speaks as the town comes into view. "You really do need a shower," she says.

"I know," Tom says.

"Even with the windows down, you've stunk up the inside of my SUV with the smell of burning."

"Yeah," Tom says. "It doesn't smell too good to me, either."

Monica laughs. "Where are you going to stay?" she says. "Where do you want me to drop you off?"

"The motel on the other side of town," Tom says. "You know the one?"

"Yeah. Is that where you usually stay when you're out of the forest?"

Tom shrugs. "Sometimes. I mix it up."

There's a silence, but it's loaded. He can tell that Monica

is about to say something else. Thinking about how to phrase the question she wants to ask.

"What are you going to do next?" she says. "Are you going to hang around and hope this all clears up and you can come back to work, or are you gonna move on?"

"I'm not moving on," Tom says.

"Yeah? You've had some guys try to kill you, Rollins."

"That's exactly why I'm not moving on," Tom says. "And they *have* killed Mateo." He shakes his head. "I don't know what he was involved in. I don't know why he was running from them, or why they've killed him in such a way, it's like they're making an example. But I do know that he was terrified. And that when I helped him, he was grateful. I can't just walk away from what happened to him."

"Even when it doesn't have anything to do with you?"

"It had everything to do with me the minute I found them chasing him."

Monica looks concerned. "I get the feeling there's nothing I can say that's gonna make you change your mind."

Tom doesn't answer.

"Look, just be careful, okay? I don't want you going and getting yourself hurt, Rollins."

"I appreciate the concern."

They reach the motel. Monica pulls to a stop in front of it, near the office.

"Well," Tom says, grabbing his bag, "thanks for the ride."

"Thanks for stinking up my ride," Monica says.

Tom laughs, then goes and checks in. The receptionist recognizes him. Tom has been a regular this last year, apart from the rare occasions the motel has already been fully booked up. "You look like hell, man," he says.

"Feel it," Tom says. He signs for the room, pays, then heads back outside to walk along to it. Monica is still in the parking lot. Her engine is idling. She's on her phone. She sees

Tom come back out, and she smiles and waves. Tom waves back, then goes to his room. It's up the stairs. To the right. Third room from the end. He pushes the door open and steps inside. As he turns to close the door, he sees Monica pulling out of the parking lot. Heading back to the forest. He watches her go. Wishes he were going back there. He has unfinished business in the forest.

It'll have to wait. He goes inside the room. Locks the door. Does his usual security checks. He's dirty, and he's tired, but that's no excuse to be lax. Only after he's checked the locks and the windows and escape routes does he allow himself to get in the shower.

20

W hen Reiko gets back to the station, Doris looks concerned.

"What's happened now?" Reiko says, trying to make sure her shoulders don't sag.

"Chief Grice has been calling for you."

Reiko lets her shoulders sag. She rolls her eyes. She knew it was coming, knew it was inevitable, but that doesn't mean she's happy about it.

"That's how I figured you'd react," Doris says.

"How many times has he called?" Reiko says.

"Three."

"What'd you tell him?"

"I told him every time that you were out, that you were busy, that you were working, and I'd get you to call him right back. He must think I'm a liar. Or else that you're ducking him."

"He sound pissed?" Reiko says, heading for her office.

Doris snorts. "When doesn't he?"

"I'll call him now," Reiko says. "Don't bother pressing

your ear right up to my door, Doris. I'm sure you're going to hear my side of things just fine."

Doris raises her eyebrows. "Good luck."

Reiko closes the door, then takes a seat behind her desk. She takes a deep breath with her hands flat on the wood. She stares at the phone. Runs her tongue around the inside of her mouth. She picks up the receiver, dials through to Saxton PD. Tells them who it is, and that the chief is expecting her call.

It doesn't take him long to pick up. "Reiko," he says. He speaks her name bluntly. Almost spits it. "You know how long I've been trying to get hold of you?"

"My apologies, sir," Reiko says. "I've been out in the field –"

"That secretary of yours not try to get you? This is important, Reiko. This whole thing's a goddamn fucking shitshow."

"I'm aware of that, sir," Reiko says between clenched teeth. "I'm trying to deal with it."

"Deal with it?" Grice says. "*Deal* with it? It's your goddamn fault it's happened at all!"

Reiko bites her tongue. She's trying not to lose her cool. Trying not to raise her voice. He's making it very hard.

"Anyone would think you'd never seen a fake ID before!" he continues. "You just let them take him away? Why in the blue hell would you let them just take him away? Huh? I asked you a question, Miller."

Miller.

Albert Miller, Reiko's father, was the former chief of police in Saxton. He was a damn good one, too. Well liked. Firm but fair. No doubt everyone was expecting great things from his daughter when she took on the blue. There was talk that she could become the youngest-ever police chief. Following right in her old man's footsteps.

Albert was more than aware of Linden Grice. *He's just some little prick*, he'd told his daughter. It was one of the only times she'd ever heard him speak ill of someone. He wasn't prone to casual name-calling. *He's barely a cop. He's a pencil pusher. A desk jockey, and that's all he's ever wanted to be. But he's ambitious about it, and you've gotta be careful of cops like that. He doesn't want to get his hands dirty, but he's more than happy to take the glory from those who do. And I'll tell you something else – he's had his eye on my job for a long, long time.*

Sure enough, shortly after her father's retirement, Linden Grice manipulated his way into the position of chief of police. He didn't stop there, though. He politicked further. Saw to it that Reiko was allocated to Oak Hills, far away from him and his newfound power. He didn't feel safe with her around. She made him insecure. Despite their difference in age, he felt that, if she wanted, she could take his position from him at any time. Her name, and her father's legacy, carried a lot of weight. It still does.

So he sent her to Oak Hills, where nothing ever happened, and where he could forget all about her.

"I'm still waiting, Reiko," he says. "I want an explanation."

Reiko clenches her teeth so tight her jaw aches. She slowly parts them and takes a slow breath. "You want an explanation?" she says. She's done biting her tongue. She can feel her temper flaring. She's done holding back. Done being respectful to a man who shows her none in return. "How's this for an explanation – you called immigration and didn't tell me. And then, when I called you with two fake agents right here in this building, you told me to commend them on their speed! You promised me backup, then held them back for almost eight hours. You left me in the dark. All any of this would have taken to avoid was a few phone calls to keep us up to date. And we called you – *I* called you. Doris called you. And no one had any answers for us. *You* never returned our calls. And now you're finally calling up and doing what you always do – shifting blame."

There's a moment of silence. Stunned silence, no doubt. Reiko can hear him bristling. He takes a deep breath. She braces herself. "Who in the goddamn *hell* do you think you are? Who do you think you're talking to? I ain't your father, Reiko – you think you can get away with talking to me like that? To the goddamn chief of police with such disrespect? Who the *fuck* do you think you are?"

Reiko says nothing. She runs her tongue around the inside of her mouth, squeezing the receiver against the side of her head, mashing it into her ear.

"This happened on *your* turf, Reiko," Grice says. "*Your* responsibility. And you've made a mess of it. You've fucked it up royally. And now you have the audacity to accuse *me* of trying to shift blame? You got a lot of goddamn fucking nerve, sweetheart."

Reiko opens her mouth, but she stops herself this time. She covers the mouthpiece and takes a deep breath. She looks up and sees someone entering the station. Notices how Doris's attention has been pulled away from whatever she was pretending to do while she eavesdropped, and now her head turns toward the new arrival. Reiko's blinds obscure his face, but she can see it's a man in civilian clothes.

"Are you still there?"

Reiko looks down at her desk. Takes her hand away from the mouthpiece. "Yes," she says.

"Good," Grice says. "Because the last thing you'd want to do in your current situation is hang up on me."

"Uh-huh."

"Uh-huh, *sir*," Grice says. "Remember who you're talking to, Reiko."

"Yes. *Sir*."

"That's better. Maybe a little less sass. Here's what's going to happen, Miller – I'm sending more people over to Oak Hills. We're going to get your mess cleaned up, and after that,

I'll maybe take a deeper look into what you've been doing with your time over there."

"Yes, sir," Reiko says. She just wants this call to be over.

"They'll be there soon," Grice says. "And I may even come with them, just to make sure things are done right." He hangs up.

Reiko lets the phone drop, then runs her hands down her face. "Jesus Christ," she mutters to herself, then remembers she saw someone enter the station. She can hear them talking to Doris outside her office. She puts the receiver back into place, then stands and looks out. Sees who has entered the station.

It's Tom Rollins.

21

Tom sees Reiko's phone call end. He must have arrived at the tail end of it. He's glad he won't have to wait around too long. He sees her stand. Sees her see him.

Doris glances back over her shoulder. "Looks like she's done," she says.

Reiko steps out of her office. "Hello," she says, but she looks confused as to why he's here. "What can I do for you?"

"I came to see how things are going," Tom says.

Reiko blinks. She looks at him. Looks him up and down. It's probably the first time she's seen him not in his ranger uniform. He's wearing jeans and a black T-shirt. A jacket.

"I've been told to take some time off," Tom says. "For my protection, apparently."

"That might not be the worst thing," Reiko says. "Whose idea was it? Ron's?"

Tom nods.

"Yet here you are," Reiko says. "And when you say you've come to see how things are going, I assume you mean regarding the gunmen and Mateo?"

"That's right."

"That's hardly taking time off for your own protection."

Doris sits between the two of them, her head swivelling as each of them speaks. She looks like she's enjoying herself.

"It's only been a few hours," Reiko says.

"A lot can change in five minutes," Tom says.

"Not in this instance."

Tom flicks his chin past her, into his office, where it's private. "Can we talk in there?"

"This is an active investigation," Reiko says. "There's nothing to talk about."

Tom shrugs.

Reiko watches him. She can see she's not going to get rid of him easily, much like when he insisted on coming along and seeing Mateo's dead body with her. She sighs, then steps back into her office and motions for him to follow.

Reiko sits behind her desk, and Tom sits opposite. She holds out her hands. "What do you think I can tell you?" she says. She looks annoyed. Frustrated after her phone call, perhaps. He saw the exasperated way she ran her hands down her face right after it ended.

Tom nods at the phone. "Who called you?"

"What? Why does that matter? I doubt you came here just to ask who was on the phone."

"No, but it looks like whoever it was has pissed you off."

She barks a laugh and rolls her eyes. "That would be an understatement."

"Your boss?"

She nods. She's not laughing now. "I don't want to bore you with internal politics."

Tom shrugs, holds out his hands. "I don't mind," he says. "Tell me all about it. Get it off your chest. Might make you feel better."

Reiko raises an eyebrow. "I'm not so sure."

Tom watches her. She looks back. He smiles.

"Maybe some other time," Reiko says. "I'm not in the mood right now."

"All right," Tom says. "Instead, how about you tell me what *you* think is happening here in town?"

Reiko shrugs. She leans back in her chair. "Oak Hills has never had anything like this before," she says.

"What are your thoughts on the men I saw you watching in the diner? MS-13 aren't to be trifled with. Mateo's murder was their style."

"We've never had anything even remotely resembling cartel activity here before," she says. "It just seems so strange that it should be happening all of a sudden. Why would they even come here? What could possibly benefit them in Oak Hills?"

"It could be that Oak Hills has just been unfortunate," Tom says. "That maybe what happened with Mateo, and the seeming presence of MS-13, are just coincidences. Could be the people after Mateo were just passing by when he escaped them, and they had to chase him into the forest."

"Do you think that's what happened?" Reiko says.

"No," Tom says. "It's just a hypothesis, but we can make a lot of those, I'm sure. Thing is, I can understand why the men chasing Mateo would come after me. I took a shot at them. They weren't happy about that. It wouldn't explain why they killed Mateo so near the town, though. Once they had him, they could just move on. Do whatever they wanted to do to him in privacy. What would they have to gain by doing it so close to here? His murder was clearly a warning." He scratches his jaw. "Whether it had anything to do with them or not, what are you going to do about the MS-13 contingent in town?"

"Only thing I can do," Reiko says. "I'm going to talk to them. I'm going to lean on them, if I deem it appropriate. But first, I'm going to watch them. If they *are* behind this, they'll slip up eventually. I know where they're staying, so I'll watch them. Around the clock. All of a sudden I'm finding myself with the manpower I was asking for yesterday."

"Shame it didn't get here yesterday," Tom says. "I'll be interested to hear your findings. Full disclosure, I'll be running an investigation of my own."

Reiko raises an eyebrow. "I can't condone that."

Tom shrugs one shoulder. "I don't expect you to."

"You think I can't do my job?"

"I think there are limitations on your job," Tom says. "Limitations I don't necessarily have."

Reiko leans forward. "Are you kidding me right now? You're basically telling me you plan on running around playing vigilante, and you expect me to be all right with that?"

"I'm sure it won't get so extreme as that," Tom says.

Reiko stares at him. "Let's hope so. I'd hate to have to lock you up."

"If it comes to that, you'll be the best-looking person to have put me in cuffs."

Reiko raises an eyebrow, but her stare softens. "Jesus Christ," she says, shaking her head and trying not to laugh. "That's some line."

"I'm sure you've heard something like it before."

"Funnily enough, no, I haven't."

"That surprises me."

"How come?"

"Because you're a good-looking woman, and I'm sure at least one person you've arrested has had a kink for being cuffed, and let you know all about it."

Reiko laughs. "All right, fine," she says, sitting back and holding up her hands. "It's happened once or twice. One of my earliest collars, in my rookie year, I got sent to deal with this guy stomping up and down a street corner in his underwear and socks. Turned out he was a perv, and he went storming around like that just to get himself in the cuffs. Didn't matter if it was a male or female cop, he wasn't fussy. He just liked the cuffs on."

"Takes all sorts, I guess."

"Guess so," Reiko says. She looks at him across her desk. "All right. When you walk out that door, what's the plan?"

"I haven't decided yet," Tom says. He smiles at her. "I *am* interested in hearing anything you might find out," he says, standing. "And, of course, I'll return the courtesy. Let you know where I end up going after I leave. Maybe we could talk about it later? Dinner?"

Reiko chuckles. "Very smooth, Rollins," she says.

"Doris was telling me, sometimes you work so hard and so long you forget to feed yourself. So why not combine the two? Work and a meal."

"Where were you thinking?"

Tom stands by her office door. "I hear Clyde's Diner is pretty quiet these days," he says. "Shouldn't have any trouble getting a booth. And I promise I don't want to wear your cuffs."

Reiko chuckles, drumming her fingers on top of the desk. She's considering his dinner invite. "I've got a long day," she says. "How about eight?"

Tom nods. "I'll see you then."

22

When Bull leaves the house, he half-expects to see a police cruiser sitting on his street, its occupant watching him. Or, at least, an unmarked vehicle with a cop in civilian clothes inside pretending to be doing everything except surveillance.

There's not, though. All the noise lately, and Reiko coming directly to see him, he'd expected perhaps a stakeout. There could still be one, of course. Maybe he can't see them. Maybe they've pitched up in one of the houses of his neighbors, and they're watching him right now. As he backs his pickup out of the driveway, he doesn't see any vehicles parked on the street that he doesn't recognize. He'll remain vigilant while he's driving. Watch his mirrors. See if anyone is following him.

He pulls out of the street where he lives. Gets on the road leading out of Oak Hills. Toward Saxton. It's a quiet evening. The sun is low, and the light is stretching. His favorite time of day.

There's no one behind him. The road is clear for miles. As far as he can see in the mirrors. Same up ahead, too. He stays careful, though. Halfway to Saxton, he takes a turn. Goes down a rarely used road. It leads to where the old mill is. The mill has been out of business for a long time, but the building is still there.

He doesn't go far. Doesn't go all the way to the mill. Not yet. He gets out of view of the main road, and he pulls to the side. He waits. If anyone *is* following, and if they were keeping a *very* big distance between him and themselves, they can only come this way. There's no other way around.

He watches the mirror and taps one finger on the steering wheel. He's turned off the radio so he can better hear the road. The only sound is the engine purring. He winds down the window. He hears some birds chirping. Not another engine. Nothing coming. He lets ten minutes pass. That's long enough. Anyone coming, they'd have had to show up by now.

There's one thing he said to Reiko Miller that he means with all of his being – he won't go back to prison. Not ever. He won't spend another second behind bars, and he'll do everything in his power to make sure that never happens.

Another ten minutes down the road, the mill comes into view. The area around it is overgrown. Nature has not been scaled back, like it would've been when the mill was still operating. The trees are thick, as are the bushes. They almost obscure the building from view completely. In the cracked and weed-strewn parking lot, Bull can see the trucks that belong to his nephews. When he gets closer, he can see them, too.

Kai, the younger and more abrasive brother, is the first to speak when Bull pulls up alongside them. "Took your time tonight," he says. They both climb inside. Kai sits in the middle.

Josh is not so loud as his brother. He's quiet. Thoughtful. He closes the truck door gently after himself once he's inside. He turns to his uncle, awaiting his response to what Kai has said. Josh can handle himself, though. Despite how quiet he can be, he knows how to throw down. He reminds Bull a lot of himself. Kai, however, reminds Bull of their father. Kurt, his own brother. He was loud, too. It got him into trouble on more than one occasion. Bull forever found himself being drawn into his brother's battles. Bull would attempt to use his brain. To think and talk their way out of trouble. That didn't always work. It became necessary to know how to use his fists, too. He assumes it's been the same for Josh.

"Had to be sure of something," Bull says. "Didn't wanna come here with any unwanted company behind me." He turns the truck around. There are other vehicles in the parking lot. Like his nephews' two trucks, they're parked far back. Obscured in the shadows beneath the canopies of low-hanging trees.

"This have anything to do with what we've heard about the forest?" Josh says.

"How'd you hear about that, out on the road?" Bull says.

"We've been waiting a long time for you," Kai says. "We were talking to some of the guys while they were on their break. They were telling us about the shoot-outs."

Bull sucks his teeth. "Yeah, it was to do with that."

"Should we be concerned?" Josh says.

Bull turns his head so both nephews can see his smile. "Not at all," he says. "I told you I'd deal with things, didn't I? Well, I'm dealing with them."

"Not like you to do things so noisy," Josh says.

"Some things can't be avoided," Bull says. "And some things get out of hand, and you can't have any control over them, much as you'd like. The gunfights were never part of the plan, but they *have* led to a whole new plan. What do I always tell you boys? A smart man can turn every inconvenience into an advantage. That's what I'm doing here."

They're both looking at him. Bull has turned back to the

road, but he can feel their eyes on the side of his face. He smiles.

"You gonna tell us about this new plan?" Kai says.

"You know I will," Bull says. "But first, how were your journeys?"

"They were fine," Kai says. "Both of them. No trouble. Without a hitch. They ain't important right now. Tell us what's happening. I hear about gunfights and bodies, I start to get worried."

Bull makes a show of turning on the radio. Putting on some music. He taps his finger on the steering wheel along with the beat, though he doesn't recognize the song. Shows them how calm he is. How calm *they* should be.

"You don't need to worry," he says when he can see that Kai is getting so worked up he's about to blow his top. "I've got everything in hand."

23

Tom walks into town. He goes to where he dropped off Gabriel and Luis. He's hoping to find them. He looks along the road to where he can see the small gathering of day laborers congregating. It's after five now, and the roads are busy with people heading home. Or, at least, as busy as they ever get in Oak Hills. He can't imagine the day laborers will hang around for much longer. He wonders where they go at the end of the day. If they have a place where they stay.

He goes to them. There aren't many, only six. They're winding down at the end of the day. Sharing cigarettes and some drinks before they, too, scatter and go wherever it is they bed down for the night. At first, they perk up at his approach. Thinking he's going to have work to offer. They don't care what time it is. They'll take any work he might have. He studies their faces. Looking for Gabriel and Luis. He can't see them. "Who speaks English?" he says.

The laborers are wary. For a start, he's approached them on foot. Most of their work will come from people with vehicles. They see how he's dressed, too. Cheap. Affordable. He doesn't look like he's got money to spend on their help. Tom's aware of how he carries himself, too. Ex-Army. Some things never go away. They see it. They could mistake it for law enforcement. Maybe for immigration. They avoid answering him right away. If they speak English, they don't want him to know just yet.

"Hablo un poco de Español," Tom says. *I speak some Spanish.* "Pero solo un poco." *But only a little.* Then, switching back to English: "I'd rather not put you or myself through that if it can be avoided."

A couple of them look up at this, but still no one speaks.

Tom sighs. "Busco dos hombres," he says. *I'm looking for two men.* Then, trying a mix of English and Spanish: "I dropped them off near here two days ago. I saw them come this way. Se llaman Gabriel and Luis. No se los nombres de familia – their last names."

The laborers avoid his eye. They look at their feet or across the road. He has no work to give. It's easy to show indifference when they know they're not about to get paid.

He thinks they understand English, though. Despite how they avoid looking at him, he can see that they're still listening.

"What about Mateo?" he says. "Mateo Garcia? Anyone here know him?"

At least two of them stiffen, then act like they didn't. Act like they didn't hear the name he just said.

One of the men in the middle starts to look at Tom. To study him. He's younger than the other laborers. He scratches his jaw. He's deliberating. Looks like he wants to speak.

Tom addresses him. "Do you know the men I'm talking about?"

The kid shrugs. "I know a lot of people," he says. He has an accent, but other than that, his English is perfect.

"Uh-huh," Tom says. "And the three men I mentioned specifically?"

"A lot of people pass through here," the kid says. "We might've seen them. Might not. Don't always take a name."

"What's *your* name?" Tom says.

The kid hesitates. He looks to the men either side of him, but they don't look back. "Rodrigo," he says eventually, figuring giving his name can't hurt.

"Rodrigo," Tom repeats. "How long ago did you come to Oak Hills, Rodrigo?"

Rodrigo shrugs. He looks bored. "Couple of weeks," he says. "I don't know. Maybe longer."

"You get much work here?"

Rodrigo snorts.

"I'll take that as a no," Tom says. "And it's funny, because that's what I figured. What kind of work can there be to find in a small town like this? Seems strange to me that you all hang out here day in and day out."

"We *heard* there was work here," Rodrigo says, pushing himself off the wall, suddenly animated. He doesn't look so bored anymore. "We heard there was a lot of work, so we come, each of us. But then we get here, and what do we get? There's no work. Just dirty looks from old white folks wondering what we're doing." He shakes his head, his face twisting bitterly. "It's all a lie," he says. "The work here is already taken. They've already picked the men they want. They've brought them in already. We stand on this corner day in and day out, and maybe we get to paint a fence, or put up a little drywall, and hope we can save up enough for bus fare to get us back to Sacramento, or maybe even somewhere south of here."

"What work are you talking about?" Tom says. "Who's brought workers in already? What are they doing?"

The man to Rodrigo's left grabs Rodrigo by the arm, pulls

him back against the wall. When Rodrigo looks at him, the man shakes his head. Rodrigo sucks in his lips. Bites them. He takes a deep breath. Calms himself down.

"Well?" Tom says.

Rodrigo shakes his head. "No, man," he says. "You must've misunderstood what you heard. That's not what I said. Nothing like that."

Tom looks at him until Rodrigo has to look away. He folds his arms and stares at the ground.

"No one can help you if you won't talk," Tom says to all of them.

No one answers. Not even Rodrigo. He's turned as mute as the rest of them.

One of them, the guy on the end, to Tom's left, suddenly straightens up and taps his watch. He says something in Spanish, and then he walks away. The rest of them follow him, until Tom is alone, standing on an empty corner.

24

Tom goes back to the station to meet Reiko when it gets close to eight o'clock. He's killed time wandering around town, on the off chance he'd come across Gabriel or Luis. He didn't. As he enters the station, he notices a couple of other officers are present. He recognizes the black one from earlier, at the scene where Mateo's body had been dumped. Greg. He looks surprised to see Tom.

Reiko comes out of her office. "I won't be long," she says to Tom. "Just wait outside. I'll meet you there."

Tom goes outside and leans against the building, arms folded. Reiko doesn't take long. She points to her cruiser and tells him to get in.

"You have a car of your own?" she says, pulling away from the station and heading for Clyde's Diner.

"Not for a while now," Tom says. "The ranger job came with its own vehicle. Now that I'm on leave, I don't have access to it."

"I hope you like walking."

"I don't mind it."

They reach the diner. The parking lot, as expected, is empty. They go inside, and Clyde looks pleased to have some customers. Every booth, every table, is free. They go to a booth in the corner. The opposite side of the diner to where the MS-13 guys usually sit.

"You cause any trouble in the few hours since I saw you last?" Reiko says. "Anything I need to brace myself for?"

Tom shakes his head. "Just spoke to some people. They didn't have anything to tell me. Claimed not to, anyway. How about you?"

"I've told you already," Reiko says. "This isn't how it works. It's my job. I can't tell you about an active investigation."

"Fine," Tom says. "Don't tell me. Feel free to bounce any theories or ideas, though."

"If I had any beyond what we've already discussed, I would. And since you've said you didn't find anything out, then I guess we're just here to enjoy a meal."

Tom looks at her. "I suppose there's worse ways to spend an evening," he says. "And with worse company."

"That's quite a line," Reiko says.

"It's not a line if you mean it."

Clyde comes over, takes their orders. Tom orders a burger and a glass of water. Reiko gets a tuna melt and a soda. Clyde hurries off to busy himself in the kitchen.

"So," Tom says, "are you from Oak Hills?"

Reiko shakes her head. "You know, before I was stationed here, I'd only ever been to Oak Hills once in my life. And even then, it was just passing through. I must've been about twelve. Dad took me and Mom to the forest. We went for a hike. Dad was always into outdoors stuff like that, in his time off. It's surprising we didn't come through this way more often, come to think of it. He took us hiking all over, though. Or fishing. Sometimes hunting. I loved it, but Mom hated it.

It wasn't her kind of thing at all. She did it, though. Because she loved my dad."

"Loved?" Tom says, picking up on the past tense, wondering if her parents aren't still together.

"My dad died," Reiko says.

"I'm sorry to hear that."

"Only a few years into his retirement, too. Five years ago, now. Despite all that outdoors stuff he did, constantly being active, you know what killed him? Heart attack. Mom says it was likely due to stress. She said he hid it from us, but he always brought his work home with him. He was always thinking about a case. Mom says sometimes it doesn't matter how well you eat, or how much exercise you get, if you aren't controlling your stress, then it's gonna kill you. I think she says it as a warning to me."

"You take your work home with you?"

She laughs. "As if I have much work to take with me around here. I guess my stress comes from the *lack* of work. Feeling like I'm wasting away here. Frittering away the prime years of my life *and* my career."

"So where are you from?"

"Saxton. Born in Sacramento, but we moved to Saxton before I'd even turned one. I grew up there. Until I came here, I'd spent most of my life there."

"What are your parents called?"

Reiko raises an eyebrow. "This is starting to feel like a subtle interrogation."

"It's just a conversation."

"Albert and Kimiko. You?"

"Jeff and Mary. My mom died when I was nine. My stepmom is called Sylvia."

"I'm sorry," Reiko says. "Nine is young. Real young. That must've been rough."

"It certainly wasn't easy."

"You get on with your stepmom?"

"Yeah," Tom says. "I'd already moved out when my dad met her. I had a life of my own."

"Any siblings?"

"A brother."

"You close?"

Tom hesitates. "We were. Once. Not so much anymore. Do you have siblings?"

"Nope. Only child. I hope it's not too obvious."

Tom grins. Clyde brings them their food. He disappears back behind his counter. He has a magazine folded over. He returns to reading it.

Tom takes a bite out of his burger. "Is your mom still in Saxton?"

Reiko nods. She's chewing. She swallows before she responds. "Yeah. I visit her when I can. She's...she's happy enough. I know she misses my dad, but life goes on. She has her friends. She does a lot of knitting." Reiko pokes at her food with her fork, thinking. "She's from Osaka, originally. My dad was in the Navy before he joined the police. That's where he met her. Recently, she's been talking about going back to Osaka. Permanently, I mean. I guess maybe she thinks she doesn't have much time left, and that she wants to see her home again before then. Or maybe everything she sees here reminds her of my father. If it weren't for me, I think she probably would've gone back to Japan a long time ago."

"You can always go visit."

"Oak Hills isn't going to protect itself, Tom," she says playfully. She sighs. "Just a week ago, that would've been a lot funnier. I could've left *Doris* in charge, and things would be just the same when I got back. Now, though..."

"You seem like a good cop," Tom says. "I don't mean that as a backhanded compliment. I can only go off what people tell me. Ron speaks very highly of you. And of your father, too. Whatever's going on here, you'll work it out. Get Oak Hills back to the sleepy haven it used to be." Tom eats some more burger. A couple of fries. "Speaking of," he says. "You mentioned feeling like you were losing the prime years of your career. What *is* a cop like you doing in a place like this? I would've thought an older cop waiting on their retirement would be a lot happier being put out to pasture like this."

Reiko sighs. "And you wouldn't be wrong. In Saxton, there's at least a dozen cops who would've killed for a cushy position like this. Wait for their pension. See in their golden years in comfort."

"Then why aren't they here?"

She looks him in the eye, and then she tells him all about Chief Linden Grice. Everything. His petty grievances, and his jealousies. His ambitions, too.

When she's done, Tom nods. "I see," he says. "So you get the shitty end of the stick all because he's scared you might take his job."

"Pretty much."

"He sounds like an asshole."

"He *is* an asshole." She shakes her head. "It feels good to get it off my chest. To rant about him to someone other than Doris, for a change."

"Well, it sounds like you've got a right to be annoyed," Tom says. "He'd undermined you. Even putting you out here, he's still sabotaging you. And because of him, Mateo is dead."

Reiko takes a mouthful of tuna melt, then sits back. She regards him while she chews. "I haven't spoken to anyone like this in a very long time." She considers this. "Maybe not ever. I don't really have anyone to talk to out here."

"Sometimes it helps to talk. I've been told that, anyway. Glad I could lend an ear."

"Ah, so it wasn't an interrogation," Reiko says. "It was counselling."

"It was just a conversation."

She looks at him. They're both nearly finished eating. "First time I met you," she says, "I got a vibe. When Ron told me you were ex-Army, I wasn't surprised. Truth be told, I'd already guessed something like that. Can see it in the way you carry yourself. How you speak."

"That was the vibe?"

"The vibe was that you're dangerous. And maybe you are. But now, after talking to you, I see that you aren't the kind of PTSD-suffering vet who could potentially snap at any moment. And maybe you *do* have PTSD. I'm not trying to diminish that. But you have control, too."

"Most of the time," Tom says.

"Well, I'm glad to hear *that*." She takes a deep breath. She reaches across the table, squeezes his hand. "Thank you for listening," she says. "I think I...I think I needed that more than I realized." She takes her hand back, then looks the table over. At their mostly empty plates. "Looks like we're done here," she says. "I'll pay. I'll put it on my tab. Let Grice deal with it."

"There's gotta be some perks to an out-of-the-way placement."

"Exactly. Where are you staying?"

"Motel on the way out of town."

"I'll give you a ride," Reiko says, sliding out of the booth and standing.

"I don't mind walking," Tom says. He looks up at her. Holds her eye.

"And I don't mind driving," she says.

25

R eiko stays over.

She comes up to his room, and by the time they're through the door, they're already kissing, their bodies locked together and stumbling for the bed.

She sleeps now. Before she fell asleep, she went to the bathroom to clean up, and emerged in only her underwear. She gathered her scattered uniform from the floor and neatly folded and piled it on the chair in the corner. Tom gathered his clothes up, too, and folded them, but he's dropped them by the side of the bed within easy reach. They keep his Beretta covered, too.

While Reiko was in the bathroom, Tom took two empty glass soda bottles from the kitchen. He'd bought and emptied them earlier in the day. He'd already tied string around both tops. One piece of string, connecting both bottles. He hung the contraption from the door handle. If anyone tries to break in, the bottles will rattle together. Reiko noticed the makeshift alarm as soon as she emerged from the bathroom. "Just in case," Tom said. After folding her clothes, Reiko got straight into the bed.

Tom doesn't fall straight asleep. It's hard to get to sleep when he knows there are heavily armed men looking for him. They found him at the station. He doesn't see how they could know he's here, but it doesn't hurt to be careful. Hence the tripwire. He lies awake, listening to the sound of Reiko breathing. She's lying on her side, turned away from him, but her lower back is pressed up against him, into his ribs. She feels warm and smooth. She twitches, moans, then settles back down.

Tom stares at the ceiling. It's quiet outside. He hears the occasional vehicle passing by, but they're few and far between. It's late. Oak Hills isn't the kind of place where people are driving around all night.

Eventually, he starts to doze. His eyes flutter shut. His breathing slows. He sleeps.

But he sleeps light. He always does. And no sooner does it feel like he's just nodded off, then the glass bottles on the door begin to clang against each other.

Tom doesn't think. He reacts. Pushes Reiko out of the bed so she hits the floor. She curses, surprised, but she'll thank him later. Tom rolls to the other side. Out of bed. He grabs the Beretta as he hits the ground. Points it at the opening door. Blinks sleep out of his eyes.

There's an explosion at the door. A flash of light as an AR-15 opens up. The sound of it is deafening in the motel room. Its bullets tear up the bed. They rip through the mattress where just a moment before Tom and Reiko lay.

This all happens in the space of a few short seconds. Tom fires before the shooter has a chance to realize the bed is empty. That his targets are missing. Tom's two shots catch the shooter – one in the chest, and the other in the throat. He goes down. Blood geysers from his neck. There's another shadow filling the doorway behind him. Armed with another AR-15.

A bullet tears a chunk out of the doorframe near the second shadow's head. It comes from Reiko's side of the bed. She's grabbed her pistol. She's returning fire, still dressed only in her underwear.

Tom fires, too. The second shadow ducks out of the door, leaves his fallen friend behind. Tom stands, keeping his Beretta raised. He hears the second man running. Down the stairs, away from the room.

Tom goes after him. He's wearing just his boxer shorts. Outside, the night air is mild. His feet are bare, and the rough ground bites at them. Tom gives chase to the second shooter. He flees across the parking lot. Doesn't attempt to turn, to fire back. His weapon is far more powerful than Tom's. Right now, all he's thinking about is getting away.

He dives through some bushes that line the parking lot. Tom follows, confused as to where his getaway vehicle is. It doesn't take long to find out. The second shooter rounds a corner. There's an idling vehicle waiting for him. The front passenger door swings open. The shooter jumps inside. Tom fires on the vehicle. It's pointing the opposite direction to where he stands. It's pointing out of Oak Hills. It roars away.

Tom goes back to the motel room. Reiko has hastily pulled on some clothes. She's calling in to the station. She looks at Tom when he returns.

"He got away," Tom says. "Getaway car waiting for him around the corner." He goes to his clothes, starts dressing.

"You get a good look at him?" Reiko says.

"Latino," Tom says. "Same as him." He points to the dead body in the doorway, his blood soaking into the carpet, thick and black. Neither man was wearing a mask.

"See the driver?"

"No. They were pointing the other way."

"They escaped that way?"

Tom nods. "North."

Reiko gets back on her radio, relays this information. She looks at him, says, "Model? License?"

"Plate was missing," Tom says. "They'd taken it off. But it was a Chevy."

Dressed, Tom steps closer to the man he's killed. Looks down into his face. Dead. Despite the blood coating him, he looks peaceful.

"Recognize him?" Reiko says.

Tom shakes his head. "You?"

"Not a damn clue. But whoever they are, they're determined to get to you."

Tom looks toward the door, then back at Reiko. "They've put a lot of effort into it now," he says. "But *why*?"

26

Chief Linden Grice gets to Oak Hills early. He summons Reiko from the scene of the shooting at the motel. Calls her back to the station. He's commandeered her office.

The station is overrun with officers from Saxton. It's never been so busy before. Reiko has to fight her way through, pushing people aside. She catches sight of Greg on the way. "Looks like he brought the cavalry," she says.

Greg grunts. "All of a sudden, he's smelling a big case. An opportunity to get his name in the papers and his face on the news."

Reiko nods. She looks through the milling bodies, to her office. The blinds are drawn. She can't see inside, but she knows he's there. "You seen him today?" she says.

"Yeah."

"How is he?"

"As delightful as ever."

"I expected as much."

Greg squeezes her arm. "Good luck. Don't let him bring you down."

Reiko continues to the office. *Her* office, regardless of who is sitting behind the desk.

Doris looks up at her as she approaches. Her face is solemn. It wouldn't surprise Reiko if Doris has already been chewed out by Grice over some minor slight or inconvenience. She pats Doris's shoulder as she passes. Gives her a comforting squeeze. Doris places her hand over hers in return.

Reiko pauses outside the door. She steels herself. Behind, it's like a hush descends upon the room. Like they've realized she's here, and what's about to happen. She can feel their eyes upon her. Watching as she prepares herself to step into the belly of the beast.

She knocks. It feels strange to knock on her own door.

"Come in." It's Grice's voice. The sound makes her skin crawl. Reiko steps inside.

Sure enough, Grice sits behind her desk. Reading glasses are perched on the end of his bulbous nose. Paperwork is spread out in front of him, a pen in his right hand, hovering over the sheets. Reiko doesn't think the paperwork will have anything to do with Oak Hills. More than likely, he's just catching up while his men work the fresh case. He's almost as old now as her father was when he died, though her father was in much better shape. She knows Grice will outlive him. It feels like a crime.

He looks up at her over the top of the glasses. "Take a seat," he says. He straightens up, removing the glasses. He folds them, then puts them into his breast pocket. His thinning hair is slicked back. He runs his hands over his scalp, checking that what little there is is still in place.

Reiko sits. She clasps her hands in her lap and squeezes them together. Concentrates on her breathing. Low, slow, deep breaths. Keeps her face impassive. Keeps herself under control.

Grice regards her for a long time. Looks her in the eye. An intimidation tactic. Reiko doesn't back down. Doesn't look away. She knows he won't like this. She doesn't care. She can't help herself.

"I understand you didn't go home last night," Grice says.

Reiko has been expecting this. She doesn't react. Not physically. Still, though, it feels like a jab to the stomach.

"This man you were with," Grice goes on, "what was his name – Rollins?"

Reiko nods, just once.

"I understand he's been a witness to what's been happening in Oak Hills, not to mention a victim of an attempted shooting. Twice now, in fact."

He stares at her again. It's harder this time for Reiko to not look away, but she perseveres. She feels cold inside. Her stomach is doing somersaults. There's a lump in her throat, but she doesn't swallow. She stays firm.

"Hardly becoming for you to have spent the night in his motel room, now, was it?"

"I realize that, perhaps, that may have –"

Before she can finish what she's going to say, Grice is waving his hands in the air. "Doesn't matter now, does it? What's done is done. Can't change it now. Much as we can't change the poor way you've mishandled and mismanaged this case from the start."

Reiko has to bite her tongue. If she blows up now, she won't stop. She'll cuss him out of the building. She won't have to worry about losing the prime years of her career anymore – she won't have a career at all.

"The attack in the motel last night wasn't just an attack on this Rollins, though, was it? Because you were present, we can't actually be sure who they were trying to get. Was Rollins their intended target, or was it perhaps you?"

Reiko has wondered this herself. She thinks it was likely

Rollins they were after – they'd targeted him already, after all – but at the same time, for them to know which room he was in, surely they'd been observing the motel? They must have seen her arrive with him. Seen how she didn't leave. They must have seen her cruiser in the parking lot. She can't be sure. Maybe they just weren't concerned about having a police officer as a collateral victim.

"We have to assume that you were at just as much risk as he was," Grice says. "That you were a target. Despite your bungling of this case, you must have done something to upset them, whoever they may be. I can't have one of my officer's lives in danger like this." He's grinning while he speaks. "For that reason, I'm going to have to bench you. Until this is all over."

Reiko doesn't want to react. She wants to stay firm, strong, as she has so far. But she can feel herself shaking. The corner of her mouth is twitching. It's hard to keep it all internalized.

"Of course, after that, we *will* have to make a formal enquiry into how you've been handling your business while you've been out here all on your own." Grice presses his fingertips together, steeples them. He's trying not to grin. He's enjoying this. "Try not to worry, though. I'm sure your record will speak for itself. And I'll put a good word in for you."

His smile reminds her of a shark. There's blood in the water, and he smells it. Ostensibly, benching her is for her safety. In truth, it's another method of getting her out of the way. To embarrass her. Another political move so he can find out what's happening in Oak Hills ahead of her. Claim the glory. Further solidify himself as the chief.

"I'm sure we'll be able to get you set back up here in Oak Hills in no time at all," he says. "And you can look forward to a long and uneventful career right here in this town I'm sure you've come to love."

Reiko squeezes her hands together. She hears her knuckles begin to pop.

"Is there anything you'd like to say for yourself?" Grice has given up on trying to disguise the fact he's enjoying this.

"No, sir," Reiko says. She pries her hands apart. Her fingers are white from lack of circulation. She smooths out the legs of her trousers.

"Then dismissed," Grice says.

Reiko stands. She's holding her breath. If she were to breathe, she thinks it would shudder. She thinks some kind of noise might escape her. She doesn't want him to hear that. She leaves the office. Her office. She walks through the crowd of other cops in the station. They part before her like the Red Sea. They avoid her eye. All apart from Greg. He follows her out.

"Do you need a ride home?" he says once they're outside, away from everyone else.

"Yes," Reiko says, speaking through her teeth. "Please. That would be good." She feels tense. Like she can barely move. In her mind, she pictures reaching across the desk and scratching Grice's eyes out. It's the only thing that can calm her down.

They go to Greg's cruiser. She holds up a hand before they can both get in. "Just give me a moment," she says.

Greg steps back. "Sure."

Reiko gets into the cruiser on the passenger side and closes the door. "*Fuck!*" she screams, bending over, her face in her lap. She straightens back up. She feels looser. She takes deep breaths. They don't shudder. No noises escape her. She checks herself in the mirror. Brushes a stray strand of hair back behind her ear. She reaches over and pushes open Greg's door. "Okay," she says. "I'm good. Let's go."

27

Tom checks into the hotel in town. He's careful going there. Looks around. Doubles back. Circles the block to make sure no one's following him. He can't see anyone. He gets a room. Requests that it's on the back of the building. The window leads out onto the fire escape. He leans his head out the window and looks down. The ladder at the bottom is drawn up. It can't be reached from the ground.

Soon after, he gets a call. It's Reiko. "I've been benched," she says.

"Shit," Tom says. "I'm sorry."

"The asshole chief I was telling you about has come to town," she says. "Obviously spies an opportunity for glory." She tells him what else the chief said. How she could be a potential target. He's benching her for her safety. It's all very similar to what Tom himself has been told. "It's a crock of shit."

"Where are you now?"

"I'm at home."

Tom tells her where he is. "Come here. Pack some things.

We'll lie low together. If you *are* a target, it's safer you're not at home."

"I'll be there in fifteen minutes."

"Be careful. Make sure you're not followed."

"Got it."

"Are you going to do what he asks?" Tom says before they hang up. "Are you going to stay on the bench?"

Reiko makes a noise. "Hell no," she says.

Tom grins. "Good."

28

Reiko sends a message to Greg Noble. They arrange to meet on the outskirts of town. Tom goes with her. They're careful leaving the hotel. Make sure they're not being watched or followed. They travel in Reiko's Honda. They find Greg's cruiser parked under a tree by the side of the road. It's late. Getting dark. They almost miss him. He gets out when Reiko pulls to a stop in front of him.

Greg regards Tom warily as they approach. "You sure it's wise having this guy attached to your hip?" Greg says. "All things considered."

"We're helping each other out," Reiko says. She nods at his car, how he's tried to hide it under a tree. "What's with all the secrecy? Meeting all the way out here?"

"Grice made it very clear you're no longer part of the investigation. No one's supposed to talk to you. You know he's got a few lackeys who would love to see me talking with you so they can go running back and tell him all about it." Greg looks back over his shoulder down the road, but it's a quiet road, and there are no other vehicles around. "How're the two of you helping each other out?" he says, turning back.

"We both want to know who's trying to kill us, for a start," Reiko says.

"And we both want to know who killed Mateo," Tom says. "And bring them to justice. From what Reiko has told me, it doesn't sound like your chief is the best man for the job."

Greg grunts. It sounds like a laugh. "There's no argument here. That why you got in touch, Reiko? See if I've got anything to share, anything you can use?"

Reiko nods. "Yes," she says. "Updates would be appreciated. And that'll go both ways – between us and *you*. And only you. I trust you not to tell Grice about what we're doing."

"You know I won't."

Reiko gives him a grateful smile. "I know it's only been a few hours, but is there anything you can tell us now?"

"One thing," Greg says. "But it's a biggie. The guy you shot." He looks at Tom.

"What about him?" Tom says.

"We got an ID," Greg says. "Santos Rodriguez. A Honduran national who's been working as a mercenary for the last ten years."

Tom and Reiko look at each other. "If it's cartel," Reiko says, "they could have hired him. You said a couple of guys, chasing Mateo on that first night, were white. Mercenaries would fit the bill. Hired to oversee whatever it is they're doing in this area."

Tom nods. "And to deal with any mess that might arise."

"Sounds like this was helpful," Greg says.

"It gives us something to go off," Reiko says. "Thanks."

"Don't mention it." He starts walking back to his cruiser. "Anything else comes up, I'll let you know."

They stay by the side of the road and wave him off as he turns the cruiser around and disappears down the road, back toward Oak Hills. They watch his rear lights slowly fade away.

"We've got a man on the inside," Tom says. "What now?"

"*Now*," Reiko says, "I want to get to bed. My sleep was very rudely interrupted last night, and I need to catch up. The adrenaline's wearing off, and it feels like I'm running on empty now."

"Back to the hotel?"

Reiko nods.

"Give me the keys if you're tired," Tom says. "I'll drive."

They go back to the hotel. They park Reiko's car a couple of blocks away from where they're staying, and continue on foot. Again, they make sure they're not being watched. Again, that no one is following them. They get to their room. Before they left, Tom tucked a small piece of paper between the door and the frame. It's still in place. No one has tried to break in.

Inside, they lock the door, then hang two glass soda bottles off the knob, re-creating the alarm that saved their lives last night. They both have their handguns out ready on their respective bedside tables, in case of disturbance. They strip down and get into bed. Reiko lies on her side. Tom lies on his back. He watches the door.

After a little while, Reiko turns over. She reaches out, places her hand on his arm. Strokes it. "I have *some* energy left," she says.

Tom leans over and wraps his arms around her. They kiss.

29

Bull rises early. There's a smile on his face. Today is a big day. It's the two-year anniversary of his release from prison.

His nephews aren't up yet. He can hear them snoring through the doors of their respective rooms. Bull has always been an early riser. Even before prison.

He goes through to the kitchen and makes coffee. Makes enough for when Josh and Kai eventually do rise. He makes breakfast. Eggs. Bacon. Sausages. Tomatoes. If there were more eggs, he'd make pancakes, too. He's in a celebratory mood. He appreciates every day of freedom, but the anniversary of his release date is like his birthday. It's like Christmas.

He remembers being released. Josh and Kai were there to greet him. They hugged him tight, then they drove him to Oak Hills. His new home. It was a long drive, but Bull barely noticed. He appreciated every sight, sound, and smell on the journey. Sat in the back with the window wound down and his arm hanging out. Watching how the cold air blowing over his arm made the hairs stand on end.

Kai had offered him a joint. "It's from your last batch," he said. "We saved it for you. Saved it for today."

Bull was tempted. "You and your brother have it," he said. "I'm done with marijuana."

Kai raised an eyebrow. "I thought you said you had something in mind for when you got out," he said. "It's not weed-based?"

Bull smiled and shook his head. "Oh, no," he said. "It's a far higher risk than that. But you know what they say about the higher the risk, don't you?" There was a gleam in his eye. "The higher the reward."

He's finished his breakfast by the time he hears the first of his nephews begin to stir. Josh comes out of his room rubbing his eyes. He's pulled on some shorts and a T-shirt. He nods at Bull, then makes himself some coffee. "Smells good in here," he says, drinking. "You make enough for everyone?"

"It's keeping warm in the oven," Bull says. "Didn't know how long it would take the two of you to wake."

Bull serves up a plate of food for Josh, and while Josh is eating, Kai finally stumbles from his room. He's in his underwear. He goes through to the bathroom and leaves the door open. They hear him pissing for a long time. Then the taps run. He splashes water into his face. He comes through to the kitchen picking sleep from his eyes. He sniffs the air, then frowns at Josh's plate of food, and Bull's empty plate.

"There's some for you, too," Bull says, returning to the oven.

"Good," Kai says, pouring himself some coffee. He scratches his crotch as he sits at the table, picking up his fork and scooping egg into his mouth.

"It's the anniversary today," Josh says, remembering.

"Happy two years," Kai says around a mouthful of food.

Bull pours himself a fresh cup of coffee, then sits down and raises the cup in a toast. "To freedom," he says.

Josh lifts his own cup, but Kai finishes what he's chewing before he does the same.

"Freedom is a sweet thing," Bull says. "May the two of you never lose it. We don't have too far to go now, boys. Every anniversary, we're a step closer. Home free. Then we don't have to worry about anything else ever again."

Kai is barely listening. He likely remembers when Bull said this last year. Bull can't help himself, though. He's looking to the future. He's excited.

"While I was inside, I realized what a mistake I'd made," Bull says. "Hydroponic weed wasn't the way to go. Didn't matter how much I grew, how much I sold, or how good the quality was. In California, it was stupid. *Everyone* was growing it. And then, while I was locked up, they went ahead and legalized it." He shakes his head, chuckles to himself. "Since I got out, I've heard a lot of the growing and distribution remains underground, but that doesn't matter. The market remains flooded. The money to be made has been diluted. And really, what money is there in weed? Not enough for me to return to it. And they'll be watching me. *Expecting* me to go back down that route. But I haven't. I've been smart about it. Went a whole other route. One they weren't expecting. The kind where there's *real* money."

"Are we gonna get this speech *every* year?" Kai says.

"You remember how long I estimated it would take us?"

Kai chews, thinking, remembering. "You said four or five years."

"Then you've only gotta hear it two or three more times," Bull says. "We get in on something California isn't expecting. Four or five years to make enough money, and then we disappear to a ranch somewhere in the Midwest, and don't worry about work for the rest of our days."

"It's a beautiful dream," Kai says.

"And we're not far off making it a reality. Me, yourselves,

and your sister. We won't have to worry about anything ever again. You won't ever have to suffer what I did. You won't lose your freedom. You're gonna get more freedom than you can possibly imagine."

"I can imagine it," Kai says. "You talk about it often enough."

"One day you'll understand," Bull says, sipping coffee. "Speaking of your sister, where is she? I thought she'd call around this morning. She knows what day it is."

"She's coming later," Josh says.

"She said she'll bring a cake," Kai says.

"Well, I can forgive her if she turns up with cake," Bull says. He sits back in his chair, clasping his coffee mug in both hands. He stares off into nothing, a contented smile on his face. Freedom. This is freedom. He refuses to lose it again.

"I hope it's a chocolate cake," Kai says.

30

Tom wants to go back to the forest. "To where I saw Mateo running," he says to Reiko. Tom is dressed. Reiko has just got out of the shower. She's drying her hair, listening.

"Why?" she says.

"To see where he ran from. There could be something there that leads us to their operation."

Reiko sits on the bed. "They benched you, just like Grice benched me," she says. "They're not going to let you in to take a look around."

"We don't go through," Tom says. "We go around. To the back of the forest. I can pinpoint the rough direction I saw them coming from. It might not be perfect, but it'll give us somewhere to start. I don't think there'll be a trail there anymore, but there might be something we can pick up on and work with." Plus, Tom thinks, if they go around the back, they don't have to deal with Freddy and Stephen telling them the area is off-limits. "The forest is a big area," Tom says. "And it's out of the way. It's not exactly right next to anything else. It's strange for them to have been chasing him through there.

If they chased him from the road, which is a working theory, he would've had to run a *long* way to get to where I saw them."

"Mateo *was* exhausted when I picked him up."

Tom nods. "He was, but was he exhausted enough? I still think it's worth checking out."

"I agree with you," Reiko says. "It gives us something to do until we hear about anything else. And who knows? Maybe it'll lead us to something worthwhile."

Reiko dresses. She wears blue jeans and a white shirt tucked into them. They head to where they parked her car. They take the same level of care and precaution as usual. Again, there's no one watching them. At least, no one they can see. If there *is* anyone observing them, they're doing a good job concealing themselves.

Tom drives. They head out of Oak Hills. Pass by the entrance to the national forest. Travel down the length of the forest, the trees thick and impenetrable to their left.

Reiko's phone begins to ring. It's Greg. "What's up?"

Tom can hear Greg's voice, but can't make out what he's saying.

Reiko frowns. She glances at Tom, then puts Greg on loudspeaker. "Say that again," she says.

"Grice read your report on potential MS-13 in town," Greg says. His voice is hushed and harried, like he's concerned about being overheard. "He's taking us out to their place."

"*Shit,*" Reiko says. The idea of Grice heading out there makes her uncomfortable. He likely has no idea what he's getting himself into with MS-13. He should be watching the house, being sure. He should only move in when he's certain.

"We're gonna go talk to them now," Greg says. "I just thought you'd want to know."

Tom slows the car. He pulls it to the side of the road.

"Right now?" Reiko says.

"Soon enough."

"Jesus Christ – what's his plan?"

"He wants to question them," Greg says. "Find out if they're behind everything, or at least find out what they know."

"They're not gonna want to talk," Tom says. "And if you try to take them in, they're going to resist."

"I know that," Greg says. "And I think he knows it, too. That's why we're all going."

"All?" Reiko says.

"Every cop currently in Oak Hills."

"*Shit*," Reiko says. "*Everyone?* What's he thinking? A show of force, hoping for an easy collar? Jesus Christ... He's gearing up for a standoff." She looks at Tom, tilts her head back toward town. Tom understands. He turns the car around. "He should be handing this subtly. He can't go in with a show of force – what if MS-13 aren't the puppet masters here? What if they're the muscle – has he considered that? Grice could blow us finding out who's in charge."

"I gotta go," Greg says. "We're leaving now."

"Keep your head low, Greg," Reiko says. "Don't get yourself hurt on account of that asshole."

"Don't intend to," Greg says, then hangs up.

Reiko is shaking her head as she puts her phone away. "He's not thinking," she says. "He's just desperate for a collar. Desperate to get this over and done with so he can go back to Saxton the conquering hero, his face front page on the papers. He should be watching the house. Observing them. See what they do and where they go. He shouldn't go charging in headlong like this – they're the only lead we have right now."

Tom nods his agreement. "It's going to be a firefight," he says. "How many cops are in Oak Hills now? A dozen?"

"About that, yeah."

"MS-13 see them turn up outside their door, they're bracing themselves for a battle. There's gonna be blood."

Reiko runs her hands back over her face and head. "What's our plan? What can we even do when we get there?"

"We see how it plays out," Tom says. "Maybe it won't go as bad as we fear." Tom waits a beat, then adds, "Though it's more likely it will."

"And if and when it does?"

Tom runs his tongue around the inside of his mouth. His Beretta is tucked down the back of his jeans. He knows Reiko has her Smith & Wesson M&P 9 on her person. They don't know what kind of weaponry MS-13 will have in the house, but they have to assume it's heavy. He takes a deep breath. "Then we help."

31

R eiko directs Tom to the street where the MS-13 members are. By the time they arrive, the police are in place. The entrance has been blocked off. The other houses in the cul-de-sac have been emptied, and now the occupants are behind the blockade. Tom and Reiko have to get out of the car and continue on foot. Reiko talks to the cops standing guard.

"Let us through," she says, motioning between herself and Tom.

"You know I can't do that, Reiko," the cop says, his expression regretful.

Tom looks beyond them. To where and how the cop cars are parked. Six cruisers in total, all aimed at the house. The cops are all armed. They're wearing vests. They're pointing their guns – a mix of pump-action shotguns and Smith & Wessons – toward the house at the end of the cul-de-sac. One of them has a megaphone, but he's not speaking into it yet. Tom doesn't know what Grice looks like, but he thinks this is him. He looks older than the other men here. A short guy with thin strands of hair slicked back on his head, and a bulbous nose, likely caused by years of secretive drinking. His waistline, too, looks like it's been topped up with many empty calories.

"Damnit, what do you think we're going to do?" Reiko says. She's up in the face of the cop standing guard. "Let us through. We'll hold back."

The cop stands his ground. "Reiko, listen – you know I would if I could. But I *can't*. Come on, don't do this to me."

Before Reiko can say anything else, Grice is speaking into the megaphone. *"We're not looking for any trouble!"* he says. *"Come on out of the house with your hands where we can see them!"*

Reiko steps off from the cop. She watches. A hush has descended upon the previously murmuring crowd. Everything is silent. It feels like everyone is holding their breath.

Tom can see Greg. He's near the back of the mass of parked cruisers. He stands by his own vehicle, his body shielded by his open driver's side door, his handgun aimed at the house, just like everyone else's.

There's no activity at the house. None visible, anyway. Tom imagines there's a lot of activity going on inside right now. Reiko nudges him. She points to the Ford parked on the driveway down the side of the house. "That's their vehicle," she says. "They're in the house. They must've heard him."

"Never mind hearing him," Tom says. "They must've seen your colleagues clearing all their neighbors out of their homes, not to mention pointing all their vehicles in their direction." Tom studies the house. Watches the windows. Can't see anyone moving around. "Has he got people around the back?"

"I've got to believe he can't be *that* stupid," Reiko says. "But he's surprised me before."

Grice is watching the house, too. He looks to the men to his left and right. He says something. He shrugs and shakes

his head. He raises the megaphone back to his lips. *"I repeat –
come out of the house immediately, with your hands where we can
see them. This is your last chance to comply. I won't ask again!"*

Again, there's a silence. Grice stares at the house with his
arms folded. He turns his head enough that Tom is able to
see the defiant look on his face, like he's already posing for
the cameras.

There's a sound. Glass shatters. There's movement at the
windows now. At the biggest window, the living room
window, a sofa is upended and pushed up against it, blocking
most of it. The glass on either side of the sofa is smashed.

"Guns," Tom says. He turns to the gathered crowd.
"Everybody down!"

Then all hell breaks loose.

32

As Tom suspected, the MS-13 are armed with heavy weaponry. The cops aren't prepared, and they're easily overwhelmed.

The crowd near Tom and Reiko quickly scatters as soon as the shooting begins. The cop manning the barricade dives for cover. Tom and Reiko get around the barricade, ducking low as they run. They get down the side of the house nearest to them.

"There was gunfire around the back of the house," Tom says. "He had men there, but I don't think it's gone well for them."

Reiko curses, shakes her head. They both have their handguns out. They won't be enough. "What the fuck are they firing?"

The bullets tear through the cruisers. They tear through the men. The cop vests are ineffectual against the rounds. Tom sees one cop's head explode in a burst of red mist. He looks to the house. Tries to catch a glimpse of what they're handling. "I think they're M82s," he says. He can only see the blazing barrels of the guns at the downstairs windows. At the upstairs window, he sees a little more of the body of the weapon. "It's hard to tell, but the damage they're inflicting matches up." He holds up his Beretta and nods to her Smith & Wesson. "These aren't any match. Especially not at distance. We need to get close."

The surviving cops have ducked low, got behind cover. Some of them are returning fire, but, as Tom has said, their firearms are no comparison to MS-13's heavy weaponry.

"How many of them are in there?" Tom says.

"I think five," Reiko says. "I've only ever seen five, but I don't know that for certain. This is why the house needed to be watched!"

Tom nods. "We have to hope it's just five, then. And we need to get them now. They're going to keep your colleagues suppressed – if they don't just outright kill them all – and then they're gonna make their escape before anyone else can be called in to help out here."

Reiko nods. Her breaths are shallow. She swallows. She's firm, though. Her nerves aren't getting the best of her. Her hands are tight around the handle of her gun. She isn't shaking.

Tom looks her in the eye. "They won't give up," he says. "Do you understand that? They won't take any prisoners, and they won't let themselves be taken, either. This is kill or be killed. Do you understand?"

Reiko's lips purse. She nods.

"Let's go," Tom says. "Stay close."

They head to the back corner of the house. MS-13 are three properties away. Tom can still hear gunfire. He heads across the backyard of the first house, to the fence separating this property from the next. He climbs over, and Reiko follows. They keep going. At this fence, the MS-13 house is in view. He and Reiko drop to the ground on the other side, in case they were spotted. They stay on the ground. They crawl to the next fence. Tom stands, peers toward the house. Only one house left between them and it. He watches. The gunfire is concentrated at the front of the house. Toward the cops. Tom counts four rifles at the front. All, he thinks, M82s. The fifth man could still be at the back of the house. Tom doesn't think there's any gunfire there, but it's hard to tell. This fifth man could be watching the side windows, too. Looking out for people like them, getting closer, putting them in danger.

Tom looks at Reiko. She's watching, too. She swallows. They're close. Very close. Nearly there. She realizes he's looking. She nods.

They hop the fence. Stay low. Crawl again. Go to the last fence. Tom peers over. Looks to the windows at the side of the house. There's only two. They're both empty. He ducks back down. "I'm going for the guy at the back window," he says. "You watch these two windows here. Cover me."

Reiko takes a step back from the fence, drops to her knee, raises her Smith & Wesson. Covers the windows.

Tom climbs over. He doesn't drop low this time. Doesn't stop moving. He goes straight to the house, presses himself up against the side of it. He moves down to the back corner. Looks around it with just one eye, keeping the rest of his body concealed. He looks into the space behind the house, too. There's a fence at the bottom. Beyond that is trees. He sees two dead cops. They lie flat on their backs. One of them is missing his face. The other has a gaping hole in his chest. Tom can hear moans. A third cop. Wounded, by the sound of it.

There's a shot from the top middle window. A potshot. It hits dirt. Tom hears the moaning cop cry out in alarm. Tom can't see him. Trees obscure where he lies. Tom hears a chuckle from the window. The shooter is playing with the wounded cop. Teasing him. He fires again. The bullet tears through a branch. It falls. The cop cries out. Tom thinks the branch has landed on him.

Tom can only see the shooter's rifle. It's an M82, as he thought. He checks the other windows, downstairs and up. They're clear. They haven't been opened, or smashed. Tom wraps both hands around the Beretta's handle. He waits. Watches. The rifle is lowered. The shooter is still chuckling. Admiring the wounded cop's predicament. He's enjoying himself. Making his own fun while his four friends get their fill of it at the front of the house. He doesn't have as many cops to choose from. He's having to make the ones available to him last.

The shooter raises the rifle. Either to taunt, or to end the wounded cop. Tom makes his move. Steps out from around the corner of the house. Gets out from under the window. Raises the Beretta. Spots the man in the window. He fires twice. The first bullet catches the shooter under the jaw. The second in the side of the head. Blood sprays against the wall behind him. He drops. The rifle falls back inside the house with him.

Reiko has seen. She climbs over the fence, joins him. They duck low past the downstairs windows. Go to the back door. It leads into the kitchen. The kitchen is clear. They can't see into enough of the house to see the rest of the men. The door is locked. Tom doesn't want to kick the door down. They have the element of surprise. He doesn't want to lose that.

They go under the window where Tom has killed the shooter. Tom laces his fingers. Reiko steps into them. He boosts her up. Lifts her high. She has a foot in each of his hands. Tom feels her weight lessen as she gets a grip on the frame. Pulls herself inside. Tom looks up. Watches her disappear into the house. Tom peers in through a window. He can see the men at the front downstairs windows. Three men. The fourth is at an upstairs window on the front of the house.

Tom can see the stairs. Reiko doesn't come straight down. Tom works out a mental route. She should be down by now. He thinks she's gone to the other upstairs shooter.

Tom grits his teeth. All he can do is wait.

She comes down. She has an M82. She creeps down the stairs. Her eyes are fixed on the three men remaining. She steps to the kitchen. As she reaches the door, one of the men turns. He sees her. Reiko dives through the door. The man opens fire. Tom hits the ground. The bullets are wild. They shatter the glass overhead. It lands on him. They tear through the wall. He doesn't know if Reiko got clear, or if she got hit.

He hears the back door unlock. The door swings open. At this point, it doesn't matter. They've lost the element of surprise. But Reiko is alive. She's unharmed. Tom grabs her and pulls her to him. He takes the M82 from her. He's pressed against the wall under the shattered kitchen window. Lies on his back and points it at the open kitchen door. He hears the shooter inside coming closer. He's only seen Reiko. A woman in civilian clothing. He's probably confused as all hell at her presence in the house, but he's not thinking too hard on that right now. He thinks she's alone. He's coming after her.

The shooting stops. Tom could stay where he is. Pick the guy off as he appears through the doorway. But he could be lucky – there could be two of them. If there is, he'll only get one chance to get both. From where he is, to the side of the door, a second man could dive back into cover. Tom rolls over, holding the rifle close to himself. He stops at the doorway, facing up into it. Stays on his back. Points the rifle. The shooter comes into view. Alone. Tom opens up. Braces himself against the recoil. It rattles through his body. It almost tears the shooter in two. He collapses in a bloody heap.

Tom is on his feet. He's inside the house. The two

remaining have heard. They're turning. Realizing they're under attack from the rear now, too. They're both on either side of the sofa at the living room window. Tom gets the one on the right with ease. Mows him down. Can't turn to the one on the left fast enough. He's already opened fire. Tom throws himself back into the kitchen. Wooden splinters from the doorframe fly across his face. One of them gouges deep. Tom feels blood running down his cheek. He shimmies back across the ground toward the rear door. Grabs the kitchen table by a leg and throws it toward the door he's just dived back through. It won't do much, but if the shooter is following, it could buy him a couple of seconds. A couple of seconds can make all the difference.

Glass shatters. Gunfire. Handgun fire. Smith & Wesson. The M82 falls silent. A body hits the floor. Tom gets outside. Reiko looks at him. Both of their ears are ringing. "I got him," she says.

33

Grice has been injured in the shoot-out. Nothing serious. Shattered glass from a windshield across his face. It's bloodied him. It also made him fall. Dislocated his right shoulder. It's currently in a sling. There's bandaging across his face. It's already soaking through with blood.

He's upright, though. And he's mad as hell. Gesticulating wildly with his good arm. "What the hell happened?" he's saying to anyone who can hear. Anyone who will listen. "What went wrong, goddamnit?"

There aren't many people who can answer him. More than half of the cops on the scene have been killed. The rest are injured, some of them badly. Early-retirement injured. They'll never be able to police again.

Paramedics have arrived, but they're stretched thin. Reiko and Tom have been checked already, but neither of them were harmed. The paramedics were quick to move on to people who actually needed their help.

Grice spots Reiko and Tom now. Sees them standing to the side. Watching him. Almost waiting for him to notice.

"Two of you," he says, waving. "Get over here!"

"You did well in there," Tom says, turning to Reiko.

Reiko smirks. "You didn't do too bad yourself," she says. She stops on her way to Grice. Looks at Tom. "I'm glad you had my back." She reaches out, squeezes his hand.

"And I'm real glad you had mine," Tom says.

They go to Grice. He looks Tom over. "Who the hell is this?" he says, addressing the question to Reiko. "Is this Rollins? What the hell's he doing here? What are *you* doing here, for that matter?"

Despite the blood leaking out of his face, his whole head still manages to turn bright red in his fury. It makes the blood soak through his bandages faster.

"If we weren't here," Reiko says, "you'd all be dead right now. Everyone. Including you."

Grice's jaw works. "I benched you," he says, jabbing a finger into Reiko's face. "You've got no right being here." He turns the finger on Tom. "And just who do you think you are? You're not a cop. You're nobody. You shouldn't be anywhere near here."

Tom looks at the finger. Stares at it until Grice takes the hint. He falters. Lowers his arm.

Tom turns away from him. He means it as a sign of disrespect, and he's sure Grice will take it as such. He's seen Grice's type before. Too many times. A pompous, officious asshole full of his own self-importance. Desperate to blame his mistakes on anyone he can, rather than shoulder his own personal responsibility.

His head turned, Tom sees Greg coming toward them. There's a bandage around the top of his head. A dot of blood on his left temple. Tom can't see what has happened to him, or how bad it might be, but he's still on his feet. He's on the phone, too. He's wrapping up his call, slipping his cell into his pocket.

Grice sees Greg, too. Greg is coming his way. Grice ignores him, focuses on Reiko again. "What brought you here?" he says. "How'd you find out we were going to bring those gang-bangers in – goddamn gangbangers. Gangbangers who are all dead now because of *you*. And *him*." He tips his head toward Tom, but doesn't look directly at him. "We can't question dead men, Miller."

Tom sees the way Reiko's jaw is clenched. She's standing her ground. She won't back down to the chief.

"Goddamnit, I'm talking to you," Grice says.

"And I hear every word you say, you little prick," Reiko says, taking a step closer to him.

Grice blinks, taken aback. His jaw goes slack.

Greg reaches them, places an arm across Reiko's chest and holds her back. Her glare is burning a hole through Grice. "I need to talk to the chief," Greg says.

Grice regains some of his composure. Manages to act tough, now that there's someone between himself and Reiko. "We're not done here," he says.

"Damn right we're not," Reiko says, standing her ground. "I'm not going anywhere."

This seems to shake Grice a little, but Greg is soon talking to him. "I've spoken to the deputy chief of police," Greg says. Tom notices now that Greg is glaring a hole through Grice, too.

Grice blinks. "What?"

"I've spoken to the deputy chief, and I've told him what you've done here," Greg says. "I've told him how all of this is *your* fault – these dead and injured men are on *you*, Grice. And I've told him all about Reiko, too, and how she saved us. Frankly, he couldn't believe she'd been benched. How was it he phrased it? Oh, that's right – *That'll be Grice chasing solo glory again.*"

The color is draining out of Grice's face. He's turning pale.

He looks unsteady on his feet. "I'm the goddamn chief," he says, but his voice is quiet. "He's just my deputy. He –"

"He's talking to the council," Greg says. "You're not going to be the chief much longer." Greg says this with a look of deep satisfaction on his face. He's trying to hold in a smirk. "He's taking over as acting chief. You're benched while an investigation is conducted into the botched job you've done here."

Grice is shaking his head. "No, no, you can't –"

"It's already in progress," Greg says. "You think anyone's going to back you after today? Oh, and before I forget." Greg turns to Reiko. "Acting chief says you're back on duty."

Reiko doesn't try to hide her own smirk. She steps back closer to Grice, who shrinks away from her. Greg doesn't try to hold her back this time. "And now you're going to shut the fuck up, for once in your miserable life," Reiko says to the soon-to-be-former chief. "Me and Tom came here because we knew you couldn't help but mess this up. And you're damn lucky we did, or else there'd be more dead bodies than there already are."

She steps closer. Grice has to back up, until he hits the cruiser behind him. He looks like he's about to collapse. "Now listen to me. I've had enough of you running this department into the ground. Because of you, because of what you've caused today, there's barely a department left. And it sounds pretty clear that I'm not the only one who's had enough." She's looming over him now. Her face inches from his. Reiko is scowling. She looks terrifying, and Grice is suitably terrified. "You've got your sycophants and your yes men, and there's the others who are too scared to stand up to you – but enough is enough. You're done, Grice."

Grice swallows. Tom hears a dry click in his throat.

"That's right," Reiko says. She steps back, like she's been close to him for long enough. She sneers. "You're not long for that uniform, Grice," she says. Her voice is low, but Tom hears. "You're not long for chief. It's time a Miller was back in that position. It's time things were done right again."

Reiko walks away. Tom keeps step with her. She motions for Greg to follow.

"Holy shit," Greg says, catching up. "The look on his face –!"

"I'll have time to think about that later," Reiko says. She's serious, but she can't help grinning. "Right now, I need to get back into uniform."

34

B ull is in the back room of the house. It's a small room. It's barely big enough to fit in a bed, and is likely designed for either storage, or small children only. It's a perfect size, however, for what he uses it for.

What he uses it for is surveillance.

Not on anyone in particular. It's for everyone. Up and down the street, hidden in bushes and trees and the STOP sign at the entrance, he has small cameras hooked up that allow him to keep an eye on daily comings and goings. Not just daily, either. Nightly. Every morning, he checks the footage. Makes sure no one has been sniffing around the house. Here, in the back room, is where all the footage feeds into. There's a desk pressed up against the wall in the corner, with three screens on which he can view live feeds from all twelve of his cameras. Each screen is split into four. He watches them now, eyes drifting over each feed. There's nothing to see. The most activity comes from the old lady who lives four blocks away, walking her little dog. She stoops to scoop up some of its shit.

One of the first things Bull did when he moved in was

install these cameras. He did it late at night, when the rest of the street was sleeping and they couldn't see him and come stick their noses in.

He's not obsessive about checking it. Just every morning, for peace of mind. So far, he's never seen anything to be worried about. He has a feeling, though, that he might need to keep a closer eye on it soon enough.

Later, he's watching television when Kai comes bursting into the house. His dramatic entrance brings Josh through from his room. Bull looks up at him. He heard him come roaring down the road in the truck and screech to a halt on the driveway. Heard his footsteps as he came running into the house. Despite only running a dozen or so paces, he's breathless. It's not bad health. Kai is fit and well. It's excitement.

"What's wrong with you?" Josh says, brow furrowed.

Kai doesn't respond. He looks at Bull. "You heard?"

Bull shrugs. "Heard what? I've been here all day."

"About the shoot-out," Kai says. "It's the talk of the fucking town, man."

"Another shoot-out?" Josh says, frowning. "Or the ones in the forest we already know about?"

"Not just any fucking shoot-out," Kai says. He's caught his breath. Gathered himself. "The cops and MS-13."

Bull sits up at this. He's smiling. "That so?"

Kai nods. "It's happened."

"How bad was it?"

"A *lot* of cops got killed," Kai says. "A lot of them got hurt, too. I took a drive by the place, and it's still chaos. Looks like a fucking war zone. They haven't even cleared up all the bodies yet, or the blood."

"MS-13?" Bull says.

"All dead," Kai says. "Cops got them. From what I heard, it was the Jap."

"Reiko?"

"Yeah. And some other guy – some people didn't know who he was, and some thought he was a forest ranger."

"You think it could be the same ranger from the other times?" Josh says.

Bull ignores the question. "How many people did you talk to?"

"There was a crowd," Kai says. "People were eager to speak."

"You weren't obvious about it?"

"Give me some credit."

Bull nods. "What about the cops? Are more coming?"

"A few more cars turned up while I was there. I think they've had to bring some in from outside of Saxton. They don't have the manpower left to clean this up themselves."

Bull sits back. Lounges. Feels the cool air from the fans upon his skin. He smiles. "Good."

Josh takes a seat. Kai remains standing. "Is this how you wanted things to go?" Josh says.

"Close enough," Bull says.

"What are you going to tell the cartel?" Kai says.

Bull shrugs. "I don't have to tell them anything. They'll find out for themselves. If they insist on talking to me about it, what can I do? I'll tell them their boys weren't as careful as they should have been. They gave themselves away. They made the cops come looking." Bull grins. "And now more cops are coming."

"MS-13 don't like to get knocked down like this," Kai says.

"Yes, and if this were El Salvador, I'm sure there would be violent and bloody retribution. But this is America. They can't be as reckless here as they are at home. They need to be smart. They can't come back to a town where they've just killed half the police force. The law isn't going to take too kindly to seeing their like for a long time. The slightest whiff of an MS-13 connection, and they're going to come down like a ton of bricks." Bull holds out his hands. "And thus *we're* able to sever our cartel connection."

"Greedy fuckers," Kai snorts. "I never liked them. I never liked their threats, either. We never needed their damn connection – we were fine without it." He looks like he wants to spit. Since he can't do that inside, he makes a noise through his teeth instead.

"That's true, but at least it's only been a couple of months," Bull says.

"A couple of months of their grubby hands in our pockets."

"You have to look at the silver lining, Kai. On the plus side, they've brought us the workers. The day laborers they brought us from Sacramento. They keep you two out of the fields. They've improved our productivity. And now, even after this, those workers aren't going to go anywhere. They don't know anything about the shoot-out. How could they? It's not like anyone's going to tell them. As far as they know, the threat of MS-13 is still hanging over their families back home."

Josh chuckles. "You did it," he says to his uncle. "You dealt with them, just like you said you would."

"Just like I said I would," Bull agrees. "And all we had to do was get our mercs to kill that runaway spic and make it look like MS-13 had done it. Send a couple of Latino mercs after that ranger no one seems to be able to kill. The cops have done our dirty work for us. Always remember that, boys – if you can get someone else to get their hands dirty for you, even if they're a cop, you do just that." Bull begins to laugh to himself. "This is an anniversary to remember, isn't it?"

Josh laughs too. Even Kai, who's been so straight-faced throughout this whole interaction, allows himself to smile. He's never liked the cartel, nor how they forced themselves upon their operation. Never wanted anything to do with them. He was vocal about this to his uncle when they first turned up, but Bull had to calm him. Explain to him that war with a cartel was a war they had no chance of winning. Relief washes over Kai now. The tension goes out of his shoulders. They sag. He starts to laugh, too.

35

It's been two days since the battle with MS-13. Oak Hills remains abuzz. Police officers from other counties, other agencies, have descended upon the town to help out.

Tom sits in Clyde's Diner. He's alone in a booth by the window. He can see out into the parking lot. It's lunchtime, and the diner looks more like its old self now that MS-13 are not coming here daily. It's busy. Bustling. There's a constant murmur of mingling voices. Clyde is behind the counter, and he can't stop smiling. He's not having to do it all by himself anymore. His waitresses are back. His chefs. He mans the till and makes small talk with the patrons who sit near him at the counter.

It feels as if Oak Hills has released a collective breath it did not realize it was holding. People keep smiling. They talk about the shoot-out. A lot of people who talk about it weren't there. Even those who were were quick to scatter when the shooting started. But everyone has a story – everyone has their own version and angle of events. Everyone has a story to tell, regardless of how tangentially it may have affected them.

Tom is drinking water. He hasn't ordered yet. He's waiting. Through the window, he sees a police cruiser pull into the parking lot. It's Reiko. She's late. He's not surprised. She's busy. The busiest she's ever been in all her time in Oak Hills. She's always running behind lately.

She comes into the diner and waves at him in the booth. Smiles as she gets closer. She drops into the seat opposite with a deep sigh.

"Hard day?" Tom says.

"Always, at the minute," Reiko says. "Sorry I'm late."

"Don't worry about it."

A waitress comes to take their order. They both order burgers.

Tom has been staying at Reiko's since the battle. He hasn't seen much of her, what with how busy she's been. They get to spend the evenings together, though. And the nights. She's loaned Tom the use of her Honda so he doesn't have to walk everywhere. Not that he's been able to leave her house much. Too many cops. Tom's had to answer questions about the battle. Luckily, he had Reiko to back up his version of events. The cops questioning him were satisfied with what she had to say. But Tom still hasn't had the freedom he'd like. There's still some things around town and out at the forest he'd like to look into, but he'd rather do it without scrutiny. He's waited two days. There are still a lot of cops around, but they're thinning. Not paying much attention to him anymore.

"Clyde seems happier," Reiko says, glancing to the counter. Clyde sees her. He grins broadly and raises his coffee mug in a salute. Reiko nods at him, then turns back to Tom. "This is the first chance I've had to come in here since the shooting."

"It's back to how it was," Tom says.

"Sure looks that way. And I'm sure his staff are glad to be back to work, too."

"How's the cleanup going?"

"I knew it wouldn't take you long to get down to business," Reiko says.

"Never does."

"The search of the house found a *lot* of weaponry. Not all of it guns. Blades, too. Some with traces of blood on them. We're getting them in the system, cross-referencing the samples with unsolved crimes here and out of state. But the search also turned up a bag of heroin."

Tom frowns. "One bag?" he says.

"Just the one."

"Personal use?"

Reiko shakes her head. "Unopened. We've ran a toxicology report on each of the bodies, too, and they were all clean, apart from alcohol, weed, and some general painkillers. No heroin. Nothing even remotely close."

"One bag is a small amount to be dealing in," Tom says. "And not worth instigating a firefight for. Left over from a previous sale, perhaps? Maybe a sample for a prospective bigger buy?"

"And what's it doing in Oak Hills?" Reiko says. "Oak Hills has never had a major problem with drugs, it's barely even had a minor problem with them, and to suddenly have heroin on the scene? That's a hell of a leap."

A cruiser rolls by the diner. It's not a Saxton PD cruiser. It's from Sacramento. Tom nods at it. "You've got a lot of help in town at the minute," he says. "What are they thinking?"

Reiko shakes her head. "They just want to clean up and move on," she says. "They're hanging around to deter MS-13 from coming back, but as far as they're concerned, that's that. The MS-13 members who were here are dead, and it's over."

"That's too neat," Tom says.

"I agree."

"And it still leaves too many questions. Mateo wasn't MS-

13. Short of coming into this country without papers, I doubt he'd ever done anything illegal in his life. So what was he running from? Who were the men chasing him? None of those I saw were the five we killed in the house. There's still someone out there. Something is going on. It's not over yet."

"Could be cartel, pulling the strings from afar," Reiko says. "But unless someone pokes their head over the parapet, we'll likely never know. For now, the MS-13 we had in the town are dead. They've lost whatever foothold they might have had. I'll keep an eye on things and make sure they can't get another one."

Their food arrives. "Clyde says it's on the house," the waitress says with a smile.

They both look over. Clyde is beaming broadly. He waves. He's no doubt heard the stories of their exploits in the battle. They both wave back their thanks. Tom picks up his burger. Takes a bite.

Reiko does the same. After swallowing, she says, "So what are you gonna do next?"

Tom stares out the window. Watches a couple of cars go by. He's never seen so much activity in Oak Hills before. He thinks a lot of the vehicles and people he sees are out-of-towners, drawn by the recent excitement, hoping to catch a glimpse of something worthwhile. "I'm not sure yet," Tom says. "I'm not convinced things are over here."

Reiko watches him. She chews. Tom turns back from the glass. He can see she's thinking about something. She takes a drink. "How long are you planning on staying in Oak Hills?" she says. "Are you settling?"

Tom shrugs. "I don't tend to stay anywhere for too long. This is the longest I've been somewhere for a long time now."

"There a reason for that?"

"I just like to move. It's in my blood. We've got a big country here – why would I limit myself to just one part of it?" He grins, remembering what Taylor called him: *Kerouac with fistfights*.

"What's so funny?"

"Just remembered something. It doesn't matter. Why are you asking, anyway?"

"Just curious," Reiko says. "You came here just over a year ago. Ron told me about you. He tells me about all his new recruits. Told me you don't have a fixed address. That you'd been travelling. Now I'm wondering if you're going to hang around long enough until you're satisfied things are resolved and then move on, or if you're going to ask for your job back at the forest and settle into your old routine."

"I've been wondering about that too," Tom says. "I liked the forest. It was peaceful. But that peace has been shattered, and I'm not sure it could ever come back." He looks at Reiko. "You gonna miss me when I'm gone?"

"Sure," she says. "But I'll live. The world keeps turning. Life goes on. One day, many years from now, I might not even remember your face. Maybe I'll struggle to recall your name. I'll just have this vague recollection of you as the guy I killed a bunch of MS-13 with."

Tom laughs. "That's a hell of a way to be remembered. I'll take it."

Reiko grins. "The forest could probably use your help," she says. "For the summer at least. Help them through the busy months. I know Ron would appreciate it. He likes you."

Tom looks down at his plate. He's almost finished eating. "I'll think about it," he says. "I might go later today. See how I feel when I'm out there."

"Who knows," Reiko says, "maybe you'll find you still feel the same way out there in all those trees. Maybe you'll want to stay in Oak Hills another year."

Tom smiles. He knows if he stays another year, it'll turn into two. Then three. Then he might never leave. He's not sure that would be such a bad thing. It's a beautiful area. A quiet town. He likes Reiko.

But Reiko won't be around here for much longer. There's no doubt, soon she'll be back in Saxton. She'll run for chief. She'll get it. Everyone knows she will – off the back of her name, her father's reputation, and her recent heroics. Maybe Saxton won't be enough. Maybe they'll want her in Sacramento. Maybe they'll want her somewhere further.

He shrugs one shoulder. "Maybe I will," he says. "Guess we'll just have to wait and see."

36

Tom waits another day for things to quieten down. He kills time in the diner after his dinner date with Reiko, then finds ways to busy himself around her house. When she gets home, it's late. They eat, then get to bed. Early the next morning, he drives the Honda out to the forest.

He hasn't been back out this way since he and Reiko were warned of the brewing shoot-out. He reaches the entrance to the forest. Doesn't use it. Keeps going. Heads along the side of the forest, passes by the spot he and Reiko had reached when they got the call from Greg before the shoot-out. He's going to the back. To where they were headed. In the rough direction of the area he saw Mateo running from. The area Freddy and Stephen watch over. The area they told him was too dangerous to enter. The area Stephen told him he'd already checked for a trail.

Tom wants to check it himself. He doesn't doubt Stephen, and he's sure Stephen is good at his job, but the only eyes and skills he trusts are his own.

He doesn't drive all the way there. He pulls the car to the

opposite side of the road and parks it in a gap in the trees. Keeps it out of view. Continues the rest of the way on foot. Sticks close to the trees. There aren't many people on the road in this area, but he's ready to duck into cover should anyone appear. He doesn't want to be seen. Wants to keep this recon quiet.

Something catches his eye. Tire tracks in the dry dirt, going into the trees. They're fresh. The ground is so dry that, if they were from yesterday, they'd have blown away by now, or been trampled by animals. They're so clear they can't be very old at all.

Tom looks in the direction in which they disappear into the forest. It's dark there, where the trees are thick, their branches joining in a canopy overhead. He considers that these tracks could have been leaving the forest, heading back out onto the road, but that still means they would have had to enter from somewhere else. They can't have gotten through the front way. Nothing on wheels can pass through the area Freddy and Stephen cover with ease. Not even the ranger SUVs can get too close without risking damage due to the rough terrain.

He follows the tracks. It's cooler under the trees. In their shade. The tracks pass through the trees in an area wide enough for a single vehicle. Tom gets off the makeshift dirt road. He travels through the trees, hiding himself there. Doesn't want to make himself obvious. He continues to follow the tracks. They go deep. The trees remain thick. It's as if someone has shaped this area to be a concealed entrance or exit. He knows this can't be the case, though. It's just coincidence. It would take decades for the trees to grow in such a way.

Then he reaches a spot where he can see the trees have been cut back. The road *has* been shaped here. Trees have been cut down for vehicles to pass through. Tom checks the nearest stump he can find. It's not fresh. Its wounds have darkened. There are patches of moss on it. This wasn't done recently. It's been years, at least.

Tom hears voices. He freezes. They're coming from up ahead. He ducks low. Creeps forward. Gets closer. Hides behind a thick tree. He peers around it. Up ahead, there are two men. They're not rangers. He doesn't recognize either of them. They're armed with AK-47s. One of them has it slung over his shoulder while he smokes a cigarette, while the other is holding his rifle loosely in both hands. They're facing each other. The smoker laughs at something. The tree tunnel ends where they stand. Tom can see clear skies beyond them. They're on guard.

He's on high alert now. He moves away from behind the tree. Stays low. Goes deeper into the forest. Away from the men standing guard. When he's clear of them, he stays low, but he goes toward the light. The treeline. Something catches his eye through the branches beyond. He can see movement, too, but it's far away. He gets close to the edge. Keeps himself concealed. He feels his eyes go wide.

It's a poppy field.

Tom looks the area over, not sure he's seeing right. He is, though. Poppies. A full field of them. A *big* field. It covers roughly two miles. There are people working in it. Hispanic, all of them. They move from plant to plant. They slice into each bulb and gather the sap that oozes out. Tom runs his eyes back over the faces he can see. Does a double take. He recognizes two of them. They're near each other. Gabriel and Luis. The two men he found wandering lost in the forest. Who refused to tell him the real reason they were out there. He'd thought then they were looking for something. Was it this? Were they looking for the poppy field?

Except Tom doesn't think they're working it voluntarily. Around the field, there are armed men. They're standing guard, watching over the workers. They have automatic rifles, but they're not all the same. Another AK-47, but also an FN FAL, a couple of G3s, and a Galil. These men wear combat trousers and plain, dark tops in grays, blacks, browns, a dark blue, and a green. They're dressed like the men who were chasing Mateo. The men who attacked Tom in his station.

Off to Tom's left, there's a shack. It's set back, away from the field, under a rock formation and behind some trees. It's in shadow, and he almost didn't see it. There's no one at it. No one going in or out. Tom wonders if this is where the workers stay. Where they're kept.

He wonders, is that where they had Mateo? Is this where he was running from?

The workers in the field look tired. They look hungry and thirsty. They look thin and rangy, just like Mateo. Even Gabriel and Luis look smaller than they did less than a week ago.

Tom sees a flash of uniform. A uniform he recognizes well. He used to wear it – that of a forest ranger. There's two of them. He almost doesn't want to look. He knows what he's going to find.

The first doesn't surprise him. Freddy Lowe. It's the second ranger that hurts. Stephen Summers. Tom grits his teeth. *Son of a bitch*. He liked Stephen. They always got along. This is a deep betrayal.

He wonders how many other rangers might be involved. Does Ron know about this? He's not so sure. Ron is just waiting for his retirement. An endeavor like this seems like too much stress for a man just waiting to kick up his feet and see out his golden years. Tom can't see any other rangers present. Just Freddy and Stephen and all their armed guards.

Tom can't linger on his feelings of betrayal. He watches the two rangers. His former colleagues. Stephen is drinking from a bottle of water. He stays back from the field. Freddy goes right up to it. He starts barking at the workers. Tom can't make out any of what he says. Freddy leaves them, satisfied now that he's thrown his weight around a little. He goes to the side. Tom watches. There's a pickup truck. It's parked down from where Tom is, by the trees. Likely this truck left the tire tracks Tom followed in here. The tailgate is down. It's being loaded with boxes. A couple of the Hispanic workers are filling it. They're being watched by another armed man. They're almost done. There isn't much space left on the truck. Just a few boxes left to load up.

Tom looks around. Checks to see if there's another exit for the pickup. It's hard to tell from where he is, but he doesn't think so. Just the one way in or out to get back to the road. The route guarded by the two men he saw earlier. Tom turns and wades back through the trees. Back the way he came. He doesn't hurry. He's careful not to make noise. Doesn't want to draw the attention of the guards.

When he's far enough away where he doesn't have to worry about noise so much anymore, he starts running. He runs down the road back to where he parked Reiko's car. He doesn't get straight in it. Keeps the keys ready in his hand, though. He hides behind the trees and bushes and peers out. Waits.

Minutes tick by. Eventually, he hears a low rumbling coming through the trees. The truck is moving slowly. He hears it idle. He frowns, but then he sees why. A man appears at the opening. He's unarmed. Trying to look casual. He steps out of the trees and up to the road. Tom takes a step back. Watches through low branches. The man looks left and right. He turns and waves the truck out. It emerges. It's covered in a tarp, concealing the boxes it has been loaded up with. The man on foot slaps the side of the truck, then it pulls onto the road. He turns left. Away from where Tom is.

The man watches it drive off down the road. He turns,

looks around, then goes back through the trees the way he came. Tom thinks it was one of the men standing guard, whom he saw earlier. The smoker. It's hard to tell at this distance.

Tom waits a count of five. Gives the man a chance to disappear back into the forest. He gets into Reiko's car. Counts another five. He's not concerned about how far the truck gets. It's a long straight road past the forest before it reaches any turnoffs. The longer he leaves it, the better. He doesn't want to spook them.

He starts the engine. Pulls out of the trees. The road is still clear. He follows the truck.

37

Tom keeps his distance from the truck up ahead. He expects he's going to be following it for a while.

It's taken one turn so far. Heading toward Saxton. There are more vehicles on this road. Tom is glad. He lets some of the others get between them. Never takes his eyes off the truck except to check the fuel gauge. The tank is more than half full. He wonders where they're going. To Saxton or beyond? Sacramento or further? Is he going to be driving all day – through the night, perhaps? Will they leave the state?

He gets some kind of an answer. It comes sooner than he anticipated. Halfway to Saxton, the truck turns off the road. It's a side road. It leads through some trees. There's nothing signposted that way. Tom doesn't want to follow them immediately. He'll get too close. There's no one else going that way. He continues on the main road. He goes a little further down, then finds a place to turn around and head back. He creeps cautiously along the road where the truck turned off. The tarmac here is cracked and overgrown with weeds. It hasn't been tended, nor travelled on regularly. He takes his time around every corner, wary of suddenly coming upon something he's not supposed to see.

Finally, there's a sign. It's old and rusted. One corner is bent. It has a couple of bullet holes in it. He can't read the first word of the name, but the second is still clear: 'Mill.' He doesn't go any further. Whatever mill it refers to must be right around the corner. He reverses the car back down the road a ways, then hides it in the trees. Continues on foot. He pulls out his Beretta. Keeps it low. He goes back to the sign, but then gets off the road and continues through the trees, like he did back in the forest.

As he thought, the mill is just around the corner. It looks old, like it hasn't been in business for a long time. He sees the truck. It's being unloaded. Two Hispanic men, carrying the boxes into the mill through a side door. The truck's driver stands to one side and talks with someone while another man, armed, watches the box carriers.

There's a smell in the air. It's sharp. It's faint, but it catches in the back of Tom's throat. Tingles in his nostrils. He thinks it's coming from the mill. He takes a long breath in through his nose. There's something familiar about it. It smells like vinegar.

Then it hits him. What the smell is. It's a chemical. It's been a long time since he last smelled it. Not since Afghanistan. Acetic anhydride. A clear liquid that smells like vinegar, and one of the only ingredients other than the sap from the poppies needed to make heroin.

Tom has seen enough. He goes back to the car.

38

Tom drives back to Oak Hills. He breathes deep, ordering his rampant thoughts.

Poppies are being grown in the national forest. They're being farmed and tended, apparently by day laborers who may not be there of their own will. Then the sap from the poppies is being transported to an old mill between Oak Hills and Saxton and refined into heroin. Tom thinks of all the faces he saw between the forest and the mill. Thinks of the men who chased Mateo, and the ones who attacked him at his station. Save for the couple who came after him and Reiko in the motel, they've been predominantly white. It *could* be cartel running things, and these men could just be hired mercenaries, but Tom isn't so sure a cartel would entrust the running of so much of an operation to outsiders.

Hence MS-13's presence? Were they here to watch over things, keep everyone in line? Except now there isn't any MS-13. They were just a part of this operation, not the whole. Just like Freddy and Stephen. He doesn't think they're behind all this. Freddy isn't smart enough. But Stephen? He's already deceived Tom about so much. What else could he be hiding?

Tom remembers when he went to speak to the day laborers in Oak Hills. Remembers some of the veiled things Rodrigo said to him. They didn't make much sense at the time. He was reluctant to say too much, and the others were keeping him in line, too. Tom wonders if that would be the case now.

When he reaches Oak Hills, he goes to their corner. Only a couple of them are there. Neither of them is Rodrigo. Tom pulls up alongside them, the window down. "I'm looking for Rodrigo," he says. "Young guy. I don't know his last name."

The two day laborers look at each other. One of them walks away. The other scratches the side of his mouth, but he doesn't say anything.

"Where's he going?" Tom says, tilting his head to the one who walked away. There's a chance he's going to get Rodrigo, but it's slim.

The one remaining shrugs a shoulder. "He doesn't want to talk," he says.

Tom reaches into his pocket. Pulls out his wallet. He slips out a twenty. Shows it to the man. "Where's Rodrigo?" he says.

The man stares at the twenty. He hesitates, then takes it. "He's around the corner," he says. "Getting ready to leave. You can maybe still catch him. Apartment number twenty-two."

Tom drives around the corner. He passes the man who walked away. The man disappears into a building. The same apartment building Tom is going into.

He knocks on number twenty-two. He can hear movement inside. It pauses. Tom knocks again. "Rodrigo," he says, "we spoke the other day."

Footsteps approach the door. It opens, just a little. The chain is on. Rodrigo looks out at him, into his face. "Yeah, I remember you," he says, nodding. "What do you want?"

"To talk some more," Tom says. "Can I come in?"

Rodrigo doesn't move.

"I don't think you want us talking out here," Tom says. He leans in close. In a hushed voice, he tells Rodrigo what he's already seen. Rodrigo's jaw works. He's thinking hard.

"Why do you care so much, man?" Rodrigo says.

"Because I'm in it," Tom says. "Because I saved a man's life, and then they cut him up into pieces like he was nothing."

There's a pause, then Rodrigo closes the door. The chain scrapes back; then the door opens wider. Tom steps inside. There is next to nothing in the apartment. No decorations. Nothing that makes it look like a home. It's tiny, too. Tom can see all of it from just inside the doorway. There's a bed to his left. A kitchen directly opposite him. A door that presumably leads into a small bathroom. There's the smell of rotting takeout coming from the kitchen area. The trash can is over-flowing with boxes.

The bed is unmade, and there are a couple of plastic bags on it that look as though they're full of clothes. Tom remembers the man back on the corner telling him Rodrigo was getting ready to leave. "Where you going to go?"

"I dunno yet," Rodrigo says. "Back to Sacramento for now. Just to get my bearings. Make a plan. After that, I'm not sure. I don't wanna hang around there too long. I wanna try my luck someplace else. That's why I came *here*."

"To try your luck?"

"Exactly. I'd heard there was work." He clams up then. Like he remembers the last time he spoke to Tom about this, how the other day laborer held his arm, hushed him.

"There's not many of you left on the corner," Tom says. "I was worried I'd missed you."

"We're all gonna be gone pretty soon."

"Why's that?"

Rodrigo doesn't answer.

Tom waits. Gives him a chance to speak. He doesn't take it. Tom reaches into his pocket again. Pulls out his wallet. He takes out a twenty. Looks at it, then at Rodrigo. He pulls out the rest. Holds it out. Sixty-five dollars. "I don't know how far it's going to get you," he says, "but it's all I've got on me."

Rodrigo is reticent. He doesn't take the cash right away. "You want me to talk."

Tom nods. "I do. But you're also a kid, and I want you to be okay."

"You don't know me."

"That doesn't matter. I didn't know Mateo too well, either, yet here I am."

Rodrigo stares at the money. Finally, he takes it. Stuffs it into his back pocket. "We're leaving because MS-13 ain't here anymore."

Tom tilts his head. "They made you stay?"

Rodrigo nods. "We came because we'd heard there was work, but then we got here and found out that was bullshit. All the folk who got here first, they were being *taken* – either from Mexico, or they were getting picked up from corners in Sacramento. MS-13 were bringing them. Then us fools who turned up of our own accord, MS-13 would come by, introduce themselves. They were real friendly about it. But they made it clear they wanted us to stick around. Just in case they needed us. They'd take our names. Ask us a lot of questions – where we came from, who our families were, that kind of thing. Then the next time we'd see them, they'd start reciting our home addresses back to us, or the addresses our families still lived at. They'd start giving us descriptions of our sisters or our moms. The implication was pretty fucking obvious, right? *If you run out on us, we know where to find the people you love.* And, y'know, sometimes they'd pick people up from the corner. I don't know why they came and got them – I don't know if they needed to expand their workforce, or if they were replacing other people. And if it was the latter, I don't wanna know what had happened to them. Not with MS-13. But it gets pretty obvious pretty quick that they're holding us in reserve. We're their backup workforce, in case anything happens to the guys they've already got."

"You know what kind of work they were doing?"

"Not totally, but, I mean, it's MS-13. It's cartel. It's gotta be drugs, right? Everyone on the corner reckons so. I reckon it's gotta be either meth, or weed. The rumor's always been that they're in the national forest, so I reckon the weed. Some guys said heroin, but I ain't so sure about that."

"Did you know Gabriel and Luis?"

Rodrigo hesitates. "Yeah, I knew them," he says, in a small voice.

"Did you see them taken?"

Rodrigo shakes his head. "It happened at night. They were staying in this building. That had never happened before. If MS-13 came for any of us, they came to the corner. But this was while we were sleeping. Think it woke half the building up. I know it woke me – scared the hell out of me. I heard them drag them away."

"You know why?"

Rodrigo nods solemnly. "Because they went looking. They were in the forest. You found them, didn't you? You brought them back here. MS-13 found out about it. They came for them." He swallows. "I figure they must've killed them. Worried that next time they went wandering in the forest, they'd maybe tell someone why they were there, and what they were looking for."

"They're still alive," Tom says. "I've seen them. They didn't kill them. They put them to work."

This news doesn't look like it relieves Rodrigo. Death is likely still an inevitability for Gabriel and Luis. Worked to death under the eye of whoever is watching over them now that the MS-13 are gone.

"Why were they looking?" Tom says. "That desperate for work?"

"No, man, that ain't it."

"Then what?"

"They were looking for their cousin. They came here from Sacramento, same as me, but at different times. They came because their cousin's family down in Mexico was getting threatened to make sure he behaved himself for them. To make sure he did as he was told." Rodrigo pauses. "Except he didn't do as he was told. He tried to escape."

"Mateo?" Tom says.

Rodrigo nods. "Mateo Garcia. That's their family name, too. I ain't surprised he tried to escape, despite the threats. He probably got desperate. Maybe persuaded himself he could make it back to his people before the cartel could get to them first, I don't know. All I know is, if those motherfuckers were working me to death, I'd probably try to break free, too. His cousins, they were trying to find him so they could break him out. I don't know how they were planning on keeping his family safe when they got him out. Maybe they were gonna get them over the border somehow. Maybe they already have."

Tom grits his teeth. "Do you know what's happened to his family?"

"No," Rodrigo says. "But they're probably dead, right? Thing I don't get is why they killed *him*. From what I hear, they'd follow through on the threat to the family first. Keep him alive and get him back to work. Torture him by letting him know what he's caused."

This strikes a chord with Tom. He considers it.

Rodrigo sees him thinking. "What?"

"I think you're right," he says. "I think that's exactly what they'd do. I don't think they'd kill him. Not right away, maybe. And they wouldn't leave his body by the side of the road. That would draw too much attention to them. They were at least trying to keep a low profile."

Rodrigo laughs, though it's without humor. "Right up until they weren't," he says, referring to the gun battle.

Tom continues: "They didn't make any noise. They didn't cause any trouble – not with locals. Why suddenly change all that with a dismembered corpse? They had to know that would get people looking their way."

Rodrigo doesn't say anything.

"Someone else killed Mateo," Tom says. "Someone who wanted MS-13 out of the way."

39

Reiko is tired, but at the same time she feels rejuvenated. For the first time in a long time, she's doing real police work. For the first time in a long time, she has a future again. And it's looking bright.

The station is made up of more than just herself and Doris. It's bustling with activity and life. Almost too much humanity, for how hot it is. All the windows are open, and fans are running incessantly, but none of it seems to make much difference.

Reiko has taken over the running of the investigation. The officers all defer to her, as if she were chief already. She's talking to a couple of them when she sees her Honda pull up outside the station, and then Tom comes inside.

He doesn't come straight to her. Lets her finish her briefing. He stands by Doris's desk, talks with her. Reiko wraps up and goes to him. "Hey," she says. "What's up?"

Tom looks tense. He glances around the room. "We need to talk in private," he says.

Reiko nods. "Sure," she says, stepping into her office. Tom follows. "What's wrong?"

"Take a seat," Tom says, taking one of his own.

Reiko does. Tom tells her what he's seen. What he's found out.

"Heroin?" Reiko repeats.

Tom nods.

"So the block we found in the MS-13 house, that could've been a sample? Proof of product."

"Probably," Tom says. "But that's not important. Right now, we need to find out who *is* behind this. I don't think Freddy and Stephen are the masterminds."

A name comes instantly to mind for Reiko. "Bull Draven," she says.

"Who's that?" Tom says.

"He used to grow and sell marijuana," Reiko says. "Got released from prison two years ago, moved in with his nephews here in Oak Hills."

"You think he'd move to heroin?"

"Who knows?" Reiko says. "But he has a prior. There isn't another person in town has the experience he does. He's kept his head down and his nose clean for two years, but what if that whole time that was just a ruse? He's probably had his nephews running things. Son of a bitch..."

"We need to know for sure," Tom says.

Reiko nods. "I'll put a detail on his house."

Tom looks unsure about this. "These cops in town right now, how well do you know them?"

"Not very," Reiko says. "A lot of them are from other counties. In the gunfight with MS-13, more than half of Saxton PD was either killed or injured. The ones left can't all be here. They need to still be in Saxton, too."

"We need to keep this small for now. In my experience, you can never be sure who an operation like this has on their payroll. Stick only to the people you trust."

"Only people I trust are you, Greg, and Doris. But I'm not

gonna put Doris on a stakeout. Me and Greg will alternate. We'll watch Bull's house. See what he's up to. Find out if he *is* behind this. What are you gonna do?"

"I'm going back to the forest," Tom says. "See what I can find out there. See if I can find out who else might be involved."

40

Tom goes back to the forest. He takes the main entrance in this time. He parks Reiko's car and continues on foot, wearing a plain black baseball cap pulled down low to obscure his face. He has a bottle of water and a couple of energy bars with him. Gives the headquarters a wide berth. Avoids any other rangers he might see.

He makes his way through the forest. Passes by his old station. The blackened remains of where it once stood. The damaged planks of wood are still scattered across the ground. The area is cordoned off.

He stays off the trail as much as possible. Travels through the trees to avoid being seen. Eventually, he gets where he's going. To an area marked off-limits. Freddy and Stephen's zone.

He finds himself a spot opposite the tunnel-like entrance. It's the best view he could ask for. Off to the right, he can see where Freddy and Stephen have parked their SUVs. They're in shade, to keep the insides cool.

The spot Tom is in is thick with trees and bushes. There is some shade, but it can't protect him from the humidity. He doesn't think about it. Pushes any discomfort from his mind. He ducks low and peers out. Watches. Waits. Takes a sip of water and opens one of the energy bars. He paces himself. He could be here a while.

There's occasional movement at the entrance, but the only people he ever sees are Freddy and Stephen. No one else goes in or out. They alternate keeping guard at the entrance. They position themselves far back so they're out of view. They only appear if anyone gets too close. Tom sees Stephen step out, all smiles as usual, and give directions to a group of hikers. He points the way they want to go. They make small talk. The hikers stand with him for a little while. Stephen doesn't try to hurry them on. Never once rushes them. When they finally go, he waves them off. He holds back, though, and watches them go. Makes sure they don't come back. Then he hides himself back inside the entrance.

It's Stephen who has upset Tom the most. Stephen's has felt like the deepest betrayal. Freddy has always been a prick. He's never liked Freddy. That's no kind of loss.

He liked Stephen. Thought he was a good guy. But good guys don't grow heroin and associate themselves with the kind of people who cut another man into pieces.

It gets into late afternoon. Tom eats the other energy bar. Drinks some more water. Wipes the sweat from his brow. It's hot. It's always hot, lately. He's so still birds land in the branches near him. Barely notice him.

Tom watches.

41

Bull is alone in the living room. It's evening, but the day isn't getting any cooler. It's starting to get dark, but he hasn't turned any lights on. He has his usual four fans pointing straight at him. They offer him respite from the heat. Josh and Kai are in their rooms. Kai is listening to music. Listening to it so loudly Bull has to listen to it, too. Some punk stuff. He's not sure what it all is. Sounds like a compilation, or a playlist. He's recognized The Damned and Black Flag, but the others have been unknown to him.

Josh comes through, passes by on his way to the kitchen. "Just getting a drink," he says.

"Sure," Bull says. He waits until Josh comes back, a refrigerated soda can pressed to his forehead. "Josh," he says. He tilts his chin toward the nearest window. "Take a look outside," he says. "Through the blinds. Don't make it obvious, just peek out. Look up the road. Tell me what you see."

Josh frowns, but he does as his uncle says. He looks around. "It's getting dark. Ain't much to see." He tilts his head, moves it side to side. "All right, I give up," he says. "What am I supposed to be looking at?"

"The cop."

"I don't see any cop."

"You're not supposed to. End of the road, behind the Chevy. The unmarked Ford."

Josh looks. "Oh shit, I see it. There's someone inside. Black guy. I almost missed him."

"That's the one. He see you looking?"

Josh steps away from the window. "I don't think so. How'd you know he's a cop?"

Bull grins. He turns the fan off. "Him? I wouldn't. Except it wasn't him earlier. It was Reiko. I caught her on the cameras. Sat in the exact same place. Exact same kind of car. Then about an hour ago she left, and that one took her place."

Josh raises an eyebrow. "Why were you watching the cameras?"

Bull looks his nephew in the eye. "Because I'm always watching," he says. "Especially at a time like this. You can never be too careful, Josh. Go tell your brother."

"What do you want us to do?"

"Nothing. Not right now, anyway. I just want you both to be aware."

Josh nods, then goes to his brother's room. The loud music silences. Bull hears muffled voices through the walls. Hears Kai make a loud exclamation. He comes storming through into the living room. He's topless, wearing shorts. He's pumped up. Looks like he's been working out in his room. He's heading for the window to see for himself.

"Cool it, Kai," Bull says. Josh follows his brother through, but he holds back in the doorway. Leans against the frame with his arms folded.

Kai spins on him. "I wanna see the motherfucker."

"Not all hot like that you don't," Bull says. "We don't want him to know we know, and you're about to give us away."

Kai hesitates. Begins to pace. "They're watching us," Kai says.

"I know that," Bull says. "I told *you*."

"Uh-huh – and why the fuck are they watching us? *Huh?*"

"Maybe they're just suspicious," Bull says. "I told you how Reiko came to see me. It doesn't mean anything. She's suspicious by nature. She's a good cop. She's considering every avenue. It doesn't necessarily mean anything."

"You saying you're not worried?"

"I'm not saying that at all. I'm just saying we need to be careful how we handle this."

"Maybe it's a sign," Josh says.

"A sign of *what*?" Kai says contemptuously.

"That the cops know MS-13 weren't running things," Josh says. "That they were just a cog in the machine."

"You could be right," Bull says. "But I don't think they know too much, or else they'd be doing a lot more right now than just watching." Bull looks to the side, thinking. He strokes his chin.

Kai looks back toward the window. He wants to see the cop. He's seething. His shoulders are bunched up. He's breathing hard.

"Could mean we're going to have to get our own hands dirty," Bull says. His nephews look at him.

"With cops?" Josh says.

"I won't go back to prison," Bull says. "I've said it before, and I'll say it a thousand times more if I have to. I mean it. I won't go back. And if I have to kill some cops, then so be it."

He sits back. Takes a deep breath. Can feel himself getting worked up. He doesn't like getting worked up. Doesn't like losing control. That's not the kind of man he is. He calms himself. Laces his fingers. Smiles.

"Besides," he says, "we orchestrated the battle between

Saxton's finest and MS-13, didn't we? We're already responsible for some cop deaths."

Kai laughs at this. "Kill 'em all," he says.

"Be a shame if we have to put a bullet through Reiko's head," Bull says. "I ain't gonna lie, I'm quite fond of her."

"Fond of her ass," Kai says.

"Nothing wrong with that, either," Bull says. "But I was talking more about her pretty little Jap face. Y'know, I've been with a lot of women, but never an Asian chick."

"I don't think you're her type. She's so straitlaced, don't reckon she'd ever be seen dead with an ex-con on her arm."

"Don't I know it." Bull laughs, shakes his head. "Though I'm not interested in being on her *arm*." He takes another deep breath. He feels better now. Calmer. How he wants to feel. "Don't worry about them watching us," he says. "I'll deal with it. I've said it, so you know I will. Just like I dealt with the cartel."

42

It's getting dark. Tom doesn't have much water left.

He wriggles his toes inside his boots and opens and closes his fists to keep the blood pumping. To stop himself from cramping up. It reminds him of being back in the Army. Of being on recon or lookout. Endless hours of sitting or lying, hoping something will happen – or not, as the case may have been. It was important to stay alert. Important to stay as loose as possible. The last thing anyone wanted to happen was needing to move fast, and cramping up because they hadn't stayed hydrated, or kept their muscles active.

There's movement at the entrance. Tom doesn't perk up. Doesn't try to get a better view. He stays exactly as he is. Lets the movement come closer. Come into view. It's Stephen and Freddy. They talk briefly, and then Stephen walks off. Goes to his SUV. He's done for the day. Freddy watches him go. Waves. Tom watches, too. The SUV starts up. Stephen pulls back, turns the vehicle around. He drives off through the forest. Leaves.

Freddy stands with his hands on his hips. Doesn't go back in just yet. Ostensibly, he will be here to stay on fire watch through the night. In truth, he is no doubt here to keep an eye on things within. To make sure no one comes wandering their way. Same as during the day. When there's not a danger of fires, there'll be other reasons for one or the other of them to stay overnight. To watch over things. In the forest, there's always a reason. Always an excuse.

Freddy runs his hands back through his long hair. He ties it into a ponytail. He turns, but he doesn't go back inside. He looks around. Checks the area is clear. He goes up to a tree and starts pissing on it.

Tom sees an opportunity. He stands. He moves in. Gets closer. His movements are fluid. He's managed to avoid any stiffness in his muscles and joints. He's fast, but silent. Freddy is pissing for a while. He's finishing up when Tom reaches him. Shaking himself off. He zips himself up. Before he can turn, Tom grabs him by the back of the head and slams his face into the bark of the tree. He should have focused the blow on his forehead, to knock him senseless. First, though, he wants it to hurt. He's never liked Freddy. He wants to take a moment's pleasure from this. It's just a moment. He's kept hold of Freddy's hair. Pulls his head back and slams him into the tree again. Tilts his head so this time it's his forehead that makes contact with the wood. Knocks him dizzy.

Tom spins him now. Can see bits of bark sticking in his face. Some cuts and scrapes. A little blood. Not as much as he'd like. His eyelids are fluttering, though. He can't get his eyes to work properly after the impact. Tom hits him in the gut. Freddy blows all the air out of his lungs. His back hits the tree. He gasps. Throws up. It lands on the bottom of his trouser legs. On his boots. Tom hits him again. Freddy slides down the tree until he's sitting in his own piss. He's coughing hard. Tom pulls the Beretta from his waistband. He crouches, presses his left forearm hard across Freddy's chest, pinning him in place. He sticks the barrel of the Beretta into his face. Presses it into his left cheek, right under his eye.

"We're going to take a drive together, Freddy," he says.

Freddy is still gasping, but his vision is working now. He can see Tom. His eyes are wide. There's fear in them.

Tom grins. "We'll take your SUV. Then we'll go see Reiko, and you can tell us all about what you've got going on with the poppy fields."

43

Tom gets Freddy to drive. He sits in the passenger seat, his gun pointing at him. The SUV stinks of piss from when Freddy took a seat in it. Tom has his window down. It delivers only snatches of clean, fresh air. The stink remains, tinging everything.

Freddy is nervous. He glances at the gun. Tom's never seen him look so unsure of himself. Never seen him look anything other than obnoxious.

Freddy licks his lips. Swallows. He sniffs hard. Smells his own piss soaked into his clothes. Turns his nose up at it. "Where you taking me?" he says. His breathing is short and sharp. Tom can imagine his heart is hammering in his chest.

"To the station," Tom says. "Shut up and drive."

Freddy shakes his head. "I ain't gonna talk," he says. "I won't tell you anything."

"We'll see."

"You'll see *shit*. I won't talk. You got any idea what they'll do to me if I talk?"

"You got any idea what *I'll* do if you don't?"

Freddy bites his lip. They're not far from the way out now. He looks at the gun. Tom sees him looking.

"I wouldn't recommend trying anything, Freddy," he says. "I don't need much of an excuse to hurt you further."

Freddy's watching the way ahead. "I'm not scared of that," he says. "And I'm not scared of *you*." He puts his foot down on the accelerator. They start bumping over the rough ground.

Tom reaches for him. Freddy throws his door open, then himself out of it. The SUV is heading for a tree. Tom can't get his door open fast enough. He braces for the crash. It won't be too hard. Without Freddy's foot on the pedal, it's already slowing down.

The SUV hits the tree. Tom hears the front of the vehicle crumple. The impact throws him into the dashboard, but, as he suspected, it's without much force. He pushes his door open and gets moving. Freddy is running. Trying to get away.

They're not far from the ranger headquarters. Freddy heads for the trees to the side of it. Tom catches up to him. Tackles him to the ground. Freddy spins onto his back, tries to strike. Tom easily knocks his blow aside, then hits him across the face. He grabs him by the throat and hauls him to his feet, then takes his right arm and pins it behind his back.

"Freddy? *Tom*? What the hell is going on here?" It's Ron. The crash has brought him running.

There are a few other rangers behind Ron. Tom checks who they are. Stephen isn't among them. He's left the forest. Long gone. Tom still isn't sure whom he can trust.

Monica is one of the rangers. Her husband, Jay, is with her.

"Tom?" Ron repeats.

"Take a step back, Ron," Tom says. "Freddy is coming with me. We need to have ourselves a little talk."

"A talk about *what*?" Ron says. "Listen, Tom, I know

Freddy can be an asshole, but this ain't the way to go about things. Now, calm down and let him go."

Monica steps forward, her hands raised in a placatory gesture. "Everyone just stay calm," she says. "Rollins, what's happened here?"

"Just step aside," Tom says. He's not telling them anything. As much as he'd like to, he can't trust them. Stephen has already let him down. If Stephen is in on this, there's no one he can be sure of. "All of you, out of my way."

Monica doesn't move. "Just tell us what's happening here."

"You'll find out soon enough."

"He's got a gun, Monica," Jay says. Tom tucked the Beretta back into his waistband when he chased Freddy from the SUV.

"That's all right," Monica says. "He's not holding it. He's not gonna hurt anyone, are you, Rollins?"

"Take a step back, Monica," Ron says. "Just give them some space. Everyone stay calm."

"Monica," Freddy says.

She looks at him.

"Monica, *he knows*."

Monica considers this. She nods once. "You hear that, Jay?"

Jay pulls a Glock from his waistband. Monica does the same. Tom has never seen her carrying a gun before. They both point them at Tom.

"Drop it, Rollins," Monica says.

Ron's eyes are wide. "What the hell –?"

The other two rangers look just as alarmed.

Tom covers himself with Freddy, reaches for his Beretta.

"We will shoot you right through him," Monica says. "Don't think we won't. Drop the gun, *right fucking now*."

"Do as my wife tells you," Jay says. Tom doesn't think he's ever heard him speak so much before.

Tom stops reaching for the gun, but he doesn't take it out and drop it on the ground, either. He keeps Freddy close, despite the piss stink. Peers over his shoulder. Makes it hard for them to get a bead on him.

"You don't care if we shoot Freddy, I get that," Monica says. "You've never liked him. What if it's someone you *do* like, huh, tough guy?" She turns her gun on Ron.

Ron holds his hands up in surrender. "Monica," he says, sounding hurt, "what's going on here?"

"What's it gonna be, Rollins?" she says. "You think I won't do it?" She's smiling. There's an almost crazed look in her eyes.

It could be another ploy. He knows this. They could be playing him. Ron could be in on this. A couple of weeks ago, they could've tried this same tactic with Stephen, and he would've thrown them the gun to keep him safe. It would have backfired on him. *This* could backfire on him. If he gives up the gun, they could shoot him dead on the spot. But if he doesn't give them the gun, they could shoot Ron. It could be a bluff, but he sees the look on Ron's face. The expression of shock, confusion, and hurt. It's too real. It's genuine. Ron isn't one of them. Ron is in danger of getting a bullet through his skull.

Reluctantly, Tom gives up the gun. He grits his teeth for what comes next.

"Let go of Freddy," Jay says.

Tom does. Freddy tries to elbow him, deal him a parting blow. Tom grabs his arm, prevents him. Shoves him away. Freddy shakes it off. His obnoxious smirk is already coming back.

"Put your hands on your head, Rollins," Monica says. She turns, motions to the other two rangers. "Get over here, next to Ron. Where I can see you all." She turns back to Tom. His fingers are laced atop his head. "Down on your knees. Don't try anything. I'm gonna be watching you like a hawk."

"Bull ain't gonna be happy about this," Freddy says, looking at the four prisoners they now find themselves with.

"Let me worry about how Bull feels," Monica says. She sniffs the air. "You pissed your pants?"

Freddy stammers.

"Whatever," Monica says. "Get a gun and help us watch over everyone here. I'm gonna call Bull – find out what he wants to do."

44

R eiko took the initial watch on Bull's house, but she was only there a couple of hours before she was called back to the station. Greg took over from her. He's been there a while now.

Still at the station, Reiko changes into civilian clothes, then pours coffee into a thermos. It's going to be a long night, and she's already tired. As much as she'd like to hope something will happen, that Bull will give himself away, she doesn't think he will. Especially not so soon after the battle with MS-13. If he *is* involved in all this, he's going to be very careful right now. Lying low, probably. Letting things play out. Letting time pass. Bull's a smart guy. That's especially true if he's been running this operation in her own backyard for the last couple of years.

No, it's more likely that she's in this for the long haul. Day after day and night after night of surveillance, until he finally gets lax. Until he finally slips up. Until he gives himself away, reveals himself to be a part of this or behind it, and they can move in.

Of course, the thought does occur to her that maybe he

doesn't have anything to do with it at all. Right now, Bull is just a theory. A strong theory, but a theory nonetheless. They could get one, two, maybe even three or four months down the line, and they could be no further forward.

Reiko sighs. Tries not to think about that right now. Hates the thought that she could be wasting her, Greg's, and Tom's time.

She says good night to the officers still in the station and then heads out on foot. Tom still has her car. She'll call him later. They can talk. She can find out what he's been up to. If he's found anything out. The conversation will help keep her awake in the deep hours of the night. For now, she walks. She doesn't mind. It's dark, but it's pleasant. There is a stillness in the air. A calm that permeates a town that is only now realizing it was not as safe as it believed it was.

It's a half-hour walk to Bull's street. She sends a message to Greg to let him know she's coming. On her way she passes only a dog walker and a late-night jogger. Counts only three cars crawling along the road, no hurry to be anywhere. She reaches the entrance to the street, and she pauses. Looks down to Bull's home. She can see a couple of lights on inside, glowing around the sides and down the middle of the closed curtains. Can see the unmarked vehicle she and Greg are using, parked in the same place as when she left it. She sticks to the shadows as she goes to it, crossing close to people's houses. Over their lawns. Behind their bushes and their trees.

She reaches the car. It's empty. She frowns. Wonders if Greg has sneaked off to relieve himself. She checks her phone. She doesn't have any messages from him. Through the passenger window, she sees something. It catches her eye on the driver's seat. A splash of it on the passenger seat, too. It looks wet, and dark. Did he spill something? Is he looking for something to clean up? Reiko feels her breath tight in her throat and chest as she opens the door.

She doesn't need to investigate further. The smell hits her first. It's blood. Before she can straighten back up, before she can turn, something is stuck low in her back. It's cold through her jacket and her shirt. And it's hard. Metal. She doesn't need to see it to know it's a gun.

"Stay right there," a low, gruff voice says. She didn't hear anyone approach. Didn't see anyone else on the street. "Nice and easy. Stay cool. You don't gotta get hurt if you're smart. Not like your buddy. He wasn't smart."

Reiko feels her blood run cold. "Is he dead?" she says.

"Don't worry about that right now. Just worry about yourself. Now, I know you've got a gun. Take it out, nice and easy. That's right. Now hold it out to the side. My brother's gonna take it from you."

Reiko feels her gun snatched out of her hand.

"Okay, *now* you can straighten up," the voice says.

Reiko does. She doesn't turn.

"You know where we're going, sweetheart. You've been watching it, ain't you? Close the car door, then let's go down to the house."

Reiko does as she's told. She can't see either of the brothers, but she knows exactly who they are. Kai and Josh Draven. Bull's nephews.

"You just stay calm," the speaker says. She isn't sure which of the brothers it is. He's close to her, the gun still sticking into her, pushing her forward. He speaks into her ear. His breath tickles on her lobe and the back of her neck. "This doesn't have to end badly for you, Reiko. Just be smart about it. Use your head. Think about your future. Let's go."

45

Bull watches through the window as his nephews lead Reiko to him. Josh holds back, carrying her gun. He's looking around, checking their neighbors. Making sure no one's seen them, that no one's watching. Kai stands close to her. A little closer than necessary, but whatever. He's getting the job done.

It's unfortunate, but this is the way it has to be. Still, they can salvage things, he's sure. He can talk Reiko around, one way or another. She doesn't have to get hurt. He meant it when he told his nephews he was fond of her. He sees promise in her. If she uses her brain, she could benefit from this whole operation just as much as they are. Back when he was growing weed, he had more than a few cops on his payroll, paid to look the other way, or send him a heads-up if a bad situation was coming in his direction. A bad situation still managed to catch up to him, but that wouldn't be the same here. This is a smaller town. Not as much to worry about. And when things have calmed down, there's still only ever going to be one cop here. He intends for that to be Reiko. They're going to become very good friends. He'll make sure

of it, whether through kind words, or dark threats. Whatever
it takes.

Bull's phone rings. It's Monica. His niece. She starts talking, fast, as soon as Bull answers. He listens as she tells him
about a ranger called Tom Rollins. How he's found out about
the heroin, but she and Jay have managed to capture him.
"Freddy's here, too," she says. "For all the fucking good he
does."

Bull frowns, his mind racing. "He knows about the
heroin?"

"Yeah."

"That's...unfortunate."

"Uh-huh. He's been spending a lot of time with the cop,
too. Reiko. I think they've been fucking. I've heard he
might've helped her out with the MS-13 shoot-out, too."

"That so? That's interesting." He's referring to the first
part of what she'd told him. Tom's relationship with Reiko.
"Has he said anything since you captured him?"

"No. He's not talking. He could've spoken to Reiko
already, though. Could've told her what he knows."

Bull considers this. Considers how the cop was still sitting
outside the house earlier. Still alive, at the time. He hadn't
looked like he was in a rush to make any kind of move. "I'm
not so sure about that," Bull says. "If that were the case, we'd
already be surrounded with blue lights. We'd be getting
hauled in. No, I don't think he's told her yet."

"All right. Good. But there's a bit of a situation out here."

Jesus Christ, Bull thinks. *More?* "What?"

"Ron and a couple of other rangers were present when we
caught him."

Again, this doesn't concern Bull too much. "Ron is an old
man waiting on his retirement," he says. "*You* told me that. He
just wants an easy life. I think we can talk him around no

problem. Hell, he might even thank us for it if he realizes how much we could bump his retirement fund."

"What do you want me to do with them?"

"For now, leave them with the mercs. They can watch them. Tell them they won't have to guard them for long."

"And Rollins?"

Bull hears the front door open. His nephews drag Reiko inside. "Take Rollins to the mill," he says. "We'll be along shortly with some company for him."

46

They tie him up and cover his eyes, but Tom knows where they've taken him. The old mill between Oak Hills and Saxton. The heroin factory. He doesn't let them know he's already been out here. Now he's going to see it from the inside.

They take the cover from his eyes once they're in the building. The vinegar stink is strong. There's more of the day laborers here. A lot of them are wearing cloths tied over their mouths and noses. They're working on the heroin. Packing it. Boxing it up. There are mercenaries, too. Standing guard. A few of them came with them from the forest.

"He's fucking dangerous," Monica says. "We're not taking any chances. I want guns on him."

They're upstairs now. An old office with nothing in it save for a long-neglected desk and a few chairs. Monica and Jay are in the room with him, along with a few of the mercs. He recognizes one of the mercs. A white guy with blonde hair. He was in the forest, chasing Mateo. Tom thinks the merc knows who he is, too. He's sitting on the corner of the desk and staring at Tom, grinning. He cleans his nails with a combat knife. Tom isn't intimidated. He stares right back.

Freddy comes up to the office. He's been in the bathroom. He's wearing a different pair of trousers, and he's cleaned himself up. He doesn't smell of piss anymore.

"That's better," Monica says, giving him a look. "You stank. No way I was letting you hang around in an enclosed area like this, smelling like *that*."

"All right, all right," Freddy says, leaning against the wall. "I didn't piss myself, damn it. How many times I gotta say that? I took a piss, and then this asshole knocked me *into* it."

"Whatever," Monica says, turning away.

Tom is seated. They took the blindfold off him as soon as he was inside. He's still bound, though. His hands are tied behind his back. Bound with plastic ties. His arms are over the back of the chair. He can't work at the tie. One of the mercs stands behind him, watching him.

Tom watches them all save for the merc he can't see behind him. Watches how the blonde merc he recognizes from the forest is still picking at his nails with the tip of his combat knife. Watches how Freddy's jaw works, how red spreads up his neck in his embarrassment and shame. Sees how Jay stands by the door, watching Tom as closely as the mercs are. This is the most time Tom has ever spent around Jay. Usually he just turns up at headquarters, picks up Monica, and they go on their way. Tom wonders now how many times they circled back and went into the forest through the other entrance he found, leading right to the poppy field.

The merc isn't picking at his nails anymore. He drags the edge of the blade back and forth along his cheek. Tom hears how it scrapes against his stubble. Freddy turns on Tom. Desperate to reassert himself after his earlier shame.

"Look at you," he says, sneering. "Ain't so tough now, are you?"

Tom looks back at him, unimpressed.

Freddy steps closer. "Who do you think you're looking at?" he says, sneering. Alpha male bullshit. Desperate to absolve himself of his earlier shame. To eradicate everyone present's memory of how he stank of his own piss not so long ago.

Tom smiles at him. "I'm looking at *you*, piss-pants," he says.

Freddy goes bright red. He steps forward, closer, a fist raised, teeth bared.

"*Freddy*," Monica barks. She's not in the mood for his bullshit. "Back off. What, you want him to kick your ass again?"

Freddy's jaw works. His embarrassment deepens. This is not the redemption he was looking for.

Tom hears someone coming up to the office. Someone else. Someone new.

"Sounds like he's here," Monica says. She hears the approach, too.

"Finally," Jay says.

At this point, Freddy is keeping his mouth shut. He stands to the side and sulks.

The person coming reaches the office. Joins them. Tom isn't surprised to see that it's Stephen. He's out of uniform now. Wearing jeans and an untucked denim shirt. "Oh, shit," he says, seeing Tom. He shakes his head. "It's true."

"What," Monica says, "you think we were lying to you?"

Stephen hovers in the doorway, still shaking his head. "This is a mess," he says. "I'm sorry, Tom. I'm sorry this has happened. It was never supposed to happen. You were – you were never supposed to know."

Tom says nothing. Stares at him.

Stephen steps into the room, hands out, earnest. Like he needs Tom to understand. Needs his forgiveness.

"Don't get too close," Monica says.

"I wanted to tell you about it, Tom," Stephen says. "I swear. I wanted to cut you in. But your background, being in the Army, I wasn't sure – *we* weren't sure – how you'd take it. We couldn't run that risk. Because if we asked you, and you said no, then we would've had to...we would've had to kill you. And I didn't want that. I still don't, Tom. I promise."

Tom stares at him.

"Well, it doesn't make much difference now," Freddy says, smirking.

"Shut up, Freddy!" Stephen says, wheeling on him.

"He's right, though," Monica says. "For once. Get a gun, and forget about Rollins. Forget about him as the guy you used to work with. The guy you thought you could take to the bar and get friendly with. He ain't that guy. This is some asshole who's trying to take everything we've worked for away from us. You got that? And he's *dangerous*. We know he's dangerous. He's a trained fucking killer. He's already killed some of our guys. Hell, from what I hear, he killed the MS-13 fuckers. You think he wouldn't kill *us*? He ain't your friend, Stephen. He's nothing to us now. He's our enemy."

Stephen listens to her. He chews his lips, but he nods. He knows she's right. He goes to get a gun.

"And if you need to," Monica says to his departing back, "don't hesitate to shoot him. I swear to Christ, you hesitate, and I'll shoot *you*."

Tom thinks about Ron and the other two rangers back at the forest that they took prisoner. Monica, Freddy, and Stephen are all present in this room – if any other rangers were involved, he has to assume they'd be here now, too. Does that mean the other rangers are all clean? Potentially. There's no way to be sure of that just yet, though.

"How come you ain't told *me* to go get a gun?" Freddy says.

"Because you're a fucking asshole, that's why," Monica says.

Tom chuckles. He sees the hurt look on Freddy's face. Can't help himself. Freddy wheels on him.

"Something funny?"

Tom doesn't respond to him. He looks at Monica. "At least we can still agree on some things, right?"

47

R eiko sits crushed between Josh and Kai in Bull's truck. The gun Kai is pointing at her is pressed into her ribs. Bull drives. They head out of Oak Hills. "Where's Greg?" she says.

No one answers.

"Where's Greg?" she repeats. She wants to know. Needs to know. It's eating her up inside. "What have you done to him?"

"Who the fuck is Greg?" Kai says. He sits to her right, by the window. He pokes the gun a little deeper.

"He's the cop you bloodied outside your home," she says, shooting him a look. "He's my friend."

Kai chuckles at this. "Oh, *him*," he says. "The black boy. He's in our basement, coated in lye." He laughs again. "That's what snoops get."

Reiko feels light-headed. Deep down, she knew he was dead. She saw the blood in the car. She knew it was too much. Now they're holding her captive, taking her some-where, but Greg is nowhere to be found. She *knew*. She knew he was dead already. But that doesn't make it any easier to hear. She closes her eyes.

"Now, now, Kai," Bull says. "Our friend Reiko here has just lost a colleague. No laughter, please. Show some respect."

"I'm not your fucking friend," Reiko says, her eyes still closed.

"You may not feel like it right now," Bull says. "But let's see where the night takes us, shall we?"

Reiko opens her eyes. Kai pokes her with the gun, just to remind her it's there. She doesn't react to him. Josh is to her left. He doesn't speak. His arms are folded. His shoulder leans against hers.

"If you've killed Greg already," she says, "then why am I still alive?"

No one says anything for a little while. Bull continues to drive. Doesn't give any indication that he heard her question. Eventually, though, he speaks. "Do you have any idea, Reiko, how hard it was to be a white man locked up in California State Prison?"

Reiko blinks at the seeming non sequitur. "That doesn't answer my question," she says.

"And that doesn't answer mine," Bull says. "But that's all right. It was rhetorical, really. I don't expect you to know. How could you? You're a woman. You're an Asian woman, and you're a cop to boot. You lock people away – white, black, brown, yellow, doesn't matter to you, I'm sure – all the time. Lock them up, walk away, don't give them a second thought. Forget all about them, I bet. But we still exist. We're still there. We're still suffering amongst the dregs of society. All I did, Reiko, was grow some weed. Is that truly so bad? So bad that I should be locked up with murderers, rapists, gangbangers, kiddie fuckers? I didn't harm anybody. I grew and sold a *plant*."

"I don't believe you never hurt anyone," Reiko says. "The amount of money you were dealing in, someone always gets hurt."

"Believe what you like," Bull says. "But the fact is, I was never much of a fighter. My brother, Kurt, he was the fighter. That's who Kai gets it from. He takes after his father in so many ways. But I was never a fighter. I've always been more of a thinker. Just like Josh here. He's got the same genes I do. But a man like me, in prison...well. There's only so much I could talk my way out of. The animals inside are all desperate for blood. Or ass. Sometimes both." Bull shakes his head. Sighs. "I needed protection. It was the only way to survive. And I *found* protection. The only protection a white man like me *could* find. The Aryan Brotherhood."

Reiko watches him while he speaks. She wonders where he's going with this story. Why he's telling it to her.

Bull keeps his eyes on the road. Doesn't turn away from it. It's dark, and he needs to be careful. "But what could I give them in turn? Like I said, I'm not a fighter. And all the money I had had been seized by the thieves in the US government. Well, I could make them a promise. I was going to behave myself. Despite the length of my sentence, I knew I'd get out early. And once I was out, I had a plan. A new plan, to make more money than I was before. The money before would look like small fry. The Aryan Brotherhood liked this plan. They liked the prospect of what I could offer them in return – a cut. But they were wary. Rightfully so. It was just a plan. There was nothing solid about it. Nothing tangible.

"Except there was. You see, back when I was selling weed, back when I was living the high life, this man came to me. He was a veteran. He'd been in Afghanistan. He had terrible PTSD. Woke screaming every single night. The only thing that kept him calm was marijuana. But he didn't have any money. Didn't have a home. He had the clothes on his back, and whatever cash he was able to scrabble together during the day, begging. Old Uncle Sam sure takes care of his own, huh?"

He barks a laugh. Just one. He doesn't look particularly amused.

"One day, he came to me, and he'd been ill. Too sick to beg. He didn't have any cash to offer me. But he reached into his backpack, and pulled out a small plastic bag. In that bag were some seeds. Poppy seeds, all the way from Afghanistan. He said they were all he could offer me in exchange. I felt bad for him, so I took them. Had no idea at the time how those little seeds would impact my future.

"He disappeared shortly after. I don't know what happened to him, but that's not important. His part in the story is done. The fact is, I had the proof. I had the poppy seeds. And I'd left instructions with my nephews and niece in how to cultivate them. How to turn our modest little seeds into a full field, in preparation for my eventual release. The Aryan Brotherhood got their proof. And so they took care of me. They kept me alive. Kept me safe, and I was able to behave myself, and, just as I always said I would be, I was released early. And I came here, and the field was ready and waiting for me."

"Have you paid them back yet?" Reiko says.

"The Brotherhood?" Bull smirks. "They don't even know where I am. Oh, I was very careful. I didn't tell them *everything*. As far as they're aware, I'm on the other side of California. I don't believe in making money for others, Reiko. Never have. That's why I've always gone into business for myself. I make money for me and mine. Only people *anyone* should make money for. I'm sure the Brotherhood aren't too happy about that, but fuck them. They're not my problem. They'll never see me again."

Reiko frowns. "Then why bring in MS-13? A cartel? I doubt they were helping you out for free."

Kai makes a noise through his teeth.

"Oh, we didn't invite the cartel here," Bull says. "They

invited themselves. Found out about our operation and insisted on moving themselves in. Sure, they helped us out a little – bringing in the day laborers was their idea, and that's certainly increased productivity – but they were asking too much in return. Far too much money for the service they were providing. A service, I hasten to add, we never asked them for. We didn't bring the cartel to town, Reiko. I want you to understand that. I never wanted them here." He turns his head a little, looks at her now, and there's a brief gleam in his eye before he turns back to the road. "And I have you to thank for getting rid of them for me."

"How do you mean?" Reiko says.

Kai pokes her with the gun. "You really don't get it, or are you just willfully stupid?"

She glares at him, twists her body to get the gun out of her side, but he just follows her with it and pokes it in deeper.

"Now, now, Kai," Bull says. "Play nice."

Kai grunts. Finally eases off with the barrel of the gun.

"It was simple, really," Bull says. "All it took was a few strategic clues to point you in their direction. Now, the real opportunity came when that worker escaped. That provided us with a golden opportunity. We got our boys to cut him up, cartel-style."

"That was you," Reiko says. "You sent those fake immigration agents."

Bull chuckles, like this is at all funny. "Our men are well trained in a lot of ways, and it turns out playing dress-up is one of them."

Kai laughs at this, too.

"How did you know?" Reiko says.

"It isn't obvious?" Bull says. "We have your phone bugged, Reiko. That's another way in which our men are very highly trained. We've known every call you've ever received or made in that station. We know exactly how frustrated you get with Saxton PD, and the recently wounded Chief Linden Grice."

"Have you bugged them, too? How'd you know they'd called immigration?"

"Oh, we didn't," Bull says. "That was a coincidence. A lucky one, because it meant you didn't question things too much. But we figured you'd assume it was Grice trying to undermine you yet again, and you did exactly that. From what I hear, turns out he *was*."

Josh speaks up suddenly. There's a look of consternation on his face. "Why are you telling her all this?" he says to his uncle.

Kai grunts. "He's got a point."

"Because Reiko is our friend," Bull says. "Maybe not right now. Not yet. She might not even realize it herself. But she will. She just needs time. And I believe a firm foundation for any friendship is a lack of secrets."

"I get it," Kai says. "Either she sees the light, or she doesn't. Either way, it doesn't matter what she knows."

"Exactly," Bull says. "But let's not say it in such a threatening tone, you think? We're not looking to threaten Reiko. We just want her to understand. Speaking of which, we're all very sorry you almost got shot at the motel with that ranger."

"That was you, too," Reiko says. "I'm not even fucking surprised at this point."

"Another strategic clue," Bull says. "Send a couple of our Latino mercs to deal with the ranger. He wasn't supposed to survive, but our would-be assassins were going to make enough noise to draw witnesses. A couple of heavily armed Latinos fleeing the scene – with everything else going on lately, what were you to think? Cartel, of course. But like I said, we apologize, Reiko. We didn't intend for you to be at risk of getting hurt, or to be anywhere near the danger. How could we anticipate that you'd be sleeping with him? But we don't want to kill you, Reiko. We've never wanted that."

They turn down a dark road. There are no other vehicles here. She recognizes where they are, and knows where they're going. To the old mill. It's not long before she sees it come into view. She sees men outside, armed, standing guard. They point their automatic rifles at the truck until Bull rolls down his window and waves to them. They let him in. Bull is smiling. He parks, and turns to Reiko fully.

"I can see promise in you, Reiko," he says. "Promise that you can see the bigger picture. Promise that, as Kai put it, you'll see the light. I believe that you can come to understand what we're doing here. I believe that you'll come to understand there is more to life than your career. You could be *rich*, Reiko. You'll never have to worry about interdepartmental politics or unworthy superiors ever again. You'd have money and true freedom. And all you'd have to do is turn your head and look the other way. To send us the occasional warning if ever you think there's something we should be concerned about."

"If it ain't you," Kai says, leaning over so his mouth is close to her ear, "there'll always be someone else."

"Please, Kai," Bull says. "No threats. I've said it already."

Kai smirks.

"But first," Bull says to Reiko, "we need you to tell us – who else knows about what we're doing here?"

Reiko looks at him.

"Your friend in the car," Bull says. "And the ranger. But who else have you told? The FBI?"

Reiko understands. Despite how calm he appears, he's panicking. Desperate to know who might be bearing down on him. She doesn't answer. She can't. Right now, it's her only leverage. "What about Greg?" she says. "Did you give him the same opportunity?"

Bull waves the mention of Greg away, like he was nothing. Like he didn't matter. "Greg wasn't from around here," he says. "We didn't know Greg, and he didn't know us. We could never get him to understand, we knew that. And so he wasn't important."

"He was important to *me*, damn it," Reiko says. "He was important to a lot of fucking people."

"But not us," Kai says, poking her with the gun again. Reiko's sure by now that she must have multiple bruises on her ribs.

"We don't need to talk about all this anymore," Bull says. "Not right now. Just think on it, okay? Think on what I've said, and what I've offered, and about telling us what we need to know. I don't expect you to come up with an answer so soon. I know you're going to need some further persuasion." He looks toward the mill. He smiles. "And I have some persuasion in mind."

48

T om hears someone else coming their way. Coming to the office. It sounds like more than one person.

"All right, all right, back it up," someone says, stepping through, making space. Tom doesn't recognize him. There's something familiar about him, though. Something in his face. "Let's make some room. What's with all the bodies in here?" He looks at Tom. "For *this* guy?"

Tom winks at him.

The new guy frowns at this. Doesn't know what to make of it.

Following him into the room comes another guy who looks similar to him. He's holding Reiko by the arm. The merc who's been playing with his knife pushes himself off from the desk and drags another chair forward so it's next to Tom. The second guy puts Reiko into it. Tom notices she's been tied up, too, but her hands are bound at the front. They exchange a look.

Tom can hear conversation beyond the office. Down on the factory floor. He can't make out what's being said. The first new guy turns to Monica. He's grinning. "Hey," he says.

"Hey yourself," Monica says. "What took you all so long?"

The guy shrugs.

Tom realizes why this guy – and the second – have a familiarity about them. They look like Monica. They must be siblings.

Reiko must notice him looking. She leans over, nods her head to each in turn, says, "That's Kai. The other's Josh. Bull's nephews."

"Who said you could speak, bitch?" Monica says, spinning on her.

Reiko sits back.

"You could've told me Monica was related to them," Tom says.

"I didn't know," Reiko says. "Long as I've been here, she's never been a Draven. Always a Boyd. Plus, she was a ranger, and Ron was always fond of her. He never mentioned any connection to Bull. Could be he didn't know. And I've never seen her with her uncle."

"That's because my uncle's a smart man," Monica says. "Told me in advance to keep my distance. I still see him – I see him plenty – but you'd never see me around."

"She doesn't have any kind of criminal record, either," Reiko says. "Unlike her brothers."

"Yeah?" Tom says. "What've they done?"

"Fighting, mostly," Reiko says. "Usually with tourists. I think Kai's the instigator, though, truth be told. Josh is just along for the ride."

Tom looks between the two brothers. "Yeah, I can see that."

"I told you to shut the fuck up," Monica says. "The both of you."

Kai doesn't look like he cares so much. "Fuck it," he says. "Let them talk. What good's it gonna do them?"

"They're pissing me off," Monica says. "I don't like it. How they're all high and mighty, like we don't have the both of them by the balls right now."

"Ouch," Reiko says. "That must be more painful for you, Tom."

"It's mildly unpleasant," Tom says.

Kai snorts a laugh at this. Monica rolls her eyes.

Another body joins them in the room. Bull. He claps his hands together. "How's everybody doing?" he says. Tom recognizes his voice from the factory floor. He was likely directing traffic while he was passing through. "Everyone comfortable? Reiko? Yes?" He looks at Tom. "And this is Rollins?" he says, directing the question to Monica.

"This is him," she says.

"Pleased to meet you," Bull says. "I'd offer to shake your hand, but under the circumstances, I get that's probably not a wise thing to do."

"Not if you want to keep it," Tom says.

"Oh my," Bull says, laughing. "He's a lively one. I see why you've got so many people in here to watch him." He raises his eyebrows.

"We weren't taking any chances," Monica says.

"That's wise," Stephen says, speaking up for the first time in a while now. "Tom has combat experience. We don't know how dangerous he is."

Freddy makes a noise through his teeth. "He ain't so tough."

"He got you to piss your pants," Monica says.

Freddy is about to protest, but Bull cuts him off. "That sounds like an interesting story," he says. "Let's put a pin in it for the time being, but I wanna hear all about it later. For now, let's clear the room a little. Give us some space to breathe. Stephen, Freddy. Monica, Jay – wait outside. I'll be with you shortly. I need to talk with our friends in the corner." He looks at the mercenaries.

Tom glances over, too. The merc with the knife, he's not handling it anymore. He's put it back in its holster. Except he hasn't been paying attention. He hasn't buttoned it back into place. It's loose.

The room is cleared. Only Bull and his nephews, and the three mercenaries remain. Bull doesn't say anything for a while. He stands in front of Tom and Reiko. His nephews stand behind him. Josh is ramrod straight, with his hands clasped behind his back. Kai leans against the wall, arms folded. There's a constant smirk on his face. Bull starts to pace. He takes a deep breath. Sighs it out. He stops. Talks to Reiko.

"We've spoken already," he says. "There's not much more I can say. I just want you to be prepared for what is about to happen next. If you would just tell us who else knows about us, none of this needs to happen." He gives her a solemn look, like he's genuinely regretful. "Now, I wish, I really do, that I could just offer you a large sum of money and that would be that. You'd take the money and look the other way, and we could just leave it at that. We could all get on with our lives. But I think we all know you're not that kind of cop." He sighs again. "And that's a shame, really." He turns to Tom. "It's especially a shame for *you*, my new friend."

Bull motions for the mercenary with the knife to come closer. "We need Reiko to get on board," he says. "Do you understand? You're gonna have to hurt Tom here. You're gonna have to hurt him real bad." Bull looks pained by what he's saying, but he soldiers through. "It doesn't matter what you have to do, or how long it takes, I'm afraid you're going to have to break *her* through *him*."

The mercenary is grinning at this. He glances back at Tom, and the tip of his tongue is pressing up into his top lip.

"Don't kill him, though," Bull says. "Make sure to keep him alive. We're gonna need him to keep dear Reiko here in check." He looks Tom over. "But don't be afraid to go heavy on him, you get what I'm saying? Don't hold back. He looks tough. Stephen certainly *thinks* he's tough. Let's see what he's made of. I reckon he can take it." Bull raises his eyebrows, then places an arm around the merc's shoulder, and they turn away. Bull says something to him that Tom can't hear. The merc nods, and then they turn back, and Bull removes his arm.

The merc is excited to get started. "You got it," he says.

Bull leans past him, talks to the other two mercs. "You get all that?"

"We heard," one of them says.

"Good," Bull says. "Contact me when it's done." He doesn't look at Tom or Reiko again. He turns, leaves the room, and motions for his nephews to follow.

The merc looks at them, though. He runs the tip of a finger along his jaw, where he was scraping with the knife. "Sounds like we're all about to have ourselves a good time."

49

"So what do we do with Ron and the others?" Monica says once they're outside.

The rangers and Jay stand together facing Bull and his nephews. Bull considers his niece's question. "What indeed?" he says.

"That's not the answer I was looking for," Monica says.

"Let me think," Bull says.

"Just waste him," Kai says. "Waste all of them. They know too much now. We can't take a risk on them talking. Waste them and blame it on this Rollins guy. Say his army past caught up to him, PTSD or whatever. He went fucking crazy."

"Ron's an old man waiting on his retirement," Monica says. "We don't need to just *waste* him. All he's wanted for a long time now is an easy life. We offer him *that*, and I think –"

"You're too sentimental about the old bastard," Kai says. "You weren't there when he used to chase me and Josh out of the trees when we were younger. He was an asshole about it, too. More than once, Dad was gonna go down there and kick his ass."

"Uh-huh," Monica says. "I had better things to do than climb fucking trees."

Kai opens his mouth, but Bull cuts the rebuttal dead. "What part of 'I'm trying to think' did you all not understand?" he says. To Kai, he adds, "We can't just go around killing off everyone we *think* might cause us a problem. You never heard that old adage, *you catch more flies with honey than with vinegar*? We slip them some honey, see if that'll shut them up. All most people are ever after is a little more honey." To Monica, he says, "We won't kill Ron or the others if we don't have to. But there might be cause for it. Like with Reiko in there. She's one of those you can't sway with just honey. They take a little more. You understand that, don't you?"

"Yeah, I get it," Monica says.

"You keep giving away honey to the flies, and there's not gonna be any left for us," Kai says.

"I know what I'm doing," Bull says.

"Whatever," Kai says.

Josh has been silent so far, but he speaks up now. "You told her too much," he says to his uncle. "In the truck. You told her *everything*. What, were you trying to scare her? Is that how you plan to get her to come on our side?"

Bull shakes his head. He sighs. "I'm fond of Reiko, I really am," he says. "But it doesn't matter what I told her earlier, because she's not surviving this night."

Josh blinks. "But –"

Bull shakes his head. "She'd never come around, no matter what we might do to the ranger. You saw me talk to our merc privately, right? That's what I told him. Torture Rollins until she gives up who else she's spoken to – the FBI or whomever – and then kill them both. Dangling the carrot of collusion was just another way to get her to speak. If she thinks we're hoping for her to join our operation, then that might get her to talk faster. Her mind will be working, you understand? Looking for a way to use this to her advantage. Trying to figure out a way to save Rollins from harm, so she can double-cross us later."

Josh nods along. "All right," he says. "I get it. I like it. I like it a whole lot better than thinking we're gonna have to worry about her loyalties the rest of our days."

"What now?" Monica says. "Ron, the others?"

"Here's what we're going to do," Bull says. "We're gonna go to the forest, and we're gonna talk with Ron. Get a gauge on his attitude. If we can resolve things with words tonight, then great. If we can't... Well. That's on them. We're gonna be our usual charming selves, and if they don't want to take us up on our more than generous offer, then so be it. But like I said, that's on them."

Stephen stands close to Monica's shoulder. Bull can't help but notice how he looks like he might be sick. All the color has drained out of him. He's practically glow in the dark. Freddy, on the other hand, looks like he couldn't give a shit. His hands are in his pockets, his shoulders are slumped. He's listening. He doesn't care what happens to Ron, or his other captive colleagues.

"And how do we cover up their disappearance?" Monica says.

Bull looks at Kai, and he grins.

"What?" Kai says, confused.

"We use your idea," Bull says. He turns back to Monica. "We don't disappear them at all. If we have to kill them – *if* we have to kill them – we don't get rid of the bodies. We arrange them nice and neat, scatter them around the headquarters, perhaps. Inside, outside, it doesn't matter. And then we put the blame on Rollins. Blame him for Reiko, too. It'll be a real tragedy. Nobody knows what set him off. What triggered him. Maybe it was all the stress lately of the strange shoot-outs? MS-13? The brutal death of poor Mateo? Doesn't matter. No one will ever know. But we put the blame on him. He's the one the authorities are gonna be looking for."

"This is all a big *if*," Monica says. "I don't think it'll come to that. Ron will acquiesce. We throw some money at him, he'll let things continue."

"What about the other two?" Kai says.

"They'll do whatever Ron does," Monica says.

"Let's hope so," Bull says. "Tonight has already gotten messier than I ever would have liked. These last couple of weeks, in fact, have been far noisier than I ever wanted things to get. It's just a shame that noise and mess are such necessities, sometimes." He turns, motions for Kai and Josh to go to the truck. "Let's go," he says. "We'll meet at the forest."

"You want us to be there?" Stephen says, his voice wavering.

Bull nods. "Present a united front. Show Ron a few faces he recognizes. Let him know he's joining an elite club." He winks. "Might help sway him."

Monica nods. She's already taking Jay by the arm, leading him towards their car.

Bull goes to the truck. Kai is behind the wheel now. He already has the engine rumbling. Josh sits in the middle. Kai turns as Bull gets inside. "I don't think we're gonna be able to keep this as neat as you'd like it," he says.

Bull looks at him. "Then we'll deal with it," he says. "If things get messy, we'll clean them up. I always find a way, don't I? You need to stop being such a pessimist, Kai. Develop a streak of optimism, like me and your brother. It won't kill you."

"Yeah, well," Kai says, looking forward and pulling away from the mill. "Neither will having my doubts."

50

The mercs don't get straight to work. They move Tom and Reiko from the office first. Take them downstairs. Lead them across the factory floor. The merc who was playing with his knife leads the way. The other two are behind Tom and Reiko, pushing them along with the barrels of their rifles.

On the factory floor, Tom notices how the workers don't look up. They keep their heads down, getting on with their tasks. They're too scared to look. Too scared to do anything but what they're told. The mercs standing guard watch them go, though. He sees how a couple of them watch Reiko as she passes, with an appreciative eye. One of them whistles low. Reiko ignores them all.

One of the guards is sneering at Tom. Tom recognizes him. The Latino who got away the night of the attack upon himself and Reiko in the motel room. Tom reckons he'll be looking to settle a score. Pissed about his dead friend. Killed by Tom. He'll likely come by looking for a chance to get in on the torture.

Of course, Tom has no intention of letting things get that far.

"Reiko," he says, speaking out of the corner of his mouth and keeping his voice low. The sounds of the workers cover what he says from the guards, but Reiko is close enough to hear.

She grunts to acknowledge him. She knows better than to turn her head, give them both away.

"Guy up ahead," Tom says, "his knife is loose in its sheath. You're bound at the front, I'm bound at the back, so you have the better chance. When I make a move, you know what to do."

She grunts again.

The merc up front leads them to a storage room at the far end of the factory. There are a few boxes around the edge of the room, with what Tom assumes to be heroin within. Inside, the merc motions them deeper into the room.

Tom eyes the sheath as he passes the merc. The sheath is still loose. If his hands were free, or bound at the front, he'd have no difficulty in getting it now. He waits for the other two mercs to get inside. For them to close the door. Waits for everyone to get into position, or at least until he has an idea where everyone is going to be. When he looks down, he sees why they've brought them to this room rather than just getting on with things back in the office. There is a drain in the floor in the center of the room. Somewhere for the blood to go.

The merc is grinning. He's eager to get started. Is going to enjoy himself. He's so desperate for bloodshed, for torture, that Tom wonders if he's the one who cut Mateo up. He was chasing him that first night, after all. Tom figures what the hell. He'll ask. "Did you kill Mateo?" he says.

The merc shrugs. "I don't know their names," he says. "They all look the same to me."

"The guy who ran away," Tom says. "Cut up and left by the side of the road."

The merc starts laughing. "Oh, yeah," he says. "Yeah, that was me. Well, couple of us. Group effort, y'know. Someone had to keep him alive, so he could really *feel* it."

"Jesus," Reiko says. "Bull ask you to do that?"

"Nah," the merc says. "Bull just said to chop him up, make it look like cartel. But we took the opportunity to get creative. Just like we're about to do now."

"Uh-huh," Tom says. He notes where everyone is. Reiko is a couple of paces to his left. To her immediate left, one of the other mercs holds her by the arm. The other merc stands by the door, guarding it. He's holding his AK-47, but that won't do him much good in here. Too enclosed a space. Runs too much risk of hitting his buddies.

The merc with the knife is four paces to Tom's right. Tom needs him closer. "Y'know," Tom says, "I've been tortured before. And the guy who did it, I reckon he was more adept at it than you. I don't know you, your background, your history, but I knew enough about him. I know he'd made a career out of it. Wasn't all that long ago, either. Not really. When you get tortured, it's never as long ago as you'd like it to be. It's always right there, on your shoulder. A reminder, whispering in your ear, of what you went through." He looks the merc with the knife in the eye. "I don't intend to let it happen again tonight."

The merc smirks. "You don't get any say in it."

Tom still needs him to come closer. The merc to his left, however, the one holding Reiko, is as close as he needs to be. "We'll see about that," Tom says. He pivots to his left, raises his right leg as he spins and lashes out with a vicious kick that catches the merc holding Reiko in the chest. It forces him into the wall behind him. Knocks the air out of him from the front and the back. He's let go of Reiko. Almost dragged her back with him, but his fingers slipped from her arm.

The merc with the knife is caught off guard. He's frozen for a moment, but then he steps forward. Tom pivots back the other way, then drops down and kicks again, sweeps the merc's legs out from under him. The merc lands on his front, his face hitting the ground. He didn't have the time to get his hands up.

Reiko knows what to do. She dives across the ground, rolls him onto his back. Reaches for his knife in its loose sheath. While she does that, Tom charges for the merc at the door. He's panicking. Not enough room to let loose with the AK-47. Instead of shooting it, he swings it. Tom ducks. Feels it brush by his temple. He barrels into the merc shoulder first, drives him back against the wall. Straightens up and plants a headbutt into the center of his face.

Reiko has the knife. She comes over, cuts Tom loose. He takes the knife from her and instantly plants it into the chest, into the heart, of the merc by the door. He moves on. Goes to the one who was holding Reiko. He's holding his chest now. Where Tom kicked him. Trying to catch his breath. He doesn't get the chance. Tom stabs him, too. Through the heart again.

He moves on to the last merc. The one whose knife he's handling. He's trying to roll onto his side. He's dazed from the fall. His nose is mashed from the impact. Tom takes a handful of his hair, lifts his head so they can look into each other's eyes. "If I had the time," Tom says, "I'd do to you what you did to Mateo."

The merc tries to say something. Tom stabs him through the eye, then lets his head drop onto the ground with a thud.

Tom pulls the knife back and stands, goes to Reiko to cut her loose. As he goes, he notices how the blood pouring from the three men runs toward the drain in the center of the room.

Reiko is stunned by what she has seen. "Jesus Christ," she says. She rubs her wrists when they're free.

"Grab a gun," Tom says. The merc who was holding Reiko had an SG 553. Tom takes this. Reiko picks up the AK-47. "There's a few more of them out there. We'll have to fight our way out."

Reiko checks the AK-47. She nods. "And then we go get that bastard Bull," she says. "And his whole fucking family."

51

It's been a long time since Bull was last at the forest. It's always been important for him to stay away from it, to not be seen anywhere near it, so as not to raise any suspicions. He's left the overview of the forest to Monica, and to a lesser extent Kai and Josh, and up until recently things have always run smoothly.

He blames MS-13 for the recent chaos. Blames the cartel. If they'd kept their nose out of his business, none of this would have ever had to happen. If they'd just left well enough alone and left them to do their thing, there wouldn't be so many dead bodies right now. Or so much stress.

They take the back way into the forest. Through the trees, to where the poppy fields are. The route the mercs use. The route Kai and Josh and the other drivers take when they're collecting the raw product. The route the day laborers are taken in. Away from prying eyes.

Kai stops the truck when they reach the two men standing guard. "How've the new prisoners been?" he says.

"I ain't heard any trouble," one of the guards says.

"Good," Kai says, then drives on. Monica and Jay are

following then, and Stephen and Freddy are behind them. The little convoy pulls to the side and parks.

Bull gets out. He looks the poppy field over. "My, how it's grown," he says. He feels a prideful swelling in his chest.

Despite everything that has happened recently, Bull is feeling confident. Things *will* calm down. They won't get back to how they were – they can't, not now – but they *can* get better. Better than they were before. Things can be smoother. No more cartel. He might have to pay a few extra people in and around Oak Hills for their silence and their compliance, but that is nothing compared to the overheads the cartel was impressing upon him.

The poppy plants sway. Bull looks out across them. The workers are locked away for the night. In their cabin off to the side. Under heavy guard. A heavier guard since the recent breakout. Bull speaks to the nearest merc. "Where are the rangers?"

"They're in the cabin, with the rest."

"Go get them."

The merc heads off to the cabin. Bull turns to the rest of his group. Stephen is shifting his weight from foot to foot. He's staring at the cabin, looking worried. It's clear he'd rather be anywhere else. He's not prepared for what Ron is about to find out.

"I'll do the talking," Bull says. "And Stephen, try not to look like you're about to piss your pants."

Stephen manages to stop himself from fidgeting. Forces himself to stand still. He swallows. "All right," he says.

"Don't look weak," Bull says. "We have all the power here. *They're* weak. They're the ones in a bad position right now."

The merc Bull sent away reaches the cabin. Another man already standing there pulls some keys out of his pocket, unlocks the door. They both go inside to get Ron and the other rangers.

Before they can re-emerge, Bull feels a vibration against his leg. His phone. He pulls it out. It's one of the mercs from back at the mill. He answers.

A cacophony sounds right in his ear. Bull has to snatch the phone away. "Jesus," he says. Cautiously, he brings it back to the side of his head, thinking it was some kind of glitch on the phone. A connection problem. An unexpected explosion of static.

"Bull? Are you there? *Bull!*"

"I'm here," Bull says. "There's no need to shout."

Then his blood runs cold. It wasn't static. It wasn't a glitch. The sound is still happening in the background of the call. It's gunfire. There's a firefight.

"What's happening?" Bull says, turning away from the group. "What's going on? Speak to me!"

The merc on the phone is breathing hard. He sounds scared. "They got out!" he says. It sounds like he's running. There's a brief burst of gunfire that once again almost deafens Bull. The caller is firing. "The guy and the cop, they got out! Jesus fucking Christ, they're armed, and they're coming after us – the guy's fucking Special Forces or something – he's cutting through us like we're nothing!"

"Get it under control!" Bull says, his temper slipping, anxiety sneaking into his chest. "Christ's sake, they were tied up! How could they get loose?"

He doesn't receive a response. He hears the caller cry out. A choked, strangled sound. There's a thud as the phone hits the ground. The caller has been shot. He's likely dead.

Bull turns. Everyone is facing him. They've all heard his side of the conversation. They've picked up on his concern. They're all just as worried as he is.

Monica steps forward. "What's happened?" she says.

Bull starts to pace. He can't answer, not right away. His mind is racing. He needs to think.

"Damn it, Bull, what's happened?" It's Kai's voice.

Bull turns back to them slowly. Takes a deep breath. He still needs to think. He'll think out loud. "Rollins and Reiko have escaped."

"How the fuck did they manage that?" Kai says.

"That's exactly what I'd like to know," Bull says. "But it's unlikely we're ever going to find out." Over his shoulder, he notices bodies coming their way. He looks. Ron Judge and the two other rangers, being pushed ahead by the mercs. "Stop!" Bull holds up a hand to halt them. "Wait right there. Hold it for now. Don't come any closer."

The mercs hear, and they comply.

"So what's happening?" Kai says. "They're getting it under control at the mill, right? Keeping it contained?"

Bull shakes his head. "I don't think so. I think Rollins and Reiko are shooting their way out. And if they do that, they'll free the workers, too. And then Reiko will call for backup..." He balls his fists, squeezes them tight as he stares off to the side and bites his lip.

"Oh, shit," Stephen says. "Oh shit, oh *shit*." He sounds like he might throw up.

Everyone is silent for a moment. Bull can feel his arms trembling.

Josh breaks the silence. "So what are we gonna do?"

"They'll be coming back to Oak Hills," Bull says. "They'll be coming for us. For *me*. Even after calling for backup, they know they can reach us faster."

"There's still some out-of-town cops in Oak Hills," Monica points out.

"Shit," Bull says. "That's right." In his panic, he forgot this key detail. "I still think they're gonna be coming for us, though. Of course, that's *if* they've been able to call anyone. They had their phones taken off them when they were captured."

"The mercs have phones," Josh says.

"With lock screens," Kai says.

"Not for emergency numbers," Josh says.

Bull runs his hands back over his head. "Whatever the case, they're coming for us. They're coming this way." He looks to his right. At Ron Judge. "They could be coming right *here*. They know we have these rangers."

"We're spending too long standing still talking about it," Monica says. "If we're gonna do something, we need to start doing it *now*."

Bull nods. "You're right." He's thinking, still. He knows what he has to do. They have to walk away. Leave this behind. There's enough money for him, his nephews, his niece and her husband to lie low and be comfortable for a while. Perhaps not so much for the others, but that's their problem. He's not their keeper. Just their boss.

It'll be hard to leave. They've built something special here. Something lucrative. But they can't stand and fight, either. Their freedom is worth far more than a field of poppies. Wherever they end up, they can always start over again. They'll find something. They'll find a way. *He'll* find a way. He always has. He's a fucking survivor. This is just another setback. Nothing can stop him.

What they need to do right now is cause a distraction. Something to keep Rollins and Reiko preoccupied so they can make their escape.

He turns to the mercs who have Ron and the other rangers. "Take them away," he says. "Lock them back up." The mercs don't understand it, but they do as they're told. Bull turns to his group. "You're not all gonna like this," he says. "But this is what we have to do..."

52

Most of the mercs at the mill are dead. A few of them ran away, likely deciding whatever they were being paid wasn't enough for them to lose their lives over.

A lot of the workers fled in the firefight. They saw their opportunity, and they took it. The ones who weren't brave enough to run ducked for cover. Kept out of the way of the flying bullets. When it was over, Reiko spoke to them in Spanish. She told them to run. She took care of them while Tom went outside and found a car to hotwire. Reiko came out to join him, talking on a phone. She got in, and they raced for Oak Hills.

"I've called it in," Reiko said. "Told them everything. Who's behind this, what they're doing. Told the officers that if they see any of Bull's crew, they need to arrest them on sight, but to be careful, as they may be armed."

Tom nodded. He drove. The weapons they'd taken were slung on the backseat. If they were fast enough, they'd need to use them again before long.

"Town or forest?" Reiko says as they get closer.

Tom has been thinking about this since they left the mill. "I think leave me at the forest," he says. "I'll get Ron and the other prisoners. You continue on to town, get Bull. If we're lucky, the other cops have already gotten there ahead of you."

"They're not gonna go down without a fight," Reiko says. "Bull has already told me as much. I'm not sure my colleagues are prepared for that, especially if Bull has the mercs with him. You saw what happened with MS-13."

Tom is about to respond when something up ahead catches his eye. Something through the trees, floating up, disappearing into the night. As they get closer, he sees something flickering. Sees light being thrown up into the sky and across the ground. An orange glow.

Reiko sees it too. She points. "Holy shit."

Tom nods. "A fire." A thick black plume of smoke rises into the night sky, blotting out the stars. They get closer, and it soon becomes clear where it's coming from. "It's the forest," Tom says.

"Do you think they've set it on purpose?" Reiko says. She fumbles out the cell phone from earlier. Dials emergency services.

"Maybe," Tom says. "I think it's coming from the poppy field. They could be trying to destroy the evidence." He stops talking while Reiko speaks into the phone, calls the fire service and directs them to the forest. He continues when she's done. "But the forest is dry. Whether they've set it or not, it's gonna spread."

"Then we'd better pray the fire department gets there fast enough."

"That's not all," Tom says. "There's the day laborers they've had working for them. You think they're going to concern themselves with evacuating them? Or do you think they're just gonna leave them there to burn with the poppies?"

"Shit," Reiko says.

"We need to get them," Tom says. "The fire guys won't get here in time. We might be the only hope they have."

"You're right," Reiko says. He can see it eats at her to potentially let Bull escape, but they have no other choice. "Let's get them. And let's hope we're not too late."

53

Tom heads to the rear entrance. As he gets halfway into it, the trees are burning. He can barely see ahead of himself. They drive into the inferno. It gets hotter and hotter. Sweat beads burst on their foreheads and run down their faces.

They break out of the tunnel, reach the field. The poppies are burning. They're blackened and dying. The fire is spreading across the dried grass, into the trees. It's mostly moving in the direction Tom and Reiko have entered. It hasn't quite reached the other end yet, where the cabin is. It's not burning, but no doubt the people inside are already hot, and panicking.

"They're gonna shoot!" Reiko says.

Through the thick smoke and the flying embers, Tom isn't sure what, or who, she's talking about. Then he spots them. Where the forest isn't burning, near the cabin, there are men. Armed men. More mercenaries. And they're pointing their rifles at the car.

Tom spins the wheel hard. He gets them out of the smoke and aims for a gap in the trees. The mercenaries have opened fire. The rear window shatters. Tom gets them into the trees, where they're obscured. Where they're covered. Thick branches snag the bottom of the car. He can't drive it any further, but that's fine. It's got them deep enough. He grabs the SG 553 again, and Reiko gets the AK-47. They push open their doors and slide out, taking cover in the bushes and behind the trees. Bullets are tearing through the undergrowth around and above them. They stay low. Move away from the car. Stay separate.

There's no smoke here. Tom can feel a breeze. It's blowing the fire away from them. He gets onto one knee and looks to where the mercenaries are. They're firing wildly. They can't see where he and Reiko have gone. They're hoping for the best. Tom starts picking them off. He hears Reiko opening up, doing the same. Tom drops three of them, then moves position before they can realize where he is. He counts eight remaining mercs. The number promptly drops to seven as Reiko hits one.

There's not just the mercs, though. Stephen and Freddy are there, though they're not shooting. They're taking cover behind an SUV, lying low with their arms over their heads. Monica and Jay are firing. Kai is, too. Bull is here. He's with Josh, but they're not armed. They're trying to get to their truck. To get away.

A chunk of tree explodes near Tom's head. A branch falls loose and hits the ground behind him. Tom gets on his stomach, and moves to a new position.

54

Bull and Josh duck low and flee from the firefight. Bull is sweating hard. It's a humid night already, but coupled with the fire they've set and the bullets flying overhead, he's soaked through.

He throws himself down by the truck, and Josh does the same. "Fuck this!" Bull says. "We need to get out of here!"

Josh looks back, toward his brother and his sister. "We need Kai and Monica!" He tries shouting their names. They can't hear over the sounds of all the gunfire, including their own.

Bull hears sudden loud screaming. He peers under the truck. The flames are spreading. They're getting close to the cabin. The people locked inside have noticed. They're starting to panic.

Josh is still calling to his younger siblings. They still haven't heard. Bull looks around. Sees one of his mercenaries catch a bullet through the throat. He counts how many are left. Five, he thinks. It's not enough. He searches the trees for Rollins and Reiko, but can't see them. Just the occasional burst of gunfire, constantly moving, never staying still. There could be a dozen men in those trees, firing upon them.

Stephen and Freddy are crouched behind a ranger SUV nearby. Stephen is covering his head with his arms. Freddy is looking around, shouting for someone to give him a gun. There's a dead mercenary near him, but he's lying out of cover of the car. Freddy doesn't attempt to leave his protected space, to get the dead man's weapon.

Monica and Jay stand close to Kai. Kai is at the forefront. He's trying to get closer. He's screaming unintelligibly toward the trees. Bull can make out some choice curses between gunshots.

"These mercenaries are fucking useless," Bull says. "You'd think I was paying them to throw themselves into the damn bullets!"

Josh doesn't hear. "Kai's getting too close," he says, shaking his head, his eyes wide. "He's going to get himself killed." He shouts his name again.

"He's not gonna hear," Bull says.

"Then I'm gonna go get them," Josh says. "You start the truck. I'll be right back."

Before Bull can say anything, Josh has already pushed himself up and is running toward the battle. He ducks low and weaves as he goes. Bull braces himself, keeps expecting to see a spray of blood. To see him fall. It doesn't happen. Josh reaches Monica. Jay is on the other side of the car, covering behind an open door. He hasn't noticed Josh at all. Josh drags Monica down behind her car. He points wildly. Points toward Bull and the truck. He's shouting to be heard.

Bull breathes a sigh of relief. He gets up and reaches warily for the truck door, pulling the keys out of his pocket. He gets it open. He's about to get inside when Kai makes a break for the trees.

Frozen, Bull can only watch. He sees Kai react as if he's

spotted something. Someone. He's seen either Rollins or Reiko through the undergrowth. He's shooting as he goes.

Then he's not shooting anymore. Isn't running. His head snaps back. There's a spray of blood from the back of his skull. He hits the ground and slides back, then stops. Dead.

Josh and Monica have seen. Monica is screaming. Josh wraps his arms around her waist and picks her up, hauls her away. Bull feels like he's going to throw up. He grits his teeth and steels himself. Jumps into the truck and starts the engine. Leans over and pushes open the passenger door. Watches in the mirror. Josh and Monica fall. Just a trip. They're still alive. Monica tries to twist out of her brother's arms, tries to get back to the fight. Josh grabs her again. They get to the truck. He bundles her in through the open door, then climbs in after her, slams the door.

Bull realizes Monica's husband is left behind. He checks the mirror. Jay hasn't noticed they've gone. He's still firing, still ducking and reloading. Caught up in the action. Monica doesn't seem to have noticed they don't have him, either. She's certainly not calling his name. She's calling for her dead brother. She's calling for Kai.

Bull starts driving. They need to get out. They need to leave this all behind. They need to make sure they stay free.

He needs to make sure he stays free.

55

Tom has heard the screams.

He knows why they're screaming, too. He's seen how the flames lick ever closer to them. The cabin looks just as dry as everything else. It'll go up like a tinderbox, with all those people inside.

He sees Bull escaping in his truck. They need to get after him. They've been lucky to find him here. They can't let him slip through their fingers. But they also need to free the captives in the cabin. There aren't many shooters left to deal with. Kai is dead. He spotted Tom, charged in. That wasn't sensible. He was firing as he came, but his rapid movement made his shots wild. Tom took his time. All it took was a single bullet to the head. All it took was a little calm. If Kai had some of that, then maybe things would be the other way around right now.

Tom checks over the opposition. There are three mercs left, plus Jay. Stephen and Freddy, too, but they aren't armed. He hasn't heard any gunfire from his right for a couple of minutes. He moves. He gets close to Reiko. She's uninjured.

"I'm out of ammo," she says. "You?"

Tom checks. "Less than half the magazine."

"Is that gonna be enough?"

"I'll make it last."

"Have you seen the fire?"

"I've seen it," Tom says.

"If you cover me, I can maybe get around, break them out."

Tom checks the distance. "I'm not sure," he says.

"We have to try," Reiko says. "They're gonna cook in there otherwise. I'm sweating *here*, and we're not as close to the flames as they are."

Tom spots movement out of the corner of his eye. It's Stephen. He's running. Trying to escape? No. He's already stopped. Kneels down by the body of a dead merc. Searches his person. For a weapon? Tom points the SG 553 at him, ready to open up should he come up armed. He doesn't, though. Whatever he's found, it's small. He starts moving again. He's running toward the cabin. Freddy tries to stop him. Tries to tackle him around the waist. Stephen hits him in the side of the head with the point of his elbow, knocks him down. He continues on his way.

"What's he doing?" Reiko says.

Stephen reaches the cabin. He leaps up onto the porch and hurries to the door.

"I think he's doing the right thing," Tom says.

Stephen unlocks the door, throws it wide. The people trapped inside come flooding out. They flee from the cabin, from the fire. Off into the forest and into the night. Tom wonders if Gabriel and Luis are among them. It's too far, and they're all moving too fast for him to be sure he sees them.

Ron emerges, assisted by a ranger on either side, his arms over their shoulders. Stephen reaches out to help, but he hesitates. He takes a step back.

The remaining mercs and Jay have been distracted by

the escape. They're looking back. Tom seizes the opportunity. He picks off the remaining mercenaries. As Jay is turning, Tom shoots him through the side of the face. He hits the side of the car, his blood spraying over its roof, then falls.

Tom and Reiko emerge from the trees. Tom keeps his weapon raised, just in case.

Freddy scrambles to a dead body, tries to drag its weapon free, but the strap is trapped under them. Tom strides up, kicks him in the center of the face. It feels good to bloody him again.

"Please," Freddy says, lying flat, holding up his hands. "Don't shoot me."

"You're not worth the bullet, Freddy," Tom says. He presses his boot onto his chest. "Enjoy your time in prison. I'm sure those inside are gonna get real excited when they see a new plaything. Especially one with hair as pretty as yours." He winks, then smashes the butt of the rifle across his jaw, knocking him out.

Stephen stands with his hands on his head. Surrendering. Dejected. Tom looks at him. Stephen can't meet his eye. Tom grits his teeth. He doesn't want to say anything to him. He does, though. "This doesn't fix what you've already done," he says.

Stephen nods. "I know."

Reiko goes to Ron and the other rangers. "Are you all right?"

"I've been better," Ron says. He's breathing hard.

Reiko looks at the spreading fire. "We need to get out of here," she says. "Until the fire department gets here, there's nothing we can do." She speaks to Tom. "We can't hang around here. We need to get after Bull before he can get too far. I'm not gonna let that son of a bitch get away. Not after all he's done."

Tom nods. "We'll get him. Either in the forest or on the road, he won't get away."

Reiko turns back to Ron, points to the two rangers either side of him. "This isn't exactly my jurisdiction, but I'm gonna have to deputize the two of you. Grab some guns off the dead, and keep an eye on them." She motions to Freddy and Stephen. "There's gonna be other cops get here soon. Just keep away from the fire, and make sure these two don't go anywhere. Once they get here, the cops will take over."

The two rangers nod, but it's clear they're nervous. They're on their way to commandeer some weapons while Tom goes to the ranger SUV that Freddy and Stephen came here in. The keys are in the ignition. Stephen hauls Freddy up from the ground. Hooks an arm over his shoulders. Freddy's legs are limp. Stephen drags him away. Stephen won't give these unofficially deputized rangers any trouble.

Reiko gets into the SUV. "Let's get him," she says.

56

The sweat is running into Bull's eyes. He's trying to get them out of the forest. The uneven surface jostles them, bumps them around. The way out of the poppy field wasn't good terrain for driving on. He felt it scrape and tear at the bottom of the truck. It almost flipped them a couple of times. He persevered, though. Got them out, though he can hear things in the undercarriage rattling and banging. Bull holds the steering wheel tight in both hands, his teeth chattering. Behind them, the smoke continues to billow up into the sky. Embers fall around them like burning red snowflakes. He needs to get them to the road. Then they're out of here. Home free. He doesn't care what kind of noises the truck is making, it'll get them far enough away. He'll drive through the smoke. Anyone following won't know where they've gone. Hell, Bull doesn't know where they're going just yet. He'll work it out on the road.

"We need to go back," Monica says. "Bull – you hear me? We need to go back, damn it!"

"We're not going back," Bull says.

"We've left Jay!" Monica seems to have finally realized they are without her husband.

"Then he can deal with Rollins and Reiko," Bull says. "And then he can catch us up."

"*We* need to get back there for Rollins and Reiko!" Monica says. "They killed Kai! They fucking killed Kai!"

"Yes, they did," Bull says through his teeth. "And there's nothing we can do about that now. We can't bring him back. He's gone."

"We can't bring him back, but we can damn well do something about the bastards who killed him!"

Josh is silent between them. He's distraught over Kai's death. His eyes are glassy. It looks like he's about to cry. He closes his eyes. His teeth are gritted.

"Damn it, Bull, stop ignoring me!" Monica says.

"I'm not ignoring you," Bull says. "I just have no intention of doing what you're suggesting."

"Fine – then what about my husband? Are you just gonna leave him alone back there?"

"He's not alone. And if those mercenaries do what they're paid to do, Jay should be fine. He'll get in touch. We'll let him know where we've ended up."

Monica stares at him for a while longer. She opens her mouth a couple of times, but she doesn't say anything. Bull hopes she's finally giving in. Seeing sense.

Josh opens his eyes. He wipes his face. He looks to the side. Looks past Bull. Out the window. He sits forward a little. "Someone's coming up behind us."

Bull looks. He sees them. An SUV with ranger markings.

"Is it Jay?" Monica says, turning to her own mirror.

"It could be Stephen," Bull says. "Or Freddy."

It's gaining on them. Getting closer.

"It's coming too close," Josh says.

Bull stares, glancing at the way ahead to make sure he

doesn't hit anything or lose control. Someone leans out the passenger window. They're pointing a rifle. It's Reiko.

"Oh, shit," Monica says. She's seen.

Reiko lets off a burst of automatic fire. The back two wheels of Bull's truck blow out. He loses control. He curses, wrestling with the steering wheel. The truck skids sideways. It flips. As they land on their side, the SUV rams into their underside. They roll. Bull's body is thrown around, and he knows it's the same for Josh and Monica. He bangs his head. He feels dizzy and sick. When they come to a stop, they're on their roof.

57

Tom knows the trail better than Bull. He didn't have to be so careful. He was able to go faster in the SUV. Was able to catch up.

The truck lies on its roof. There's movement, though. The vehicle jostles as the people inside attempt to get out.

"They're probably dazed," Reiko says. "Reckon they'll just give up?"

Tom doesn't answer. He watches.

They soon get their answer. Monica and Josh emerge from behind the truck. They're firing handguns. "Not dazed enough," Tom says. He puts the SUV into reverse as they approach. He and Reiko duck as their bullets shatter the windshield. Tom grabs the handbrake and spins the steering wheel so the rear of the SUV is pointing at Monica and Josh. The rear window shatters, just like the front. Tom puts it into reverse.

"Grab the gun and stay low!" he says.

Before Reiko can respond, he slams his foot on the accelerator. They fly back. Reiko scrambles for the SG 553. It's in her footwell. She used it to blow out the tires on the truck.

She dropped it as Monica and Josh opened fire. She has it now. She keeps her head down.

Tom turns his head a little. Looks into the mirror. It's hard to see. He makes out a figure behind them. He swerves the wheel, and he makes contact. It's Josh. He can see him clearer now as he crushes him between the SUV and the overturned truck. Can hear his choked-off cry as his chest caves in. Sees blood burst from his mouth.

Reiko pushes open her door and rolls out. Comes up on one knee, SG 553 raised. She fires. Tom can't see if she makes contact. He jumps out of the SUV and hurries round. Reiko is standing up. Monica is fallen. Reiko's fire strafed her across the chest.

"Where's Bull?" Reiko says. They haven't seen him come out of the truck. He wasn't with his niece and nephew, wasn't firing at Tom and Reiko.

Tom ducks down, checks in the overturned truck. Bull isn't inside. Tom can see him, though. In the distance. Can see him running away.

Reiko has spotted him now. Tom doesn't need to tell her. She's after him. Sprinting. She's slung the gun over her shoulder. Tom follows. Reiko dives through the air when she gets close enough. She tackles Bull to the ground.

Bull cries out. He twists and battles. He manages to push Reiko off, but Tom is there to kick him in the face, to keep him down. Reiko is promptly off the ground. She slams her forearm into Bull's face, then rolls him onto his stomach. She takes the gun from her back and removes the strap from it. She uses the strap to bind his hands together.

"No!" Bull is screaming. "I won't go back! I won't go back there, damn it!"

Reiko keeps him pinned.

Bull twists, tries to see her over his shoulder. "I told you – you know what they'll do to me! You know what they'll do if

you send me back! It's a death sentence! You're sending me to
die!"

Reiko stands. "I don't care," she says. She kicks him in the
ribs. "That was for Greg, you son of a bitch."

Tom can hear sirens. The fire trucks, finally here. They
won't come through the forest this way. They know they won't
be able to get their trucks through. They'll go to the back.
Directly to the flames. Tom looks to where the fire is. He can
see it in the treetops. It's still spreading. The forest is so dry.
He clenches his jaw.

Reiko stands beside him. She watches. She's concerned,
too. "Do you think they'll be able to stop it?"

The flames lick up toward the few stars that are still
visible through the black smoke. They cast long flickering
shadows on the dark ground. He looks away from the fire. To
the rest of the forest lit up by its glow. This place he has come
to love. This place that has, until recently, brought him such
peace.

"I hope so," he says.

58

The town remains busy with cops. Disaster tourists, too. Tom isn't sure why this latter group has come. There isn't much for them to see. They can't get into the forest. The closest they can get is the road, and the most they can see from there are some blackened trees.

The fire service managed to stop the fire. They battled through the night, and it took them a further day to ensure the whole thing didn't burn down. Tom stayed at the forest. Helped out where he could.

It's been a few days since then. It's reminded him of the time after the battle with MS-13. Reiko has been busy. Busier than before. He's hardly seen her, despite staying at her place. Some nights he's gone to bed alone, only to wake up with his arms around her. Unlike after the battle with MS-13, however, there is not a feeling of incompletion. It doesn't feel like there is still someone behind the scenes, pulling the strings. It feels as if Oak Hills might actually be cleaned up.

Tom sits in Clyde's diner and sips from a glass of water. It's loaded with ice. The heatwave has not yet broken, though there are darkening clouds on the horizon that signal a thunderstorm may be headed their way. Tom is sure it will come as a relief. He sees Clyde sitting behind the counter. Clyde has been watching him. Now he has his attention, he raises his mug in salute. Tom nods, then turns away. When he first arrived, a half hour before, Clyde came out from around the counter, vigorously shook Tom's hand.

"You and Reiko," he said, "the two of you, you've saved this town. There was a poison in it most of us didn't even realize was there, but the two of you saw it, and you saved us all from it."

Tom had to take his hand back. He didn't bother explaining to Clyde that it wasn't quite so straightforward as that. That people had to run and suffer and die for them to notice something was happening. Clyde wouldn't hear it anyway. He'd already made up his mind who the heroes of this story were.

"Don't get me wrong," he went on, "I was always fond of Bull, but you can't let fondness blind you. A wicked man is a wicked man, and turns out he was one of the worst. Real shame, but that's how it is, I guess."

The diner is busy again. Tom has a booth by the window. He realizes it's the booth where he first saw the MS-13 members. That day feels so long ago now, the day everything started to change, but really it was barely a couple of weeks ago.

He's waiting for a couple of people he's not sure will turn up. He passed a message on to the couple of day laborers he found still hanging around on their corner, but he has no idea if they've been able to pass it on to the people he's hoping to talk to. Has no idea if they'll have even seen them. For all he knows, they may not have hung around. They may have fled straight back where they came from.

While Tom stayed at the forest to help with the blaze, Reiko handed Bull over to the other cops who eventually arrived on the scene. She would have taken him in herself, but she had somewhere else she needed to be. Bull's house. Down into the basement. To see if it was true. If Greg's body really was there, covered in lye.

Unfortunately, he was.

The autopsy revealed they'd stabbed him first. Through the ribs, which would explain all the blood Reiko found in the car. What the autopsy couldn't reveal was how they got so close to him. They hadn't smashed the window in order to get at him. She asked Bull what had happened. Bull was reluctant to answer at first. Tom isn't sure how Reiko eventually got him to talk. Turned out Kai had approached from the rear of the vehicle, pretending to be drunk. It was dark, and Kai was wearing a hat and had the collar of his jacket pulled up so Greg wouldn't recognize him. He knocked on the window, pretending to be asking for directions. As soon as Greg wound it down, Kai struck. Stuck the knife into him.

Bull had apologized, not that it meant much. "I didn't tell him to kill him," he said. "I told him to take him prisoner. Josh got that. He understood. Josh always understood. But Kai... Kai was impetuous. It was difficult to get him to do what you wanted – to get him to do the right thing. He was hard to control."

Tom looks toward the door. Two men enter. The two he's waiting for. Gabriel and Luis. He waves to get their attention. They come to join him. They look wary. He remembers the first time he met them, in the forest. Gabriel wore a trucker cap. Luis wore a bandana. They're both wearing plain black caps now. He assumes their former headwear was lost while they were forced to work in the field.

They slide into the booth opposite him. "Thanks for coming," Tom says. "I wasn't sure you'd get my message."

Gabriel shrugs. "We're leaving soon. There's no reason for us to stay here anymore."

Tom notices they both look thinner than when he first met them. Their cheeks look hollowed out. They couldn't have been working in the field for long, but they must have been getting worked *hard*. "I'm sorry for what they did to your cousin," Tom says.

Luis grunts. Gabriel says, "We're sorry, too. Now we have to go back and tell his family we weren't able to find him. To tell them...to tell them what was done to him." He purses his lips. "I know the people who did it are dead, and some of them are going to prison, but this will be of little consolation."

Tom nods. "Is there anything I can do?"

"I don't see what."

"Neither do I. But if I can help in any way, I will."

Gabriel shakes his head, but then Luis nudges him, says something in Spanish. Gabriel turns back to Tom. He raises an eyebrow. "We need a ride to Sacramento," he says.

"Done," Tom says. "I'm looking to move on soon, too."

"How soon?"

"How soon are you planning to go?"

"Today," Gabriel says.

"I'll take you tomorrow," Tom says. "I'll need to say a goodbye first."

Gabriel nods. "Okay. Thank you. You know where to find us." They start to get out of the booth.

"You already ate?" Tom says.

They pause. "We don't have any money," Gabriel says. "They weren't paying us to work in their field."

"Sit back down," Tom says. He gets the attention of one of the waitresses. She grabs a couple of menus and comes their way. "It's on me."

Reiko gets home earlier than usual. Tom is in the bedroom, packing his bag, when she comes in. She sees what he's doing. "You weren't just trying to slip out, were you?" she says.

"No," Tom says. "Just getting my things ready. I wouldn't go without saying goodbye."

"So you *are* leaving?"

"Figure it's time."

"That's a shame," Reiko says. "You know, the forest won't stay closed forever. Ron could do with some good men to help him out."

"I'm sure he won't have any trouble finding them," Tom says. "All the bad ones are either dead or on their way to prison now."

They stand and look at each other for a moment. "You've said goodbye," Reiko says. "So what now? You leave?"

"Not until the morning," Tom says. "We have one more night together, if that's all right with you."

She grins. "It's permissible."

"I'm glad to hear it."

"Shall we eat?" Reiko says. "I've got a frozen pizza, and to be honest, I don't have the energy for anything else."

"Sure," Tom says. "Get changed. I'll deal with dinner."

Reiko comes through to join him in the kitchen a little while later. She's out of her uniform now. Wearing a loose blouse and a pair of tracksuit bottoms, her feet bare. She takes a seat at the table. The pizza is almost ready.

"How was work?" Tom says.

"Busy," Reiko says. "Same as it always is, at the minute. But I can't complain. This is what I wanted. This is what I'll need to get used to, when I make it back to Saxton."

"That's happening?"

She nods.

"And then you're going after the chief?"

"I don't think it'll be too hard to get his position," Reiko says. "I've heard he's not coming back. Begging off, on account of the injuries he sustained in the shoot-out with MS-13."

"Sounds more like he took your words to heart."

Reiko laughs. "I hope so. Though I would've liked the satisfaction of taking his position away from him. Still, we'll see. His pride might get the better of him. He might try to come back to work. Might kid himself that he could fend me off for the position." She shrugs. "I'm not scared of him. This is something I should have done a long time ago."

Tom takes the pizza out of the oven. "Next time I'm passing through this way, I'll be sure to check in on my old friend Chief Reiko Miller." He cuts the pizza into slices. Puts half on a plate for himself, and the other half on a plate for her. There's a bag of salad in the refrigerator, still fresh, but only just. He fills the rest of their plates with this, then joins her at the table. Reiko forks up some lettuce leaves while the pizza cools. She sighs before she puts it in her mouth. "I met with Greg's family today."

Tom raises an eyebrow. "That wasn't them just finding out, was it?"

Reiko shakes her head. "No, but I wanted to give them a few days with their grief." She shakes her head again. "They were still grieving. His mom, his aunt, his sister and nephew. I went over to Saxton to see them. It was a long drive there... A long drive back, too. His nephew's only six. They were close. Greg's sister's partner is in the Navy, and he's away a lot. Greg was almost like a surrogate father to the boy while his dad was gone." She closes her eyes, rubs them. "It almost tore me up, the whole thing. So much grief..."

"There's probably been a lot of that going around right now."

"Yeah. And for a lot of *young* men and women, too. That'll make it hit the hardest – when it's so unexpected. We just can't plan for these things. We just don't know when or how or if they're gonna happen."

"Death doesn't have any mercy." Tom knows he's quoting a song, but the sentiment is true. He's seen enough of it firsthand.

Reiko nods at this. "Yeah," she says. "That's right. It's damn right."

They eat in silence for a while. Reiko is lost in her thoughts. Likely thinking of her visit with Greg's family. Tom is thinking about where he might go next, after he drops off Gabriel and Luis. Might just see where the road takes him. Get a full tank of gas and see where it runs out.

"They said they were glad I'd come, though," Reiko says, referring back to her visit. "There's that, at least. They said they knew Grice would never do such a thing, not unless it was an opportunity for a photo op."

"Sounds like Greg told them all about him."

Reiko grins. "I'm sure he did. And I'll bet he didn't sugar-coat it, either."

Tom didn't have many interactions with Greg. It feels like a loss that he didn't get to know him better... He seemed like a nice enough guy and loyal to his friend Reiko. Tom doesn't have much to contribute to Reiko's reminiscing about him. He wishes he'd had the chance to get to know Greg better.

"Anyway," Reiko says. She picks up a slice of pizza. "It's your last night in town. Our last night together. My last night with a house guest before I return to solitude." She grins. "What do you want to do?"

"You look tired," Tom says. "What do *you* want to do?"

Reiko lets her shoulders sag. "In all honesty, I just wanna watch a movie and then go to bed."

"Then that's what I wanna do, too."

Reiko smiles. She reaches across the table for his hand. Tom takes it. She squeezes his palm. "Good luck with wherever you go next," she says. "And whatever you end up doing there. I hope you find whatever it is you might be looking for."

Tom isn't sure he's looking for anything. He'd thought, briefly, for almost a year, that he might have found it in Oak Hills. Peace. Solitude. A little like Thoreau, but with occasional casual friendships. But if that was enough, he'd stay. Things could go back to how they were. The poppy field is destroyed. The workers are free. Bull is going to prison.

He knows it can't be how it was, though. Not really. It's tainted. Too many betrayals. Too much death and bloodshed.

Sometimes, it worries him. That no matter where he goes, he finds trouble. He can't turn away from it. He can't back down. If someone is in trouble, if they need help, he'll give it. But this isn't what worries him. It's that he's good at it. It's that when the fists and the bullets are flying, when instinct takes over and plans must be made on the fly, that this is when he feels most comfortable. That in these moments of violence, he feels home. His true self comes out. A true self that can only be kept in check by his moral code.

It worries him that maybe he'll never find peace.

It worries him that maybe it isn't peace he's looking for.

He looks at Reiko, and he returns her smile. "I hope I find it, too."

EPILOGUE

The bar is nearly always quiet on a Tuesday night. The regulars are in. A couple of older Hollywood burnouts who live nearby and these days are content to nurse their drinks, and an aspiring scriptwriter with his latest girlfriend in tow, filling her with promises that when his movie gets made, he'll make sure they cast her in the lead. The girlfriend looks bored while he pounds at his laptop keys. She chews a maraschino cherry and glances around the room at its run-down décor. The writer tells her he needs this authenticity for his art.

The bar is on the outskirts of Los Angeles. At the end of a run-down, but quiet, neighborhood. The bar used to have a reputation. It was known for being loud. For being rowdy. People had been stabbed here. They'd been shot. Then, about three months ago, they hired a new bartender. No one else would take the job. Shortly after that, things began to calm down. People behaved themselves. It took a few broken bones and fractured skulls, but word got around. This wasn't the place to come looking for trouble anymore, unless you were prepared to deal with what you'd find. And what those people most often found was a trip to the ER.

Tonight, however, seems to be an exception from a usual Tuesday. A group has come in. There's four of them. All guys. Young guys. They settle in, and they start to drink. It doesn't take them long to get drunk. That's when they start to get loud.

The bartender watches them closely, but they're not causing any trouble yet. He hasn't seen them before. He's not sure why they've come here. He knows some people come here specifically to see him. To find out if the stories are true. To put themselves to the test. See if they can walk out with bragging rights.

He doesn't think that's why these guys are here. Doesn't think they've come to look for trouble specifically, but he gets the impression they're not concerned if they start it. There's four of them, after all. Even though they're drunk, they're confident they still have the strength in numbers.

One of the regulars sits at the bar nearby. He's watching the bartender. Watching the group, too, occasionally glancing back over his shoulder. "They're getting awful loud," he says to the bartender.

The bartender nods. "Yeah," he says. "They are."

"A bit *too* loud." The regular has been around long enough to know what this kind of noise, this kind of obnoxious display, is usually a precursor to.

One of the four gets up from the table. He scrapes his chair back. He didn't need to do that. Just another noise to add to the cacophony. He comes to the bar. There's a swagger in his step. He plants both hands down on the counter and grins at the bartender. Before he can speak, the bartender cuts him off.

"You've had enough," he says.

The drunk blinks, caught off guard, suddenly not so sure of himself. "What?"

"You and your friends have had enough," the bartender says. "You don't have to leave, but you're not getting any more drinks here."

The drunk blinks again, then shakes his head. Recovers himself. Leans in a little closer. "Listen, buddy, my friend over there, today's his birthday, and we came here looking to get *real* drunk. Not buzzed, like now, but *drunk*. We're gonna have a good time, you understand? And we're gonna spend a lot of money in your shithole establishment. Hell, only reason we wound up in here is because we printed off a list of all the bars in the area and got the birthday boy to stick a pin in it. Little tradition we have. We could be anywhere right now. Think yourself lucky that we're *here*."

The bartender is impassive. "I don't care," he says.

"Man, I –"

The regular turns on his stool, reaches out, places a gnarled old hand on the drunk's arm. The drunk glares at him. The regular motions for him to come closer. He whispers something into his ear. He's whispering for a while. The drunk's eyes go wide. He looks back at the bartender like he's seeing him in a new light.

The regular lets him go. The drunk straightens up. He deliberates, then he turns, goes back to the table. He talks to his friends in a low voice. They're all suddenly very quiet. The three others look back at the bartender. They stand, and they leave.

The bartender turns to the regular, raises an eyebrow. "What did you say to him?"

The regular chuckles, then takes a drink. "The truth," he says. "But mostly I told him about that time that guy came at you with a switchblade, so you took his eye out."

The rest of the night passes in its usual Tuesday pattern.

The regulars all gradually drift away home, saying goodnight to the bartender as they go. When he's alone, he tidies up. It doesn't take much. Then he locks the door and walks to his place. It's not far from the bar. A small upstairs apartment at the end of the nearest block. It's a calm, warm, clear night. He takes his time walking back. It's nicer outside than it is in.

The apartment is small. He's stayed in bigger motel rooms. There is water damage on the wall that leads through to the bathroom. He turns on the television and sits on the bed with his back propped up on the headboard. It's late. He flicks through the channels. There's an old monster movie on. A real B movie, with rubber suits and cardboard sets. He lets it play out as background noise. He reaches down the side of the bed and pulls up his bag. Takes out a notepad and a pen. He puts them to one side. He needs to write a letter. It's overdue.

Before he does, he reaches back into the bag and pulls out the phones he keeps inside. It's a nightly ritual. No one ever calls him, or messages, but that's a good sign. If they try to get in touch, it's more than likely with bad news. So he goes through the phones, makes sure their homepages remain blank.

Except tonight, they're not all blank. One of them has four missed calls. He double-checks the name he's taped to the top of it. *Cindy*. He dials her number. She answers like she's been waiting for his call.

"Tom," she says. "I need your help."

The End

ABOUT THE AUTHOR

Did you enjoy *No Quarter*? Please consider leaving a review on Amazon to help other readers discover the book.

Paul Heatley left school at sixteen, and since then has held a variety of jobs including mechanic, carpet fitter, and bookshop assistant, but his passion has always been for writing. He writes mostly in the genres of crime fiction and thriller, and links to his other titles can be found on his website. He lives in the north east of England.

Want to connect with Paul? Visit him at his website.

www.PaulHeatley.com

ALSO BY PAUL HEATLEY

Blood Line

(A Tom Rollins Thriller Book 1)

Wrong Turn

(A Tom Rollins Thriller Book 2)

Hard to Kill

(A Tom Rollins Thriller Book 3)

Snow Burn

(A Tom Rollins Thriller Book 4)

Road Kill

(A Tom Rollins Thriller Book 5)

No Quarter

(A Tom Rollins Thriller Book 6)

Made in the USA
Monee, IL
05 August 2022

11053754R00184